The Evil That Men Do

Boson Books by Robert D. Rodman

The Evil That Men Do

Where Evil Lurks

THE EVIL THAT MEN DO

A Dagny Taggart Jamison Mystery

Robert D. Rodman

Boson Books
Raleigh

Published by Boson Books
An imprint of C&M Online Media Inc.

ISBN (ebook) 978-0-917990-89-2
      (print) 978-0-917990-87-8

For information contact
C&M Online Media Inc.
3905 Meadow Field Lane
Raleigh, NC 27606
Tel: (919) 233-8164
e-mail: cm@cmonline.com
http://www.bosonbooks.com

Designed by Meagan Williford

Prologue

I was running dead out when the bell rang and I wondered why they kept chasing me. Recess was over—that's what the bell meant—but still they chased me and I was afraid. I sprinted into the school building. They pursued me relentlessly through empty, crisscrossing, unending corridors.

The ringing changed to a growling. I was my adult self on a beach at night—barefoot and naked, and my body was whole—rushing to reach the red beacon and safety of a lifeguard hut. The sand was loose and deep. It yielded beneath my feet and oozed between my toes. My legs churned in the slow motion of dreams; my guts ached and my chest heaved with exhaustion.

The growling drew closer, grew louder. Over my shoulder, their apish faces—sickening blobs of flesh—bobbed in the sickly green moonlight. Desperately, I launched myself at the red light and I was afloat in midair. I touched the blessed light. The growling faded, and then it merged with the buzz of my alarm clock.

I awoke terrified, drenched in sweat, my heart pounding. The Dream, again. Would it never stop plaguing me? Same plot, different scene. The school was new, but the matrix of corridors factored naturally into The Dream. Freud would have loved it, and he could have the damn thing.

Time had passed. The case was closed. The bad were punished, the good rewarded. More or less. Still, I couldn't quite close the psychic curtain on the final scene, where I had sprinted so desperately for my life, in an Oz-like world complete with flying monkeys.

"Write up the whole case, little sis," urged big brother John, when I complained bitterly to him about the nocturnal reruns. "Wallow in it. Share it with friends. Psyches are like vampires; they abhor the light. Maybe yours will tire of the dream game."

Not a bad idea, so here's what I did last summer.

Chapter 1

I'm Dagny Taggart Jamison. Nine months out of the year, I live and work as a private investigator in Raleigh, North Carolina. But in the summer, when business slows and kudzu grows, I flee the soggy, sullen air of the North Carolina piedmont and fly to breezy Santa Barbara, California. There I live with, and work for, my brother John, who owns and runs a P.I. firm.

I got my start as an apprentice in John's private investigation firm while attending UCLA. "The profession needs more women," John said. "Half the female P.I.s in the world are fictional." To John's disappointment, I moved to Raleigh to open my own practice after one year at the UCLA law school. It was a guy thing. By that I mean I was fool enough to follow my law professor boyfriend when he took a job at the University of North Carolina. He dumped me for a Carolina coed with big boobs and long vowels. Ouch!

The summer of the flying monkeys, as I've come to think of it, I went to Santa Barbara in June, a month shy of my 30th birthday. (I was born on the day that Neil Armstrong took a giant leap for mankind.) I was barely inside the door of John's house, and still gasping from a brotherly bear hug, when John laid my first assignment on me. I had to interview a Chilean witness to an automobile accident. This required a Spanish interpreter, who was to come to John's office at 8:00 the next morning.

I woke eagerly at six, my body under the illusion that it had slept late. I jogged on the beach to the beat of the Pacific surf and by 7:30 I was fighting Monday morning traffic in my rented blue Ford Taurus.

John's office is located in a narrow three-story downtown building with a rust-stained stucco exterior. The sparse, wilted landscaping gives the building a lean, mean look, the perfect location for a knuckle-cracking P.I. to hang out and obsess over curios from the Isle of Malta like crosses and falcons. Neither John nor I fit the stereotype, but we'd once been to Malta with our parents, so maybe that counts.

I parked the car in John's stall beneath the building, took the stairs two at a time to the third floor, and walked briskly along the dully lit corridor to the office. John had proudly stenciled both our names on the door when I got my California P.I. license some years back. He said he didn't have any reason to change it since I worked for him summers, so there it was:

John Galt Jamison, P.I.

Dagny Taggart Jamison, P.I.

I'd just gotten out my key when someone stepped out of the elevator at the other end of the corridor. She came toward me, checking office numbers as she neared. "Oh, damn," I thought. I'd gotten to work early because I wanted to have some minutes alone to get my act in gear, but this, I feared, was a too-prompt Spanish interpreter.

I figured I'd make the best of it, so I stood by the office door. When she drew near I tried some Spanish I'd learned in a night class, just to be friendly.

"Buenos días. Cómo está usted?"

She looked quizzically at me and fired back some Spanish. Leastwise, I thought it was Spanish. She sure didn't say "Muy bien, gracias, y usted?" the only answer I'd ever heard in class. Hell, she might have been speaking Maltese.

"I'm sorry, but I didn't understand you. I've only had a bit of Spanish, in night school, actually."

"I know I look Latina, but we'd do best in English," she said in the flat, unaccented English of a native Californian. She adjusted her shoulder bag and shifted her weight to one leg.

I'd been so preoccupied I hadn't actually looked closely at her. She was beautiful. She had light brown flawless skin that exaggerated the size of her dark chocolate eyes. Her hair was ebony, straight, and shining with good health. She wore it in a natural cut, parted in the middle, flowing over ears and shoulders, a perfect frame for a lovely, oval face. She did look Hispanic, as she said, but there was something else there, maybe some Asian.

"Oh, I can't do much with Spanish, but I thought given your profession, I'd see if I'd learned anything. I guess I haven't."

Again the quizzical look, and the trace of a smile, and a twinkle that brightened her somber face for an instant. "You're funny. Sparky didn't mention a sense of humor. Can you figure out what I do just by looking me over? You know, like Sherlock Holmes could do."

A flashbulb went off in my head. "Wait a sec. I think I'm confusing you with someone else—someone I was expecting to meet. You're talking about Elaine Sparks, right? Goes by Sparky, and hates the name Elaine?"

"Yeah, that's her. She's a good friend of mine from the university. She said you practically saved her life last year. According to her, you're the best private detective in California. She said you found the man who murdered her parents and killed him in a fight, but I don't know…"

Her tone of voice said, "…but you look too scrawny to win a fight with a man."

I said, "It wasn't a wrestling match. I'm afraid I had to shoot him."

She grimaced. "Anyway, you're her hero."

"So Sparky sent you, which means you're not the Spanish interpreter I'm supposed to meet." I looked over my shoulder hoping the real Spanish interpreter would materialize and make me look less of an idiot, but no such luck. "Can we start over? I'm Dagny Jamison." I held out my hand. "You caught me off guard just now."

She gripped my hand firmly. "I'm Lucy Navarro."

"Let's go inside." I unlocked John's office. "Why don't you sit down while I put on some coffee?" I nodded toward a chair reserved for clients. I opened the blinds to let in the morning light, and busied myself with the coffee maker. "How did you know I'd be here? I just got into town last night."

Lucy put her bag down beside the chair, sat down, crossed her legs, and tried to relax. I could read tension in her face now. She said, "I thought you were from here. You're in the phone book, you know."

I didn't know, but it was all part of John's ongoing schemes to get me to work with him full-time. He calls the agency Jamison & Jamison though I have no idea how he accounts for the missing Jamison nine months out of the year.

"I'm just here for the summer," I explained. Boiling water began drizzling over the coffee, filling my nostrils with the aroma of the brew.

Lucy fidgeted in her chair. I took my seat behind the desk, propped my forearms on the desktop, and leaned toward her. "How can I help you?"

She began to speak staccato-like, taking short breaths as she ran her phrases together. "I'm sorry if I acted like a smart ass. I'm just so upset— something awful's happened and I don't know what to do. My friends can't help me and my parents think I'm crazy but I know I'm not. I tried to make an appointment with you. I called your office all weekend, but all I got was the machine. I was going to leave a message, but whenever I think of Judy I start to cry, and I didn't want to leave a snively message so I hung up."

She sniveled, sucked in a deep breath, and exhaled with a sigh. "I figured you went to work early, so I came over here to wait for you. You're my only hope."

The coffee finished brewing just as she wound down. The edge was off her and her shoulders slumped.

"Would you like some coffee?" I offered.

She shook her head, took a couple more breaths, and dabbed at her eyes.

"Why don't you go ahead and tell me what happened?"

"You probably figured out I go to UC Isla Vista. I'm a graduate student there, in Anthropology. I study the Churok Native Americans, you know, Indians. It's a natural for me because my grandfather is Churok."

"The Churoks, don't they have a big reservation along the Yacuma River?"

"Yeah, that's right. Anyway, my best friend and roommate is—was—Judy Raskin. She was studying the Churoks too, only she was way ahead of me. She actually went to live on the reservation for a couple of years. The Churoks really loved her; she was so good to them. She worked in the schools, and helped the boys and girls study for college. Everyone loved her so much…"

Lucy began sobbing and reached into her bag for a tissue.

"I'm sorry," she said between sobs, "I can't help it when I think of Judy, but I want to tell you something about her, so you'll understand why I want you to help me."

"Take your time. I want to hear your whole story," I said.

"Okay, here's what she did," said Lucy, composing herself. "She got the chief to let her tape record the Churok rituals. Nobody was ever allowed to do that before, and they aren't written down. And that was so important that she could get her degree from it, you know, her Ph.D."

"So, that's a lot of work, I guess."

Lucy shifted in her chair, now composed enough to speak earnestly. "Oh, it is. She recorded dozens of hours, and had to write it all down, too, afterwards. It was brilliant research—for all the good it did her!"

Her face lost some of its animation. She tucked her feet under the chair, looking more and more uncomfortable with every tick of the large clock on the wall behind her.

"Judy completed her research and wrote her dissertation. The final requirement for the Ph.D. is to give a talk about the research in front of all the faculty and students, who may then ask questions. The talk is called 'the defense,' because you have to defend the originality and worth of the dissertation."

I knew about that because I once had a teacher at UCLA who was actually a graduate student. He told us weenie undergrads about oral exams—we had some jokes about that—and about defenses. The week of his own defense, he was so freaking nervous he couldn't lecture, so he read from the textbook.

"Judy's defense was last Friday. Everyone came to the large lecture hall for her talk. We friends of Judy came to hear her, and to rag her a little, calling her 'doctor,' and stuff. But really we were there to support her. The advisor is usually the last to arrive, and comes all smiles to the defense to share in the glory. When Professor Akrich entered the room, he wasn't smiling—he was nearly snarling. He had both Judy's dissertation and a sheaf of papers with him. He didn't waste any time. He stepped to the rostrum and began speaking real quietly."

Lucy had her lower lip between her teeth and was worrying it like a puppy at the fringe of a rug.

"I have a tape recording of what happened," she said. "I wanted to record Judy's defense so when mine came up, I could review how she did. I thought she'd be brilliant, and I'd pick up some pointers. But just from the way Dr. Akrich looked, I could see something unusual was coming down."

She pulled a small tape recorder from her purse. It was gold in color, and about half the size of a paperback book. She set it on the desk between us, switched it on, and adjusted the volume. After some seconds of audience noise, a man's voice that I at once found whiny began to speak.

"Ladies and gentlemen, until a few moments ago I was prepared to welcome you to one of our university's oldest traditions, the defense of the doctoral dissertation. For those of you not familiar with Miss Raskin's work, it would have been a compelling story of ancient Churok history, as recounted by the Churoks themselves. Candidate Raskin collected, organized, and analyzed an extensive oral history, transcribing it meticulously as it was spoken in the language of the Churoks. Hers was a Brobdingnagian task, executed brilliantly in this dissertation."

The light had shifted and Lucy was squinting into it, her hand cupped over her eyes. I got up and adjusted the ancient Venetian blinds to mute the light, appalled at the dust that had accumulated on the slats.

She smiled her thanks as the professor's voice continued.

"Less than an hour ago I was handed these papers."

There was a slight pause and then a rustling sound as he apparently brandished the pages.

"These are photocopies from a journal of Native American history that appeared twenty years ago. On these pages can be found, word for word, much of the material that appears in this dissertation."

There was a sound of a flat hand striking a book, then silence except for the sound of people breathing and the low hum of the player's motor.

"What we have here is plagiarism. These proceedings can continue no longer. Miss Raskin, I'm sorry. Please meet me in my office as soon as you're able."

The sounds of the professor leaving were interrupted by the scraping of a chair leg. A voice, a female voice, quavering, full of bitter emotion, cried out: "You, you of all people. How can you, how dare you…?" The sound of a woman in heels…tap, tap, tap…receded in the background. Then much scraping of chair legs, a cacophony of voices, a staticky click, and the hiss of blank tape.

Lucy reached over and turned off the machine. "I never saw Judy, or anyone, look like she did when she said those words. Her face was white. She was trembling and fighting to speak. She fixed Akrich with so demonic a glare, it was like she was a different person, not one that I knew, not my best friend and roommate."

Lucy's fidgeting turned to uncontainable agitation. She stood up, her right hand clenched in her left, and walked over to the window to look out through the dusty slats. I was hoping she wouldn't hold the poor housekeeping against me. Still looking out the window, her back to me, she went on in a low voice: "At first there was silence, then everybody was standing up and talking at once. The students were looking at one another in disbelief. None of us had ever seen such a spectacle. I tried to follow Judy, but by the time I'd squeezed my way through the crowd and run into the hall, she was gone."

Lucy turned to face me, her slatted shadow stretching across the room to the chair where she had been sitting.

"I hurried up the two flights of stairs to the floor where Akrich had his office, hoping to find her there. The corridor was deserted. I waited by his office door until I heard voices in the stairwell. A gaggle of professors with Akrich at the center was approaching."

The phone rang. I flapped my hand at it and said, "Let the machine take it," but when it clicked on the volume was up. It was the Spanish interpreter saying one of her kids was sick and she couldn't make it, and asking me to call her back. I turned the volume off and asked Lucy to go on.

"It dawned on me that Judy wouldn't come straight to his office. She'd have to collect herself somewhere. I thought maybe she'd gone back to our place, about ten minutes from campus. I headed away from the jabbering group and went down the other stairwell. I wanted to find Judy real bad. When I got downstairs I ducked into the ladies room and took off my heels and pantyhose. I could make better time in bare feet. Do you want to return that call? I can wait."

I shook my head and motioned her on. I wasn't sure where she was going, but I could tell by the tension rising once again in her demeanor that when she got there, I'd be interested.

"I made it back to our place in under five minutes. I had my keys out but the door was unlocked. I went in. I knew Judy was there because her pocketbook was on the table by the sofa. I called her name. There was no answer. I walked through the living room and poked my head into the kitchen. No Judy, but the back door was ajar. I walked through the kitchen and I took a quick look out back. Not there, either."

Lucy was pacing up and down, almost as if reenacting her movements in the house. I shuddered at her brashness. I'd have kept going out the back and found reinforcements, and I'm usually armed.

"I went back inside to check out her bedroom. I turned into the hall and something made me hesitate. I sensed movement, not directly, but reflected in the pattern of light and shadow coming from the bedroom. I called to Judy again. I was starting to freak out big time. I knew I should get the hell out of there. The last thing I needed was a rapist, but I had to find Judy. I retreated and opened the front door wide. That gave me an escape route. I went back into the hallway and listened. All I could hear was our electric fan blowing. There was no other sound. I moved closer to the bedroom door, and then I saw her feet."

Lucy had stopped pacing now. She sat down. She was gnawing her lower lip so hard I was afraid she'd draw blood. Her eyes were filling with tears; her voice barely a squeak.

"They were not touching the ground. I closed my eyes and shook my head real hard to chase away the vision. When I opened them the feet were pointing in a different direction."

I put my hand to my mouth, seeing now all too clearly where the tale led.

"I wished I hadn't hesitated earlier. I rushed into the room and Judy was hanging by an electrical cord buried in the flesh of her neck. Her face was swollen beyond recognition. I jumped up on the bed, grabbed the light fixture above her head, and swung. The weight of our two bodies broke it loose from the ceiling. We ended up in a heap. I clawed at the cord to loosen it but it was hopelessly embedded. I tried to remember my first-aid class. Mouth-to-mouth, I kept thinking, but what was the use with the cord so terribly tight around her neck? She was gone, and nothing I could do would bring her back."

Lucy was sobbing again, tears brimming from her eyes and tracking down her cheeks. I found a box of tissues and walked around my desk to hand them to her. I forced myself not to give in to my own emotions. I leaned down next to her and put my hand on the arm of her chair. She wiped her eyes, then cupped her hands over face and lowered her head. It was a full minute before she could speak again.

"I called 911. Within minutes there were campus cops, city cops, a fire engine, the EMT truck. Some plainclothes cops showed up a short time later. Then the crime lab people, the ones with the orange jump suits, came. They scoured the place, took dozens of photos. The plainclothes cops asked me a zillion questions about what had happened earlier. I was in a daze, drained, but I guess I told them what they needed. It was nearly five o'clock when they finished. A crowd had gathered and dispersed. My neighbors from two doors down, a married couple, took me in, gave me brandy in milk, and put me to bed. I slept until noon Saturday."

She paused, thinking, and then she suddenly regained her composure. To my surprise, she grinned, and it was like the sun breaking through clouds of rain.

"When I woke up, I was lucid. Lucy was lucid."

She emitted a sound that was half-snort, half-laugh. I managed a smile, and reached out to her, gently squeezing her shoulder.

"My mind had been at work while I slept," she said, adding, "I do this all the time. Lots of students do. You stay up late and bandy about a bunch of facts and theories. Then you go to bed. When you wake up, you're able to make a lot more sense of them."

No stranger to this phenomenon, I nodded in agreement.

"I woke up knowing Judy didn't kill herself," Lucy said emphatically. "She wasn't that type of person. She wasn't impulsive or flighty or highly emotional. Judy *might* kill herself, but she'd reason about it for days, weighing the pros and cons. And she'd leave a note. In fact, she'd probably leave an essay. But the cops didn't find anything."

Lucy thought for a moment. In the silence I stood up straight and stretched, then half sat, half leaned on the back of my desk, still close to her. She was fingering the little crucifix that hung about her neck, her eyes cast down. Then she raised her head and looked straight at me, her jaw set, her eyes flashing. "Miss Jamison, someone murdered Judy."

Chapter 2

Lucy's earnestness was compelling, but the play of events that she'd described didn't seem like murder. "Please call me Dagny, okay?" I said, and with a reassuring smile that I hoped didn't betray my skepticism asked, "Why'd someone want to kill her?"

Lucy dropped her gaze. "Okay, Dagny, then. I don't know about a motive, if that's the right word. I just know she didn't kill herself. I spent the whole weekend arguing about this with everyone. No one believes me, not even my own mom. She says I have a lurid imagination. 'Now Lucy, with all you've been through...'" She spoke the words with a falsetto twang that caricatured her mother's voice.

"Sparky was the only one who took me seriously, maybe because of what had happened to her parents. She didn't think I'd get too far with the cops, since they'd already been there and made up their minds. That's why she suggested I see you."

"The coroner's office will order an autopsy," I said. "If there was foul play, one of the medical examiners will find it. They're competent."

"Would they have done it over the weekend?" asked Lucy. "How could I find out?"

"She'd have been examined at the scene to fix the time of death, although that was hardly necessary since she was seen alive, what, half an hour before?"

"About that."

"At the same time, they'd look for evidence of a struggle. They'd examine her for signs of bodily harm such as bullet holes or knife wounds, head injuries, ligature marks on her wrists and legs, stuff like that. A person can be murdered by hanging but they have to be disabled somehow. It's hard to disable a person without leaving a trace."

"What are ligature marks? I thought those occurred in music."

"Sorry, it's cop talk for the marks left after a person's been tied up."

"Oh."

"She'd be taken to the morgue and scheduled for an autopsy today or tomorrow, I'd guess."

I walked over to bookshelves and pulled down a well-used volume.

Lucy's eyes followed me.

I leafed through the book while speaking. "Even if they're sure it's suicide, they have to do the autopsy because it's a—" I found the right page "—'sudden, violent, or unexpected death that may not have had a natural cause.'" (I was quoting the appropriate legal code. Not great literature but very practical.)

"What if they don't find anything?"

"Then that's it. The body can be claimed by her family." I paused for a moment. "I'm sorry, Lucy. It's dreadful business, but to be honest, I just don't see what I can do."

"Could I hire you to tell them to look extra carefully? I'm not even sure where to go or where her body is or who to talk to. Even if they don't find anything, I want to hire you to look into it. I should get my fellowship check today. I can pay your fee."

I checked my watch. Quarter to nine and I had to interview this witness for John, except I'd be without a Spanish interpreter. I acted impulsively. "Look, I'll make you a deal. I need to interview this Chilean man, Fernando Mendoza Vareta." I read the name with my best Spanish accent. Lucy was unimpressed. "He witnessed an accident and I need someone to interpret. You do that for me and we'll talk in my car on the way over. Afterward, we'll go over to SB General and find out who's doing the autopsy. What do you say?"

"You mean right now?"

"Yeah, if you have time."

"Whenever you're ready." She stood up and grabbed her handbag.

"Frankly, if there's no sign of murder and no motive for a murderer, I'm not going to waste your money or my time," I added.

She looked at me blandly and didn't say anything.

"Vamonos, then," I said. I was getting in the mood for this Spanish gig. Lucy rolled her eyes.

We got in the Taurus and headed for the 101. We needed to go to Goleta, the bedroom community west of Santa Barbara. I got out the directions and handed them to Lucy. "You navigate, and while not getting me lost, tell me about Judy."

She studied the paper, checked the street sign, and when she was satisfied I wasn't getting myself lost she began talking.

"Well, we met at UCLA, I guess in some classes we took at the same time. Then, when I came up to Isla Vista, she turned up in the same dorm as me, even though she'd been there longer. And we just sort of hit it off, you know how that happens. One day we were just talking and saying how tired we were of dorm life, and wouldn't it be cool to live in an apartment or even a small house. Turned out, there are these little rental houses for graduate students, so we applied for one, and I guess we were just lucky to get it."

"Where's she from?" I asked.

"She grew up in L.A., Beverly Hills actually, but she wasn't your typical rich, spoiled Beverly Hills brat. She always worked and studied hard. I think her father would've spoiled her, especially after her mother died, and let me see, that was when she was fourteen or fifteen when it happened. Her mother was young when she had Judy. She was his second wife, maybe a trophy wife. I never asked. But she had mental problems and—wow, I hadn't thought of this before—she killed herself, I'm almost sure by hanging. Judy didn't much like to talk about it, but anyway, Judy, she wasn't ever depressed or anything."

"What got her interested in the Churoks?"

"She liked to have friends from all different backgrounds and countries. She took anthropology out of curiosity for other cultures, and she took linguistics because through languages she gained access to those cultures. With the Churoks, she combined…Whoa, you need to get over a lane, sorry."

I blinkered the Taurus to the left and nearly cut off a police cruiser. I made a quick palms-out shrug of apology. The officer waggled a finger in my rearview mirror, but the blue light stayed off.

"Anyway," resumed Lucy, "since Isla Vista has Dr. Akrich, who's one of the leading experts on the Churoks, she opted to go there to study with him, just as I did. She was a straight A student. And here's the thing. She was completely honest. She wouldn't even fib to a professor about a toothache if she hadn't finished some homework on time, let alone copy someone."

"Did Judy have any ex-husbands or lovers?"

"She'd had the usual flings, maybe slept with half a dozen guys. For the past year, until last Easter, she had a pretty serious boyfriend, Troy Stanton."

"What can you tell me about him?"

"For some reason he stopped working on his dissertation about six months ago. He was living off his fellowship but wasn't really doing any work. I think it bugged Judy. It seemed dishonest to her. He said he was staying on to be with her, that he loved her. That worked for a while—we women are such suckers for that line—but eventually Judy bit the bullet and broke it off."

"How did he take it?"

"Not too well. They argued. He made some vague threats about what he'd do if he saw her with another man, but she didn't take them seriously. He tried to hang out around our place but Judy wouldn't have it. He was jealous of her because she was smarter than him, and about to get her degree."

"How about drugs?"

"Judy was squeaky clean. Didn't smoke, hardly drank. Troy smoked a little dope and maybe did some coke too, which didn't help their relationship."

"So she didn't run up a big drug bill or sell stuff? Dealers might have got nasty if they weren't getting paid."

"No way. I'd know, believe me."

"Are there any siblings?"

"She has a half-brother who lives in Houston, I think. He's married with a couple of kids. But I don't think they're close."

"Same father?"

"Uh-huh, by the first wife."

"Do they stand to share an inheritance?"

"Probably. Her father's pretty rich, but he's still not that old. He's not fat, doesn't smoke, and works out. He's actually a cool dude for a dad. He'll probably marry someone younger like the first time, and she'll get all his money. You need to get off at Buena Vista, according to this."

I changed lanes, taking particular care not to cut off any police cruisers, and glided down the off-ramp. While Lucy navigated, I briefed her on the subject of the impending interview.

"About a month ago two guys, brothers, lost control of their '79 Cutlass and smashed through the plate glass storefront of an auto parts dealer. The vehicle shattered display cases, annihilated the service counter, and took out a dozen shelves of spare parts. From the photos, it was a god-awful mess, though by some miracle nobody was hurt. The brothers were suspected of switching places after the accident to cover for the one that had a suspended license. Their insurance company hired us to find out who was really driving. Insurance companies are picky about those kinds of details. An unlicensed driver might save them from having to pay out."

"And this Hispanic man—he saw it happen?" said Lucy.

"Apparently. It went by so fast that the people in the shop were too busy scrambling to see much, but Vareta was on the sidewalk a few feet away and had a good view of the accident and its aftermath. So we go to this address—he's expecting us—and find the man. I'll ask questions, you translate into Spanish, he answers, and you translate into English. Got it?"

"Totally," said Lucy.

Vareta lived on Via Verde, a couple of blocks west of Buena Vista Avenue. Via Verde is one block long, with single-family dwellings built in the 50s. Zoning laws must have been lax in those days, as the houses were barely eight feet apart. They were separated from the roadway by a weedy, turf-filled strip two feet wide, a sidewalk cracked and buckled with age, and tiny, unkempt front yards. Much of the grass had suffered neglect, as had the sparse trees on the block, half of which were dead. A few cars—none less than 10 years old—were parked alongside the curb and in driveways, and more than one yard had jalopies up on blocks in various states of disassembly.

"This is more like Via Parda than Via Verde," remarked Lucy. "More brown than green."

I found the address in faded paint on the curb. The house that it belonged to was typical of the neighborhood, with a filthy, streaked, white clapboard exterior and a roof of warped wood shingles. We parked, got out of the car, and walked up to the door, stepping around various children's toys. I knocked.

Señor Vareta answered almost immediately. The TV behind him blared a Spanish language station. He didn't know us from the Virgin Mary, but he produced a smile, showing tobacco-stained crooked teeth with numerous gaps. His smile grew broader as he cocked an eye at Lucy. I knew he was married with children, but his kids were probably in school and his wife at work. I really didn't want the kind of trouble his leer suggested.

I said to Lucy, "Please tell him we're from the Jamison detective agency and we want to ask him some questions about the accident."

Lucy translated into Spanish.

The only word I recognized was my own name.

He motioned us in. I put my paranoia aside and stepped in, with Lucy just behind me. I turned to Lucy. "Would you explain that you're going to ask him some questions for me?" Then I added, speaking rapidly and running my words together, "Blinktwiceifyou'renervous."

Her eyes opened a little wider. She stepped forward, turned her gaze on Vareta, and began to speak in Spanish.

He spoke back, his beery breath permeating the smoky room.

After a moment she turned to me and said, "I explained what you wanted, which he seemed to know. I hinted that you were working with the police. That should keep him in line."

I told Lucy what to say. She asked, he answered, she translated, I wrote. The upshot was that he'd seen the brothers switch places. "Ask him if he's willing to testify in court." Some Spanish followed.

"He wants to know what we'd pay him."

"Tell him in America we never pay witnesses."

"He says in Chile they always do."

"This isn't Chile," I said between clenched teeth. "Tell him that he can be required to testify in court. He can be subpoenaed."

"I don't know the Spanish word for subpoena," said Lucy. "Oh well, I'll fake it." She spoke more Spanish.

Vareta looked unhappy but he shrugged and said something.

Lucy said, "He doesn't want trouble with the law. He'll come to the court and tell the judge what he saw."

"That's great." I could pass this on to the insurance company. "Tell him that's all for now—someone will contact him later."

We got back in the car. "Gracias for helping me out with this."

"De nada," said Lucy. "I think it'll work out. I made it clear this was important business."

I got back on the 101 heading for Santa Barbara and SB General, the city's main hospital. We had to pass the old county hospital where they keep an overflow morgue, but I was pretty sure Judy's body would be at the morgue in General's pathology department.

"Let's see, what were we talking about?" I asked Lucy.

"You were suggesting that Judy might've been murdered for her inheritance," said Lucy.

"Hold on. I'm not suggesting Judy was murdered at all. I don't know if she was murdered. I'm looking for a motive for murder, that's all."

Lucy was unmoved. "If her half-brother's in Houston he couldn't do anything to her, so what's the point?"

"He could hire someone, but we're getting way ahead of ourselves. Before I devote any more brainpower to this problem, I want an autopsy report." We proceeded in silence.

I parked in the visitors' lot of the hospital. Within minutes we were stepping out of an elevator into the bowels of SB General where the Pathology Department resided. The receptionist greeted me with a smile of recognition. She's a gorgeous woman of African descent whose friendship I won several years back when I found out where her estranged husband had secreted his winnings from a lottery ticket. It wasn't one of those Power Ball monster payoffs, but my investigation netted Lisa about a quarter of a million dollars, after which she got her divorce. Lisa grew up in North Carolina, which meant nothing to me at the time, but a year later I attended law school and made my home in the state, so we had this additional bond. She'd been helpful on several occasions when matters macabre brought me to the morgue.

"Hey, Lisa, how's it going?"

"Hey, Dagny, what's up, girl?" We North Carolinians always say hey when we meet, and call each other girl well into our nineties.

"This is Lucy Navarro. Her roommate comm—uh, died on Friday under suspicious circumstances. I'm wondering if she's here, and if she is, when the autopsy is scheduled. They'd've brought her in from the university."

"Yeah, she here. They brought her in Friday. Sad thing, that, so young. They said she was real smart, very pretty and, uh…" She broke off when she saw Lucy's eyes filling with tears. "Oh, I'm awfully sorry, hon, truly I am."

Lucy took a proffered tissue and wiped her eyes.

"They'll do her today, for sure," continued Lisa. "We had a power outage in the morgue Friday. The fridge went out and we couldn't keep the body cold. We're not on auxiliary, you know. Twice over the weekend they wanted to move her to a nearby mortuary, but the engineers kept sayin' 'power any minute, power any minute.' Every time the power came up and the 'frigeration kicked in, down went everything. It's a pain moving bodies, 'specially when there're unusual circumstances. The paperwork is a heap of bother. She been ripening for three days now and they got to autopsy this afternoon. I'm sure the smell by now…" She broke off as she glanced in Lucy's direction. Lisa had a tendency to be a bit jaded about her job.

"Do you know who's scheduled to do the autopsy? I thought maybe we could talk to whoever it is for a minute." I hadn't the foggiest what I was going to say, but I owed this much to Lucy.

"They just hired a new assistant medical examiner, Dr. Charles Clarke," she said with a wink. She pronounced his name Chaaahles Claaahke, with long vowels and no trace of an *r*. Southerners have little use for *r*'s anyway. Lisa wasn't given to exaggerating her southern accent unless it was to charm some man she was flirting with, but no male prey was in the vicinity.

"Any chance we could talk to him, just for a sec?"

"Let me see if he's in his office. He's a nice guy, but a little reserved." She keyed in a number. Someone picked up and Lisa explained our wishes.

"It's cool. His office is 225 south. Go down the main corridor, take your first right through the double doors. His office is second on the left."

We followed her directions, and a minute later we were peering into an office and seeing the back of a blond-headed man who was seated at a computer terminal. The computer was on a long table that extended the length of the rear wall. On either side of it were books and journals, some opened facedown to keep their place. A smattering of papers, pencils, diskettes, and various other *objets de* desk accompanied them.

The office was windowless with floor-to-ceiling bookshelves on two of the walls. In the center of the room was a desk on which stood a calendar, a telephone, a Rolodex, a pad of paper, and a pen in one of those fancy holders that you get when you graduate from somewhere. Its orderliness contrasted with the chaos of the table behind it.

Just as I was about to rap on the open door, the man swiveled around and stood up in one easy motion. He was just over six feet tall, with straight, shiny, blond hair that lapped ever so slightly over his collar—a bit of a retro style in these days of short hair. He was dressed in a pair of gray slacks with a coordinated vest and necktie. The sleeves of his white shirt were rolled halfway up sinewy forearms. He exuded physical strength and would have looked as natural on a playing field as in a lab coat. He had an angular face with a strong chin and intelligent blue eyes. He looked about thirty. His ring finger was naked. I felt a hormone jiggle.

He stepped around his desk, stuck out his hand and said, "I'm Chaaahles Claaahke. How may I help you?" Now I saw what Lisa was up to when she pronounced his name. He sounded as English as tea and crumpets.

I started to introduce us but the first syllable came out as a squawk. I stopped, cleared my throat, and reminded myself that I was a professional woman and not a flighty girl. I began again, more mindful of my appearance than I wanted to be.

"I'm Dagny Jamison, and this is Lucy Navarro. I'm a private investigator here in Santa Barbara. Lisa told us you were going to autopsy the woman who was brought in Friday. I'd hoped we could talk about that a little. We have some concerns."

"A pleasure to meet you." He glanced at both of us but fixed his gaze on me. This was a higher compliment than any words could express. Most men would spend a little more visual effort on the stunning Lucy. "There isn't any place to lounge in here. I don't entertain much in my office. There's a break room down the hall where we can get some coffee, if you'd like."

"That's fine, thank you," I said. I was watching his mouth when he spoke, wondering how, with the same tongue, teeth and lips as any man, he could produce this marvelous-sounding English. That's as far as I permitted my imagination to stray tongue- and lip-wise.

There was a half-filled coffeepot in the break room next to which was a column of Styrofoam cups, sugar, and powdered cream. Charles served and we took our coffee to a table with a Formica surface and aluminum legs. With encouragement from Charles, Lucy told her story much as she'd told it to me. Charles listened quietly, his expression remaining neutral.

He gave Lucy a few seconds to make sure she was finished. When he spoke, it was to say a little hesitantly, "We know Miss Raskin died from asphyxiation, which is consistent with death by hanging." He looked from me to Lucy, who was blanching and gnawing her lower lip. "I'm sorry, Miss, uh…"

"Navarro," she provided. "I mean, call me Lucy."

"Right, Lucy." He looked at a loss. "Shall I carry on?"

"Please," said Lucy. "I'm okay."

"Her preliminary didn't suggest anything other than suicide. Autopsy procedures are well standardized and hard to improve on. But you know what?" Without waiting for an answer, he continued, "I trained in England under a close family friend who was a coroner all his adult life, and was actually descended from the great fourteenth-century Coroner of London, Sir John Cranston. In fact, I was named after him—my middle name, that is. Dr. Cranston always stressed how important it was for a pathologist to observe details. To test us out, he used to make small, subtle changes in the cadavers we students practiced on, such as painting a fifth toe with nail polish, just to see if we'd notice."

He said to Lucy, "I'll give it my best go. If I find anything remotely suspicious, I'll report it to the coroner."

"Would you mind letting me know, too, Dr. Clarke?" I asked, reaching for a business card. "If you don't get me at the office, try me at home." Hoping his sharp eyes wouldn't spot my shaking hand, I jotted my number down on the back of the card. "I'll pass the information on to Lucy."

"I'll be glad to, and please call me Charles (Chaaahles), uh, Dagny, right? I'm a bungler at names."

"Dagny is right. We really appreciate this."

We stood up, shook hands, and moved towards the door. As Charles ushered me out, I could swear I felt his eyes on my butt, but I chalked it up to wishful thinking.

On my way back to the office, I dropped Lucy off at her car with a promise to call when I knew something. She gave me the phone number of the neighbor she was staying with, and we parted.

When I got home that evening, I found a note from John, saying he had had to fly to Vegas on some unfinished business, and asking me to hold the fort. Just then, the phone rang, and while I hated to scare off any of John's girlfriends, I thought that "holding the fort" included answering the phone. I picked up.

"Dagny?" inquired a voice, "Charles Clarke here. I left a message at your office. I thought it would be okay if I rang your home, since you left me your number."

"I'm glad you called. Did you find anything?"

"I think so. If I hadn't spoken with you two earlier, I might have missed it." He paused as if choosing his words. "I found what I believe to be an irregularity. Maybe you ladies are onto something."

Chapter 3

I looked at the clock. Nearly six. I blurted, "Why not meet when you're off work? I'll buy you a beer."

I couldn't believe I'd just asked this man out. It was more than a nothing-ventured-nothing-gained kind of thing. It was a small victory in my battle to heal my self-esteem, much battered by the aforementioned ex-boyfriend.

Ordinarily, getting dumped—and that hadn't been the only time— didn't affect me so deeply. But this boyfriend, this professor of law, whom I'd loved enough to follow across the country, was special. Several years before I met him, I was serving in the U.S. Army when a routine mammogram turned up a lump. A follow-up examination revealed an aggressive malignancy that required a mastectomy and a withering regimen of radiation therapy. An honorable, but unwelcome, discharge from the military followed.

My trauma and its psychological shock waves kept me out of relationships for years. I felt ugly. Sex was out of the question. A prosthesis (read *falsie*) and intensive counseling put me where I could be responsible for growing back my self-image. By then I'd completed a degree at UCLA and was in law school.

The professor was the first man to touch me in nearly half a decade. He loved me and accepted me as I was, or so I felt. But I don't think I accepted myself as I was. Even when we were together, when I dreamt, the missing breast was always present. To lose him to a "whole" woman, as I thought of that chesty belle, slashed open old psychological wounds—deep, traumatic wounds that were only partially healed. It had taken me years to come to terms with my lover's rejection of me. I hadn't had a relationship since the break-up—but, hey, who was to say that I couldn't ever have another one? There's something about the balmy California air that encourages thoughts of love.

Charles answered immediately, "Capital idea. I'm not well acquainted with Santa Barbara, though. Where would you suggest?"

There's a pseudo-English pub called The Fox 'n' Hounds just off State Street between John's place and SB General. I gave Charles directions and we agreed to meet at 7:00. This gave me time to screw up my courage as I freshened up for my date—if it was a date—with Charles Cranston Clarke.

Furthermore, Charles's words had alerted my P.I. senses. He didn't strike me as the type to make cavalier remarks about autopsies. I couldn't imagine what he'd found, and by the time I got to Foxies, as the locals call it, my curiosity was as great as my romantic interest.

I had mixed feelings about a possible romance. Not only did I experience a fear of intimacy—which, thanks to my therapist, I could *call* a false fear, in the hope that it might one day prove to *be* false—but I also had guilt pangs over mixing pleasure with business. On the other hand, I didn't have a contract to investigate Judy Raskin's death, so it was my own time. Not only that, but if Charles did find evidence of foul play, the coroner would alert homicide. I still didn't see a professional role for me, but I had hopes for a social one.

The Fox 'n' Hounds is Santa Barbara's concession to local anglophiles. Having been once to England, I could testify to its authenticity, given the limitations of beer and ale available in the States. It has plenty of clients who speak ear-bending varieties of non-American English, from southern New Zealand to northern Scotland.

The main room contains a massive bar of polished wood; behind it, a floor-to-ceiling mirror makes the room seem larger than it really is. Tables and chairs are scattered throughout, and are so arranged as to accommodate parties of differing sizes. The walls are covered with coats of arms and with paintings of hunting scenes. The lighting is of the pseudo-gaslight variety, subdued but sufficient for one to read a menu or recognize a person across the room. It doesn't quite have the womb-like warmth of a true English pub, but then it hasn't had five centuries to mellow, like some of the more homey pubs I had visited in the U.K.

Charles was sitting at a small table beneath a picture of a retriever scrambling out of a pond with a duck in its mouth and water dripping from its coat. We saw each other at the same moment. He stood up as I came over. We shook hands.

He said, "Nice to see you. Please, sit down."

"Same here. Thanks for meeting me."

We exchanged smiles and sat down facing each other. "What will you have to drink?" asked Charles.

Pub etiquette permitted you to fetch your own drinks, which worked out well since the wait staff was perpetually short-handed. Charles had a glass of what appeared to be dark ale in front of him. I figured an Englishman in an English pub, even a pseudo-English pub, would know what to drink, so I asked him, "What are you drinking?"

"Newkie Brown. They said they'd just got it on draught."

"Newkie Brown?" I repeated. It sounded like the street that Senor Vareta lived on.

"Newcastle Brown Ale. It's not bad, if you like a dark ale. Here, try a sip."

"Aren't you afraid you'll get something?" It was a poor joke but I wanted to break the ice.

"Dagny," he began—my name sounded musical on his lips—"I'm a pathologist and believe me, nothing dangerous could live in this stuff."

"Charles, don't ever do beer commercials. What kind of a recommendation is that?" I took a sip. Not bad, indeed. Within moments there were two glasses of Newkie Brown on the table between us.

We made small talk for a while, neither of us particularly wanting to get around to discussing the autopsy. Eventually, at a convenient moment, I broached the topic.

"Can you tell me what you found?"

"Let me pose a question first. Did you know Judy at all?"

"Everything about her I learned from Lucy this morning."

"Was she training athletically for some kind of competition?"

"Lucy never mentioned it."

"Did she do drugs at all?"

"No. Lucy was adamant about that. Can you tell me what this is all about? Maybe if I knew I would remember something more helpful."

"Of course. Sorry. I'm trying to fill in some blanks. My manners go missing when I think too hard. I forgot you're a consulting detective." He added whimsically, "You don't look much like Sherlock Holmes."

"Haven't I told you that I tracked the Giant Rat of Sumatra to Santa Barbara?" I countered.

He laughed. "You're a fan of the great detective?"

I was. As a kid, I quickly outgrew the Nancy Drew mystery stories. Instead, I read and reread the many adventures of Sherlock Holmes written by Arthur Conan Doyle. I read them still—comfort food for the mind. Years ago I copied down a passage describing Holmes that struck a chord with me. I keep it in my wallet, and I dredged it out in a shameless effort to impress Charles.

"'Keen observation, first-class memory, attention to detail, ability to concentrate long hours without distraction, logical and methodical thinking, total commitment to the job,'" I read, stumbling at the end when I realized how show-offy I was being. "Even though that was said about a made-up person, it's what I think it takes to be a good P.I. today."

"Bravo, Dagny. You have high ideals." He reached across the table for a high-five, our fingers interlocking for a moment. We finished our ale and Charles went to fetch two more pints. When he returned he was more serious.

"I hope I haven't misled you into thinking I've solved the problem of the young lady's death. The autopsy of Judy Raskin showed nothing inconsistent with her having hanged herself. I examined her minutely before the actual procedure. There were no signs of physical coercion on her body."

He paused to sip his ale.

I was hanging onto his words.

"We had some problems in the morgue with our refrigeration. We never did get her body on ice. In fact, it was bloody hot in the morgue. Every time we'd go to move her, the engineers would say they'd fixed the problem. But they hadn't. It never got fixed that weekend. A lot of biochemistry takes place at 80 degrees. Ordinarily, this is bad. We lose information about the state of the body at the time of death. But in this instance, it may have been serendipitous."

"How's that?" I asked. "And what would her athleticism have to do with it?"

"There was one peculiarity that led me to wonder whether she'd been taking steroids. You see, her fingernails had...well, let me explain. After death, without refrigeration, certain parts of your body continue to grow, such as the hair and fingernails."

This touched off an ugly memory and I interrupted. "Oh, I read about one of the Hillside Stranglers' victims. They'd forced her to shave herself before raping and strangling her. When her body was found several days later, her pubic hair had begun to grow back. It made an impression on me, to say the least."

"I was a boy in England but I remember that nasty business. Had people in California in near hysteria for months. They must've killed over a half dozen women, the buggers. Gave the coroner's office fits, as I later learned."

He shook his head to clear the memory. "Anyway, a healthy fingernail in a young female grows about 75 millimeters a year, if it's filed down regularly. In three days one grows about half a millimeter, the width of a pencil lead. At the root of several of Judy's fingernails, about half a millimeter in thickness, was a whitening of the nail that occurs typically when a certain body-building steroid called Nandrolex is taken. It may or may not be an immediate reaction to the steroid, but if you take it long enough, your fingernails will begin to show these striations. In

Judy's case the whitening must have begun at the time of death, which is a suspicious coincidence, but it may be just that: coincidence."

"Could she have been drugged with a large dose and then hanged?" I asked.

"Not really," said Charles. "Large doses of steroids are harmful, but the effect's not immediate. At worst you'd get sick and throw up. Besides, there weren't any traces of pills in her stomach, and I couldn't find any injection sites, though in three days at room temperature they'd heal over somewhat."

"I'll get up with Lucy and try to find out more about Judy's personal habits."

"To be honest, I don't think there's enough to suggest foul play. I don't see a connection between the striations and her death, and I don't think the coroner will either. It might just be something natural we don't understand. What we don't know about the human body far exceeds what we do know. Still, I don't like unexplained details. I asked the lab to test for steroids. We'll have the results tomorrow."

Charles stopped and rubbed his chin, then took a long pull of the Newkie Brown, looking at me over the top of the glass. The look suggested the business part of our meeting was over.

We stayed and talked until midnight, exchanging stories from our respective professions. He told me more about his training under Dr. Cranston, his middle-namesake. The talk about names brought mine to light.

"Dagny Taggart Jamison," mused Charles. "Of course. I wondered about the *Dagny* but I couldn't place it until now. No doubt your parents were readers of Ayn Rand?"

"You got it. My brother John's full name is John Galt Jamison. We are the *Atlas Shrugged* kids."

"Most singular way to name one's children," commented Charles. "When you read *Atlas Shrugged*—as I assume you have done—did the Dagny character make you feel as though you weren't your own person?"

"Not really. She's an admirable figure and it'd be unrealistic for a real person to try to live like a fictional one. And you know, Ayn Rand was very much a realist. It's more like, maybe, a Hispanic family naming a kid Jesus." (I gave it the Spanish pronunciation—Hey Seuss—and was quite pleased with myself.) "He's not expected to become a religious leader and get himself crucified. I think we sibs understood the high standards of our namesakes and tried to live by them the way a person might want to have the charitable qualities of a Mother Teresa or the leadership qualities of a George Patton."

Charles said, "I certainly hope my parents didn't expect me to be as successful and famous as Sir John Cranston. But anyway, it doesn't hang me up, so I guess I understand. I gather that you've never been tempted to run a railroad." He winked at me when he said it.

"Naw, business isn't for me like it was for Rand's Dagny. I like to think small, pick at one or two problems at a time, turn them over until I know everything about them, and then come up with solutions that fit the facts. That's why I like what I do, though to tell the truth, a lot of P.I. work is routine and boring."

"So's a lot of medical practice," agreed Charles, "but the several interesting cases that come one's way make it worth the while."

"What I admired in fictional Dagny as a character, what I strive for, is her dedication to her principles, her bravery, her toughness, and how she didn't let adversity damage her."

Charles gave me a penetrating look as if he understood the emotion between the lines of my words. I was embarrassed for a moment, feeling as though I'd been melodramatic, but I'd expressed what I felt. We continued talking about our lives and ourselves well into the third (or was it the fourth?) round of Newkie Brown.

It was six in the morning when I realized that Newkie Brown is really Nukie Brown. My head felt nuked. I skipped the jog in favor of two aspirin and two more hours of sleep. By eight I felt pretty good, and by nine I was in the office, sipping coffee, combing through mail, and updating the files in my laptop computer.

When John trained me to be a P.I., he had me write all the facts of a case on three-by-five index cards. These could be pinned to a large corkboard, and arranged and rearranged, in the hope of discovering relationships that would propel the case forward. Nowadays I accomplish the same end by entering everything I know about a case into a database on my laptop. The computer does the work of displaying the data in various configurations. John still likes the corkboard because he can pace in front of it. He feels as though the pacing contributes to the thought processes and one cannot, after all, pace in front of a computer screen, leastwise not the kind I can afford.

I was entering the facts surrounding Judy Raskin's sad death when the office phone rang. It was Lucy. She'd had a sleepless night, increasingly convinced that Judy's death was foul play. I filled her in on my "date" with Charles, particularly mentioning the fingernail oddity.

"That clinches it," she said. "You have to do something." Then, as an afterthought—she couldn't resist the romantic side of the picture—she added, "I think he likes you."

I wasn't sure how she could know that. I had only related the parts of the conversation regarding Judy. Nonetheless, it pleased me for her say it.

"I like you too, Dagny, even if your Spanish is a little rough." In a more serious voice, "I want you to take my case. Puhlease, por favor!"

I had to admit that the one loose end intrigued me. I've never been a believer in coincidence. I said, "Okay, Lucy, here's the deal. I'll take the case only until the cops get involved. We don't know what the lab reports will look like, and we don't know what Charles, I mean Dr. Clarke, is going to recommend to the coroner. I charge twenty-five bucks an hour plus expenses."

"You don't, either! I know you charge seventy-five. I don't want a discount."

"Twenty-five's my student rate, take it or leave it. The point may be moot, anyway."

"Thanks, Dagny. I'll take it. I want you to start today. Would you be willing to drive out to the university so I can show you our apartment? I'll set something up with Troy, you know, Judy's boyfriend, and I'll try to get you in to see Dr. Akrich, too."

Lucy certainly wasn't going to waste a moment, but I didn't mind. It's nice to be out and about in the California spring sunshine, so a visit to the university in Isla Vista didn't seem like such a bad idea. A conspiracy of motivations moved me. I was curious about Judy, even if it turned out she really did kill herself. It was morbid curiosity, plain and simple—a little weakness of mine. It was also an excuse to stay in touch with Charles. Finally, I'd grown to like Lucy. I liked her determination and forthrightness—a quality the fictional Dagny had possessed and that I admired. I liked the depth of her feeling for her dead friend. I liked the freshness and vigor of her youth. Though our ages were only a few years apart, I felt old compared with her, and if not that, certainly more experienced—and I don't mean with guys—but with life. I believe my affection for her was in part my wanting to play big sister.

I said, "Whew, you get right on it, don't you, but okay. I'll drive out there if you'll give me directions."

Lucy told me how to find the home of Doris and Ernest Worthington, where she was staying temporarily. Isla Vista is the other side of Goleta. If you take freeways and traffic cooperates, it's about a twenty-minute drive from downtown Santa Barbara. I prepared a contract for Lucy, penciling in the twenty-five dollar rate.

I found the apartment without difficulty. Lucy met me at the door. She wore a pair of Calvin Klein jeans and a short-cut, unbuttoned Levi jeans jacket. Underneath was a T-shirt with the logo of some cosmetics company, ironic since she wasn't wearing any make-up. An inch of midriff was exposed, predating a style that was soon to become *de rigueur* for the young and flat-bellied (and, lamentably, for the old and flab-bellied, in some cases). A small, gold crucifix dangled from around her neck over the front of the T-shirt.

"Hi Dagny, thanks for coming. I guess the first thing to do is have a look at where it happened. I haven't been back. I asked Doris to get me a few things, but she didn't want to go in there, either. She was going to ask Ernie, but I didn't want Ernie fumbling through my underwear, so I've been borrowing stuff."

Lucy was nervous, spurting out her phrases in short, rapid bursts. She wasn't looking forward to visiting her former digs. She didn't really need to, as I could look around myself. Later, when she had other living arrangements, she could have someone else move her belongings. But before I could volunteer to go alone, she was leading the way.

To relieve her anxiety Lucy launched into a history of the surroundings. "Graduate student housing consists of several dozen 4-plexes erected during World War II as living quarters for coastal defense workers. They were supposed to be temporary but after the war the University purchased them, fixed them up, and now rents them to graduate students. They cost the same as a dormitory, but food's not included. Still, a lot of us students prefer the peace and privacy not found in a dorm, and we've learned how to shop cheap."

"You'd make a good docent," I quipped, as we strode up to our destination.

The apartment was ordinary throughout, except for Judy's bedroom. Even there most of the signs of death and investigation had been removed. Only the light fixture leaning against the wall in a corner, and some bare wires dangling from the ceiling, bore mute testimony to the tragedy. I wondered what Judy had stood on, or what her captor had stood her on, to raise her to the ceiling. I put the question to Lucy.

"The bed, I guess. There wasn't the usual kicked-over chair like in a soap opera."

The bed was queen-sized with a firm mattress. It might have worked.

"How tall was Judy?" I asked.

"Five-nine."

I got out the measuring tape on my key chain. The ceiling height was 89 inches—just under seven and a half feet. I had Lucy stand on the edge of the bed and stretch as far as she could toward the hole in the ceiling, while I stood on a kitchen chair and measured the distance from her neck to where the light fixture had hung. Her lower lip had slipped under her upper teeth.

We both got back down. "I'm sorry I have to ask this. How far off the ground were her feet?"

Biting her lip, Lucy considered for a minute. "At least a foot, maybe a foot and a half."

"Hmm. Her height at the neck is about five feet. Suppose she was a foot off the ground. That's six feet. So the wire she hung from was at most a foot and a half long. But your neck was a good three feet from where you stood on the edge of the bed to where the light fixture was hanging."

"Oh wow! She couldn't have used the bed."

Before I could say it, Lucy had done the arithmetic and drawn the conclusion. The excitement of discovery overcame her horror.

"It's hard to see how she could have," I said. "Are you sure there wasn't anything else around she could have climbed up on, like this chair? I'll check the police photos in any case."

"I'm positive about that. I thought she'd used the bed just as I had when I pulled her down." She shuddered at the thought of clasping the corpse to herself.

"Do you want to get anything while we're here?" I asked. She nodded. While she was collecting her things from the other bedroom, I explored the bathroom that the girls had shared. The drawers had the expected female stuff in them—multiple hairbrushes, toothbrushes, a loose tampon or two, various containers of makeup. The medicine cabinet had a few pill bottles whose labels indicated antibiotics, decongestants, something for diarrhea, and, pointedly, no steroids. The usage dates on most of the vials had expired. I looked in each one to make sure it contained what it said on the label. Each appeared to.

Lucy had an armload of clothes and was standing at the door to the bathroom. I asked, "Is there any other place where Judy might have kept pills?"

"No, I don't think so."

"Did she ever take steroids, possibly for some illness or injury?"

"Judy was healthy as a horse. She didn't even get PMS."

"Did she work out?"

"You mean with weights? No, she jogged and swam."

I couldn't think of anything else to do. In a minute we were outside, our faces less somber. The blue sky and bright late morning sun belied the horror of a few days ago. The scent of the Pacific floated in on a breeze.

I reminded Lucy about the whitening at the fingernail root. "Think hard. Could she be popping pills without your knowing it?"

"I don't think so. I knew Judy fairly well. There were some things about her undergraduate years at UCLA that she alluded to kind of vaguely but never spelled out. But not drugs, I'm sure of that."

"Did she have a family doctor?"

"Maybe back in L. A. Here we use the infirmary because it's free to students. I can't remember Judy ever going there, or maybe one time for a cold."

I changed the subject. I could check out the steroid business more carefully later. There are all sorts of tricks for getting information from a person's medical or pharmaceutical records. "Did you arrange something with Troy? I'd like to talk to him if I could."

"He said he'd meet us at noon at the co-op. We can walk over there as soon as I put my things away."

We were on our way shortly. Lucy led us unerringly through a maze of buildings and grounds. We entered the student union on one level, climbed up a flight of stairs, and navigated corridors past pool tables, video games, and food and drink machines. We finally arrived at the co-op, which was a large fast-food restaurant, a blend of Burger King, Taco Bell, and Pizza Hut, but with distinctly institutional odors. It was less crowded than I'd have expected, considering the noon hour. Lucy looked around briefly, spotted her quarry, and ten seconds later I found myself shaking hands with Troy Stanton.

Chapter 4

He reminded me of a young Harrison Ford. Not terribly handsome—
no Brad Pitt, he—but with rugged good looks. He was about five ten,
sandy brown hair, and an athletic build on the stocky side. His light
brown eyes darted about avoiding direct contact. For a strong man his
handshake was weak, perhaps in deference to my gender. He wore the
student standard issue of jeans, T-shirt, and running shoes. His only
jewelry was a stainless steel Timex. His demeanor was one of discomfort.

"Thanks for meeting with us," I said, after Lucy's brief introduction.
We all sat down around a table ostensibly wiped clean, but with stains
and graffiti still visible. I settled into my chair, crossed my legs, and
leaned forward. "I'm sorry about Judy. Lucy told me you used to date
her."

"That's right. For about a year and a half. I can't believe Akrich did
this to her."

"It was terrible," I agreed. "Would you've expected a reaction like
this from her?"

"Honestly, no. Judy was mostly cool-headed. I never thought she was
suicidal. But she suffered a shock that would flip anyone out. She must've
gone ballistic. But, anyway, why are we having this meeting? What's with
the investigator?"

The last question was directed toward Lucy, whom I had asked while
we were walking over not to reveal what we had discovered. Nonetheless,
she joined in with her opinion of the "suicide," and her reason for hiring
me, which I suppose she had to do. I did manage to catch her eye to
warn her off saying more, either about Charles's discovery or the results
of our measurements a half hour earlier. She took the hint and shut up,
but Troy could see the implications.

"Are you saying someone killed Judy?" he asked incredulously.

"Well, I suppose if she didn't kill herself, somebody must've done it,"
answered Lucy, with an accusatory tone that put me on edge. I wanted to
defuse the situation but I could sense matters reeling out of control.
Before I could think of what to say, Troy had replied sharply.

"I find that hard to believe. What a grotesque idea! And if you're
thinking I had anything to do with it, forget it. I may have argued with
her and said some things, but I was upset and angry at the time."

"Several times," interrupted Lucy.

"Okay, several times, but I still wouldn't harm her, or anybody for that matter. Anyway"—his voice cracked—"I loved Judy, and you know I loved her."

"And you weren't at her defense. Where were you?" continued Lucy in the same tone.

Troy's eyes flashed, but he didn't answer. Lucy was not helping the cause by grilling the boy. I finally managed to kick her under the table, and she went silent. I wanted information from Troy, not this anger that was boiling up in him.

I addressed Troy in my most soothing voice. "Nobody is accusing anyone of doing anything. Judy's manner of death is still unanswered, at least in my mind. I'm just trying to collect information. So let me ask you, do you know of anyone who might have wanted Judy dead, or would benefit from her death?"

He thought a moment, running a hand through his hair. "Not really. She has a half-brother but I don't think inheritance is at stake." He pondered for another moment—and I was glad to see he was cooling down. "She used to make allusions to a former lover she had at UCLA. 'He's a gangsta,' she'd say in a New Jersey accent. I always thought she was jerking me around. She knew I was a little jealous of her ex-lovers."

"Was he also jealous of her?" I asked. One could fill Arlington National Cemetery with the victims of people who were "a little jealous."

"Maybe. I don't know. I don't know a damn thing about him, not even his name."

I figured I could check this out later. Troy shifted in his chair and glanced at his watch.

"Look, I gotta run. I don't have to answer any more questions. Man, Lucy, I thought you were my friend." He got up to leave.

I stood up as well and said, "Would you let me know if you think of anything else?" I said, fishing out a business card. "I'd appreciate it."

"Yeah, sure." He took the card and sauntered off.

"I'm sorry. I got a little carried away," said Lucy. "It won't happen again. Anyway, Troy and I fight all the time. It'll all blow over in a day."

"Don't worry about it," I said. "If it's any comfort, I don't think he's telling everything he knows, and your point about his not being at the defense is worth looking into, leastwise if we can learn more about Judy's death."

"I'll get us some orange juice," said Lucy, hopping up. She returned with the drinks and we chatted until it was time for the next meeting. I followed Lucy out of the Student Union building, passing several buildings, including the library, until we reached Pearson Hall. We took a side entrance and climbed two flights of stairs to the third floor. Halfway down the hall was the office door of Professor Julius David Akrich.

The top half of the door was heavily frosted glass with the professor's name stenciled in two-inch high, black, glossy letters. Lucy knocked on the glass. I heard a chair creak, some footsteps, and the door opened.

"Lucy, how nice to see you." Professor Akrich then turned to me and held out his hand. "I'm Julius Akrich. Please come in." He ushered us into his office.

It felt like stepping into the curator's study at a museum of natural history. There were Native American artifacts everywhere, some mounted on the wall, some leaning against the wall, some on top of filing cabinets, and others lying about on the shelves of bookcases, mixed in with the books. There were elaborately painted masks, elegantly dressed dolls, bows, arrows, spears, headdresses, articles of clothing, small drums, and long, flute-shaped objects that appeared to be blowguns.

Stacks of books and journals covered the top of the professor's desk. A computer sat in the midst of this sea of paper. On a credenza off to the side was heaped more paperwork, and in its midst was some large object covered with a vinyl dust cover. The middle of the office was relatively free of clutter, containing instead a circle of several chairs, two of which we were invited to take; Akrich took another of the chairs for himself.

He was a portly man, pear-shaped, narrow in the shoulders, large in the waist. His hairline was ebbing, leaving behind a broad forehead. Thick glasses and an ample nose dominated a small, weak mouth and chin. A beard might have helped but he was clean-shaven. He was dressed in a rumpled suit, white shirt, and paisley necktie. Shoes that could have done with a polish completed the sartorial disaster.

"Lucy, my dear," he began mournfully, "I'm so, so sorry about what happened. It truly breaks my heart. Mrs. Akrich and I were up all night Friday after services. I felt so guilty, and poor Sylvia—well, Judy was like a daughter to her. Our rabbi tried to console us, but I know that I handled the whole business thoughtlessly. If only Judy were here, I'd beg her forgiveness."

Lucy retained perfect control, nodding and murmuring sympathetically while he spoke. When he had finished she said, "Professor Akrich, we both know that Judy was level-headed. She didn't get emotional over her work. She never acted impetuously."

"One of her many strong points," agreed Akrich. "She was always contemplative."

Lucy continued. "So I can't get over the feeling that she wouldn't kill herself. And if she did, I want to understand more about what happened, which is why I asked Ms. Jamison here to help me. She's a private investigator."

"I'm Dagny Jamison, Professor." I handed him a business card.

"Shouldn't any investigation be conducted by the authorities?" Akrich asked, a little less warmly.

"The coroner will determine whether further investigation by the police is warranted. If there's a 'questionable death' inquiry, I told Lucy I wouldn't take the case."

"And if there isn't?" said Akrich.

"Then I'll do what my client asks."

"Professor," said Lucy in a conciliatory tone, "it'll make me feel better to know I'm doing something about this dissonance between Judy's personality and the act of suicide. Haven't you always taught us to pursue and eliminate inconsistency in our work, and in our lives?"

"Yes, I suppose I have. If it will ease your passage through this unspeakable calamity, by all means." He turned to me. "Please, Miss Jamison, I shall endeavor to be as helpful as possible, consistent with the integrity of the department and the university."

"I don't have many questions, Professor, but I was wondering why you couldn't have told Judy in private about the problem with her dissertation."

"The answer is simple. I wasn't handed the material she plagiarized until the last moment."

"Would you mind telling us who gave it to you?"

"That I may not do until the university completes its own investigation."

"Why wasn't the plagiarism discovered sooner? Surely someone read and approved her dissertation?"

"Certainly. I read it. Her committee members read it. But the material she copied came from a little known journal that's been out of print for fifteen years. It's unfortunate, but nowadays there's so much scholarly work in our field that it's not always possible to read everything."

"Well, someone did," I said.

"Yes, someone did," he agreed, "and we couldn't grant a doctorate based on work we knew to be plagiarized. Obviously we had no way of knowing the disastrous consequences that would result, and I'm not responsible for those. But I am culpable for letting my indignation interfere with my sensitivities. I was terribly hurt that my student would commit such a breach of ethics. I wanted to castigate her with public exposure. I perceive now that I should have dismissed her from the room, canceled the defense, and offered explanations later. 'The moving finger writes, and having writ, moves on.'" He sighed, shaking his head sadly.

"Is there anything you can add? Something from her private life that you're aware of?"

"I'm sorry, but no, I am unable to provide you with any further information."

We sat in silence for a moment. I thought it was time to leave. I caught Lucy's eye. She said, still soothingly, "Dr. Akrich, thank you for seeing us. We won't take up any more of your time." I made nice-to-meet-you sounds and added my usual request to call me if he thought of something more. He opened the door for us and let us out into the hall, still maintaining his decorum.

"I would like to know what son-of-a-bitch, fuckwad gave Akrich that shit at the last moment," Lucy said fiercely as soon as we were out of earshot. I'll kill his ass, I'll cut his…" She stopped venting to let some people pass.

I took advantage of the pause to interject evenly, "How do you know it's a he?"

"A woman wouldn't do that to another woman," she snapped.

I didn't want to argue the point. She'd learn soon enough what women are capable of doing to other women. Her temper had ebbed by the time we got outside.

More people were on campus now, sitting in clumps in the grassy areas, or standing around talking. Others were walking this way or that, preoccupied with personal errands.

We were a couple of minutes into the trek back to my car when someone called out to Lucy. The voice was vaguely familiar, but the face I knew instantly. The young woman trotted over to us. "Yo, Sparky," said Lucy with delight. The two girls touched cheeks. Elaine Sparks looked at me and recognition dawned. "Dagny," she cried, and threw both arms around my neck. I returned the hug. I hadn't seen Sparky in years. She'd outgrown the teenage look I remembered, and had blossomed into an attractive young woman. She still had the long dark hair and dazzling green eyes, but the once sallow complexion and pudgy cheeks were now tanned and taut. She'd given up her cowboy boots for tennies, and of course jeans and a T-shirt. The T-shirt bore a picture of an endangered animal, the Tasmanian Devil.

"Sparky, you're looking terrific. How are you? How's life treating you? Have you been able to get on without, you know...?" She'd gone to live with an aunt during her rehab, since her parents were dead.

"I'm doin' fine. I mean, I miss my folks every day. I want to succeed for them and for me. I'm in school now—I guess you can see that—working on a degree in anthro. I may even go to grad school. Can you see me, ex-dope pusher, as a doctor?"

I could, and I said so.

"You know, Dagny, I owe all this to you," she said, taking in the campus with a sweep of her arm. "You showed me respect even though I was a punk and a druggie. So when you said you wouldn't turn me in if I went straight and kicked my habit, I knew I could do it. And when I kept my promise, you kept yours."

Sparky walked us back to my car, catching me up on the news, and giving Lucy sympathy and encouragement. She exaggerated my abilities in finding her parents' killer to the point where I jokingly told her that if she didn't quit I'd have to raise my rates and that would cost Lucy.

When I reached my car, I hugged the two girls goodbye. I told Lucy to call with any news, and promised I'd do the same. I drove back to Santa Barbara feeling melancholy about Judy. Counteracting that was the joy in seeing how well Sparky had turned out; I made a mental note to remember this transformation the next time I was feeling blue about my work.

I drove to the office. There was some mail on John's desk, courtesy of Celia May, an all-efficient secretary shared by several of the building's small businesses. The light on the answering machine was going blink-blink-blink, pause, blink-blink-blink, pause, which meant three messages. With John away, I was in charge. I put the mail in the in-box, grabbed a note pad, and played back the messages. The first one was a request for money from the Fraternal Order of Police. Back in North Carolina, it seemed the more I gave, the more they called, but being an ex-military cop, I was a sucker for it. They also gave me a sticker for my car with their logo on it, announcing to the world that I was a contributor. They admonished me that "the decal won't get you out of a ticket, ha, ha," but in truth it could, when embellished with courtesy and deference.

The second call was a hang-up, probably a telemarketer. The third call was from Charles. The lab reports were all negative. The coroner had signed off on suicide. And, could he take me out to dinner that evening?

We got back to John's place around eleven. We'd talked a lot of shop. We were both interested in each other's line of work. He was as interested in investigation as I was in pathology. We'd gotten intimate enough to exchange ages and hold hands briefly. He was six years older than I was—not the two I'd thought. We'd discussed our families, personal histories, education, sports, movies, and politics.

Charles had talked about what it was like to attend one of England's finest private schools—not all it's cracked up to be, according to him. He'd told me of his fellowship to Harvard Medical School, and what fine training he had received there. He'd been genuinely impressed with my career successes and sympathetic towards my failures. He'd given no hint that he found his work any more or less significant in the world than mine.

I'd wanted to tell him about my cancer and my fearful wait for five symptomless years. He was a medical doctor, after all, but I wasn't ready to do it.

I was, however, ready for a touch more intimacy, so I was scheming for a goodnight kiss as I put the key in the lock. The blink of the answering machine greeted us. One of John's girlfriends, no doubt. I nearly let it go, but it could be business. I gave in and pressed the play button. A highly agitated Lucy blared out of the speaker. Akrich had revealed that it was Troy who'd handed him the photocopies minutes before Judy's defense. Troy was last seen loading a duffel bag into his car and driving off.

Chapter 5

The sound of tires on gravel awakened me. I'd been asleep in the cramped front seat of a small Honda. My eyes were dry and sticky. One arm was numb and the rest of my joints ached from the confinement of the long overnight drive. I blinked hard a few times to adjust to the brightness of an early morning sky, and to squeeze up some moisture.

We were in a parking lot near a one-story structure of glass and wood. Its front and rear walls were mostly glass, exposing the interior and making the building seem transparent. Within, some people were sitting at tables, while others were up and moving around. A red neon sign in Greek-styled letters proclaimed the establishment to be The Pantheon.

"Good morning," sang a pleasant voice. "What do you say to a hot drink and a bite to eat?"

"Where are we?" I croaked. I focused on the driver who'd turned off the engine and was withdrawing the keys from the ignition. I twisted the rear view mirror for a look at myself and immediately wished I hadn't.

"Don't worry about it," said the voice again. "Most of the people here have been tripping for days. You'll do fine. Welcome to The Pantheon."

"Why do you look as though you just stepped out of a L'Oréal commercial? Am I mistaken, or have you been up driving all night?"

"Oh, I'm used to it. All-nighters are part and parcel of my work."

"Mine, too," I said, "except I look like shit when I do it."

"C'mon, Dagny, The Pantheon has its own coffee bean designed with the espresso purpose of bringing Quaalude freaks back to life," grinned the voice.

"I am not a Quaalude freak," I grumbled.

Lucy was irrepressible, and I couldn't help smiling as I eased out of her Honda, planted both feet solidly on the ground, and drew a breath of sweet and salty morning air deep into my lungs. I did a 360 to take in my surroundings. The restaurant was perched on a ledge overlooking the Pacific Ocean. The highway sign at the entrance to the parking lot answered my earlier question: The Pantheon, Big Sur, California.

Lucy led us across the parking lot to the entrance, where the hostess who greeted us was adorned with rings in her eyebrows, tongue, lower lip, and navel. She was a pretty girl, cheerful as a robin, and no more than sixteen years old. She led us to a table by a window overlooking the ocean and left us a single menu.

"Here, go ahead," said Lucy politely, pushing the menu towards me.

I opened it upside down in front of me and pushed it to the middle of the table. "I like to practice reading upside down—it's a useful skill in my profession."

"That figures," said Lucy.

I ordered the coffee that Lucy recommended, and passed over the granola with fruit that I knew I should have, in favor of bacon, eggs, hash browns, and white toast. There are times when I need grease to sustain me.

"They shouldn't serve that shit here," admonished Lucy. "This is supposed to be a health food restaurant."

I ignored her remark. Age has its privileges, and I was a good four or five years older than Lucy. The coffee, thank goodness, arrived quickly. I fortified it with three packets of sugar and took a sip. My heart revved into second gear and I could feel my blood begin to circulate as I came fully awake. After several more sips I became aware of a full bladder. Lucy pointed out the restrooms.

I regarded the two doors, each adorned with an abstract icon that was supposed to distinguish boys from girls, but I found myself baffled. "Let's hope this is the ladies' room," I murmured, and grabbed an arbitrary knob. I was about to turn it when the other door opened from the inside. This should have settled the matter, but I found myself unable to guess the gender of the person who emerged. I decided to stay with my original choice. A quick scan failed to turn up a urinal, so I entered one of the stalls. Sitting on a john will every so often invoke deep thoughts in me. On this occasion all I could muster was, "What in hell am I doing here?"

Only a work-shift ago I was having dinner with Charles, feeling romantic and sexy for the first time in ages. I could deal with Lucy's phone message in the morning. What was I supposed to do at midnight? Go chasing after Troy? Lucy's personal phone call five minutes after I'd lured Charles into my lair was not, however, so easily put aside.

"Dagny, at last. I've been calling you every five minutes for I don't know how long. Did you get my message?" I indicated that I had. "I know where he's going. We have to go after him!"

Reminders of the hour, reminders that I preferred to work alone, reminders that Troy was not a fugitive requiring immediate pursuit: none of these fazed Lucy. "C'mon, Dagny, I thought you were working for me. He's either in Big Sur or at U.C. Santa Cruz. I have to know his part in Judy's death. I can't sleep while he gets away."

In the end I gave in. Lucy insisted on driving. I gave her directions to my place and she gave me half an hour to get ready.

Charles had followed the conversation from my side and was eyeing the door. I made him sit down on the sofa and plunked myself onto his lap, facing him, by straddling his legs with mine, and putting my hands behind his neck for balance. (I was *not* wearing a mini-skirt.) This he seemed to find pleasurable. I took the opportunity to get the first kiss behind us, which, judging by the distinctly non-British sound he made deep in his throat, he also found pleasurable. "This is a down payment," I gasped. "The first installment will follow when I get back."

Charles found this, too, agreeable. He actually said "Cheerio" as he was leaving and I couldn't suppress a chuckle. I followed that up immediately with one last kiss to show that I found him charming, not silly.

The door to the restroom opened as I was pulling up my jeans. Masculine, feminine, or neuter, I wondered as I emerged from the stall. Definitely feminine. It was Lucy. "You figured it out," she said.

"The urinal was a dead giveaway,"

"What urinal?" She looked around.

"Precisely," I said as I vacated the room.

Breakfast came piping hot, perfectly cooked. I dug in while Lucy outlined her plan for locating Troy. "I'll find him, you grill him," she said.

"My clients usually hire me to do the finding so they can do the grilling."

"I know I can find him," said Lucy. "But you'll know the kinds of questions to ask when we catch up with him. There's more to this than an ex-lover's revenge. Troy is no angel, but—" She broke off and thought for a moment, chewing her lip. "I mean, was there any sign of guilt when we talked to him yesterday? No. Arrogance maybe, but not guilt. Am I right, Dagny? You P.I.s, you're good judges of people."

I had to agree with Lucy's take on Troy, though I still believed he was concealing something. In any event, my curiosity was still piqued. First, I had real concerns about the circumstances of Judy's death. Second, why did Troy wait to be fingered before he fled? Surely he knew that his role in the affair would come out sooner or later, so if he was going to hide until matters cooled, why not slip away sooner? He had the whole weekend to affect his escape.

We finished breakfast and lingered over our respective drinks: my second cup of coffee, Lucy's herbal tea. Day was fully broken. In the

Pacific, blue was winning over green as the sky reflected off the water, urged on by the bright morning sunshine.

I paid the check, parrying Lucy's protestations by reminding her that these were expenses, and she'd eventually get the bill. We stepped out into a morning awash in sunshine. As I reached into my handbag for my sunglasses, my fingers touched my semi-automatic handgun. It seemed out of place in Big Sur, but I had promised my brother never to leave home without it when on business.

The rest of the caffeine kicked in as we walked to the car and I was beginning to feel positively jaunty. Lucy got on Route 1 heading south, back the way we had come.

"Isn't Santa Cruz the other way?" I asked.

"Yeah, but I want to check out SHR in case he stopped there to crash."

"SHR?"

"It's only six miles or so back this way. Troy used to work there and he may have stopped to visit, or even to stay."

"What is it, though? I mean what do the letters stand for?"

"Oh, sorry. I just assume everybody knows of the Saint Helena Retreat in Big Sur. People come from all over to take classes in Gestalt psychology, meditation, yoga and the like. Corporations send executives there for management training and team-building. They're a self-contained institute with a hotel, eating facilities and a permanent staff ranging from doctors of psychology to dishwashers. Lot of druggies take the menial jobs in exchange for room and board and enough cash to buy pot, acid, ecstasy, or whatever floats their boat. If you're gonna spend your life stoned, SHR's a great place to do it."

The retreat was perched above the most breathtaking stretch of Pacific coastline I'd ever seen. The ocean was a deep, rolling blue that stretched unbroken to the horizon. The beaches in both directions were dotted with craggy outcrops, streaked with patches of different colors undulating under the warmth of the morning sun.

"By noon it'll all look different, though still awesome. At sunset it's another show altogether," said Lucy, sharing my wonder. "But to business." She pointed the Honda down a narrow dirt road, carefully executing several hairpin turns. We debouched into a broad parking lot with the ocean on one side and various buildings on the other three sides. "We'll try the restaurant first. That's where Troy used to work. He probably still has some friends there."

We entered a one story, flat-roofed building of slate gray. The staff was clearing away breakfast. A few late starters were scattered about the large, plain dining room nursing their last cup of coffee. Lucy spotted a young staffer she either knew or was about to charm the socks off of. I tagged along, imagining the room full of corporate executives, housewives learning yoga, ex-hippies taking a review course in transcendental meditation, all forced to rub elbows at the long Formica tables where family-style eating was compulsory.

Lucy didn't know the young man but his socks were off in a moment. Yes, he'd heard of Troy Stanton. No, Troy hadn't been here. Yes, he was positive because in the communal living arrangements, no one came or went without everyone knowing about it.

Oh, and he was about to go off duty and would Lucy and her friend (me) like to bathe in the hot springs, no clothes required. Lucy said she couldn't think of anything we'd rather do if only Troy could join us, because her friend (still me) was in love with him. This last ploy, designed to squeeze out any forgotten bits of information, yielded nothing. We left the young man to contemplate us naked in the hot springs as best he could, though I'm sure his imagination would have fallen short in my case.

"He's got to be at Santa Cruz," said Lucy, meaning the University of California at Santa Cruz.

We continued our northerly trip on Route 1. The scenery was to die for. We skirted the cliffs overlooking the California Sea Otter Refuge, an expanse of Pacific now punctuated by whitecaps, making the colors yet more vivid by contrast. Our route took us by Castroville—the self-proclaimed artichoke capital of the world—and finally put us in Santa Cruz, a Spanish-founded mission town perched on the northern arc of Monterey Bay.

Lucy drove us through the city, then north into the hills. UCSC lies amid a redwood forest. The architects had taken great care to preserve the natural setting and, despite the necessity for roads and buildings, they had never failed to emphasize the primacy of the wooded areas.

We found some metered parking by a building with the uninspired name of Social Sciences I. Lucy wanted to check out the anthropology departmental office. We climbed to the second floor, walked down a long hallway with various artifacts displayed in floor-to-ceiling glass cases, and passed through a set of double doors at the hallway's end.

A squeal of recognition greeted Lucy from behind a desk on which rested the nameplate of Annabelle Hinton. I was introduced to "Annie" after the girls had gone through the requisite cheek touching. Annie hadn't seen Troy but knew he was on campus somewhere. "He bummed a couple of joints off o' Doug Steele," she'd heard, "and is going to crash at his place over in Grad Student Housing."

Annie had heard about Judy, as had the whole department, but no one, apparently, was aware of Troy's role. Lucy didn't let on what she knew. She explained to Annie that she'd hired me to investigate the circumstances surrounding Judy's death, and that I insisted on interviewing Troy. She evaded Annie's questions deftly. "I just want to know more about what was going on in Judy's head before I let her go," explained Lucy.

The girls hugged goodbye. We retrieved the Honda and headed west across campus to Graduate Student Housing. Lucy parked in front of a one-story stucco-fronted apartment building. "We need to find apartment 6A," she said. Its entrance was off to the side. Some knocking roused a sleepy young man dressed only in a pair of jeans. Doug Steele recognized Lucy and invited us in. Lucy got right to the point.

"Yeah, he's here. That's his stuff," said Doug, flicking a glance at a duffel bag propped against a wall. "He seemed real upset—I guess about Judy. But he seemed anxious, too. He didn't want to talk, just asked me for a little dope. Said he wanted to sit in Sleepless Hollow and think things out."

"In where?" I interjected.

"Never mind," said Lucy. "I'll explain in a minute. How long ago did he leave?"

"About an hour ago."

"We'll go look for him. When he gets back will you tell him I need to talk with him. He'll understand." Doug accepted this without any show of curiosity.

"Are you in the mood for a hike?" asked Lucy. There was a pervasive hint of woodiness in the air that was invigorating. A hike didn't seem like a bad idea. I assumed it would be in search of Troy.

"Sure, let's go."

Within ten minutes we were among the redwoods on a well-worn footpath. "Sleepless Hollow is a clearing overlooking a stream," Lucy explained. "Kids gather there to smoke dope, drop acid, or munch buttons, or do 'shrooms."

"I thought ecstasy was all the rage nowadays," I said.

"It's all the *rave*," said Lucy. "Ecstasy is for partying all night. It makes people real social. The all-night ecstasy parties are called raves. The psychedelics like LSD are more suited for all-night contemplation, and that's what they do in Sleepless Hollow."

I knew that acid meant LSD. I learned that "buttons" were pieces of peyote cactus containing the psychedelic drug mescaline. "'Shrooms" is short for mushrooms and refers to a species of the fungus containing another psychedelic drug, psilocybin. The "Sleepless," Lucy explained, is for the insomnia that accompanies the hallucinogenic drug trips, which may last 24 hours. I learned a lot about drugs that summer, and this was my first lesson.

As we trudged deeper into the woods a silence descended. We could no longer hear the sounds of campus life. Only the desultory chirping of a lethargic forest bird, and our own footsteps, broke the perfect stillness of the afternoon. The long shadows cast by the tall trees hinted at an impending twilight, though several hours of daylight remained. Lucy had unconsciously moved closer to me. The vast height of the redwoods now felt oppressive rather than wondrous.

"The trail will cross a stream," said Lucy, "then there's a narrow path off to the right that leads to the hollow." We were descending and the trail soon bottomed out at a little gully with a few scattered puddles. As I picked my way around the water, my peripheral vision caught a movement. I paused to look up the gully to my right.

I'd have made a lousy dentist. They never say things like *uh-oh* or *oops*. My uh-oh burst forth spontaneously. Lucy stopped suddenly, grabbed my arm for support, and looked in the direction of my stare. "Oh my God," she whispered, "Oh dear sweet Jesus, not again."

Fifty yards away, from a log across the gully, hung a body, the feet turning slowly, very slowly, like two unhurried compass needles. "Troy Stanton, I presume," I muttered under my breath. I broke into a run.

Chapter 6

I sprinted down the gully to the body. I wrapped my arms around his legs just above the knees and lifted with all my might to take weight off his neck. I yelled to Lucy to get the rope. She scrambled up the bank, crawled out on the log above me, and began frantically to untie the knots. I willed her to hurry. Finally the knots came undone. She unlooped the rope from around the log. At the last loop, the rope slipped and Troy's body slid into my arms. I let him down as gently as my strength would allow, guiding his head to a dry patch of the streambed.

It was my turn to undo knots. The rope was not as deeply embedded in the flesh as I had thought it might be. I got the knots out and freed the rope. On my hands and knees, I straightened his head and tilted it upward to begin resuscitation. But his neck and head didn't move the way they should have. I let him go. I saw now why there wasn't the typical bloating of a person who dies from the strangulation of hanging. His neck was broken. He'd apparently jumped off the log, suffering the less agonizing death of a snapped spinal cord.

Lucy was standing beside me. "He's dead, isn't he?" It was a rhetorical question.

"His neck's broken. Wait here, I want to have a look around." Lucy turned away from the body, sank down on her knees, crossed herself, and began to sob.

I walked some yards up the creek, stepping around the various pools of water that remained from the last time it had flowed. I didn't find anything of interest. I repeated the venture downstream, walking past Lucy who was still weeping over Troy. While I knew there had been no love lost between them, this was a heart-rending sight.

I climbed up to where Troy had spent the last moments of his life. I didn't know what I was looking for. Perhaps some clue as to how those moments had passed, or some sign that other people had been present. Sleepless Hollow was little more than a clearing among the redwoods, to which logs had been dragged for seating. Remarkably, the container-empties, paper trash, and other jetsam that often litter the sites of youthful convocations were absent. These were environmentally sensitive druggies.

I found no clues. The ground was too well trafficked to pick out Troy's footprints, or to determine if anybody had been with him. There was no suicide note, though it occurred to me that I ought to search the body.

With this in mind, I rejoined Lucy who was sitting cross-legged, and dry-eyed now, by the corpse. "What are you doing?" she exclaimed, as I dug my hands into Troy's pockets.

"Looking for a suicide note," I replied.

But there was none. I found the usual things: wallet, keys, knife. The contents of the wallet were unremarkable. I put everything back. The investigators would repeat this activity and I preferred that they should remain unaware of my having rifled through the corpse's trouser pockets.

We jogged out of the woods without encountering a soul. I remembered passing some greenhouses about a half-mile from the trail entrance. We continued our jog, Lucy loping easily alongside me. In a small, temporary building beside the greenhouses, we found an office with a couple of students. We explained briefly and let them give directions to the 911 operator.

"I hope you're up to answering a lot of questions," I told Lucy.

"I've been there before, remember? I can handle it." She bit her lower lip. She must have been without sleep for 25 or 30 hours by now, but it didn't show. Lucy was resilient and it would serve her well.

I was also thinking about Judy's hanging. I could explain the discrepancy of the position of the bed and the length of the rope. Judy might have first moved the bed under the light fixture, affixed the rope, and kicked the bed back as she hung dying. Or the bed may have moved under the impetus of Lucy's rescue attempt. It was possible that the EMTs had pushed it back when treating Judy. Even the cops might unwittingly have moved it.

No, it wasn't the bed that bothered me so much as the white lines. In that, we had the coincidence of the altered fingernails, with no apparent cause, occurring at the time of a suspicious death. Coincidence is a red flag for me. What her fingernails had to do with her death, I hadn't a clue. That's what kept me intrigued.

"What are you thinking about?" said Lucy. "You look a million miles away." From a distance the sounds of sirens floated over the redwoods. They would get louder soon.

"I was thinking about Judy's fingernails. I was thinking that if it weren't for them, I'd let it go as a tragic double suicide. Boy wrongs girl. Girl kills self. Boy overcome with grief and guilt. Boy kills self."

"What about: boy kills girl; boy overcome with fear and guilt; boy kills self same way he killed girl," rejoined Lucy.

"What about: girl kills self; unknown avenger kills boy in same style," I said, abashed at the unintended coldness of my voice.

"What about: two young people with their whole lives ahead of them murdered because, because…I don't know why." Lucy's eyes filled with tears.

I took a deep breath. "I'm sorry. That was insensitive. I don't mean to be." I reached out to hug Lucy and we held each other until the black wave of despair that hovered over us passed.

"Let me go think about this," I said. I walked through the office out the back door. In front of me was the entrance to one of the greenhouses. I slipped under the plastic flap. It was like a North Carolina summer inside, hot and steamy. I walked slowly down a leafy aisle trying to gather my thoughts. Thoughts, like cats, are difficult to herd. I grabbed a stray one anyway. It was about Charles. Not a lusty thought, but a desire for Charles to examine Troy's body.

The sound of the sirens had peaked and was rapidly winding down. I hurried back to meet the onslaught. We led the various EMT and law enforcement personnel back to "Death Valley," as I had mentally rechristened Sleepless Hollow. Troy had indeed died of a broken neck caused by hanging. Easy as falling off a log, I thought bitterly.

I answered every question forthrightly. I didn't bridle at my interrogator's transparent ploy of asking the same question in ten different ways to check my consistency. My patience paid off when I asked where Troy's body would be taken. An officer pointed out an official from the Santa Clara County Coroner's office, who gave me the pertinent names and phone numbers.

It was dusk by the time they had finished. A goodly crowd had assembled. Eventually all but a couple of campus cops departed. They stayed to answer questions from the shocked and dismayed crowd of students. These cops really were connected to the community. Perhaps it's easier within the confines of a college campus than on the city streets.

Exhaustion finally caught up with Lucy. She was emotionally and physically drained, a picture of misery. I led her to the car and helped her into the passenger seat. She gave me a wan smile, leaned back, and closed her eyes. With Lucy settled, I got out my flip-phone and punched in Charles's number at home. He picked up on the second ring. "Hi, it's Dagny." I explained what had happened. He was warm and concerned and sympathetic, and I needed that. It bolstered my own sagging spirits. "Do you think they'll let you take a look at Troy? Are medical examiners territorial?"

"Not usually. I'll call them straightaway. I'm going to ask them not to refrigerate the corpse. I want to check the fingernails."

"Will the method of death have any effect? He didn't strangle; his neck was broken."

"I shouldn't think so. When are you coming back?"

"I'm feeling okay to drive. If we take the 101, it'll take about five hours. That'll put us in around two a.m. I'll call you at work in the morning, if that's all right."

"You'd better have done. Don't drive if you're too tired."

"Okay, I won't. I'll call you in the morning from wherever."

I got back in the car on the driver's side. Lucy had tilted back the passenger seat and was sound asleep. She'd had the presence of mind to leave the keys in the ignition. We left our names, ranks, and serial numbers with the cops. There was no need to remain in Santa Cruz. I gassed up in the city and made the 300-mile drive in just under five hours. Drowsiness hadn't been a problem. There was plenty to think about.

One thing I decided to do was to interview Judy's father in Beverly Hills. He might know something that would shed some light on the deaths. I particularly wanted to know about the "gangsta" boyfriend. I knew something about the L.A. Mafia. In one of his early cases, my brother John had fingered the murderer of a don's fiancée. Retribution had been swift and sure, leaving John a bit queasy about seeing the justice system circumvented. Troy's death might be a similar act of vengeance. It wasn't a gangland modus operandi, but it had a certain eye-for-an-eye flavor to it that might have appealed to an overlord.

I also decided that if Troy's death turned out to be a suicide beyond reasonable doubt, I would drop the case, Lucy not withstanding.

Lucy awakened around Santa Maria. She spent most of the last hour staring glumly into the darkness. I told her I wanted her permission to talk with Judy's father. She brightened momentarily. "I'll give you his number," she said. "He was in Santa Barbara today, I mean yesterday, to claim the body. Let me call first. I don't know how he'll feel. Would you rather have your daughter commit suicide or be murdered? Some choice!"

I drove directly to John's house. "Are you okay? Do you want to sleep here?" I asked Lucy. She said she'd prefer to go back to the Worthingtons, and slipped over into the driver's seat as I got out. "I'll call you when I get up, then," I said.

I walked unsteadily to the front door, let myself in, and debated briefly whether to shower or crash immediately. Grime was the final arbiter. I showered, brushed my teeth, wrapped myself, still wet, in a terrycloth quilt, fell into bed, and slept dreamlessly.

The phone woke me at the decent hour of 9:30. "Dagny, Charles here."

I murmured a good morning.

"I'll be in the laboratory until this afternoon. I want to let you know what's happening. I guess you got home safely."

"No sweat. I was pretty wired. What's up?"

"I called the Santa Clara County medical examiner. Turns out I know the chap slightly, a Dr. Bob Peters. We met at a conference last year. I explained as much as I knew. He was intrigued. He agreed to let the body cook and suggested I come up and we'd autopsy together on Monday."

"You'd have to take Monday off. Do you mind?" I was being polite. I was glad Charles could be there.

"Not a bit. I've some holiday due me. I've actually been thinking of visiting San Francisco one weekend."

"You should," I agreed, and a thought popped into my head. Before I could decide what to do with it, Charles continued.

"I don't suppose you'd want to show me around, would you?"

I wasn't aware of the telepathic capabilities of the telephone network. Most convenient, leastwise in this case, for I might have lost my nerve. I forced myself not to sound too eager. "I've got to drive down to L.A. today to interview Judy's father. If I get that out of the way, I guess I could leave tomorrow."

"Wonderful! I'm glad you're going with me. I'll arrange to take holiday Friday and Monday. Would you ring me when you're back from L.A.?"

I said I would. I clicked the phone off, then on, and punched in the Worthington's number. Ernie answered. I identified myself and asked to speak with Lucy.

"I called Mr. Raskin half an hour ago," said Lucy, when she got on the line. "He's pretty upset. He thinks the cops ought to investigate if there's anything suspicious. He may give you a hard time."

"Did he agree to see me?" I was half hoping he wouldn't. Interviewing a grieving parent even before the child is laid to rest ranks right up there with bamboo splinters under the fingernails. And didn't I remember Lucy saying that he'd lost his second wife under similar circumstances?

Lucy said, "I told him the cops wouldn't follow up based on my suspicions, but that you would. I think he'll see you because of my friendship with Judy."

I got Raskin's address and phone number from Lucy, who promised to call ahead to tell him what time to expect me. I'd have to stop by the office for an hour to fend off any pressing matters. I'd get to Beverly Hills by around one in the afternoon.

There is no freeway to Beverly Hills. Maybe that's why it's so exclusive. If you come in on the 101, the best route is to take the 405— the San Diego Freeway—across the Santa Monica Mountains to Sunset Boulevard, and then wind east on Sunset with the estates of Bel Air on the left and UCLA on the right until you finally reach the northwest side of Beverly Hills.

On various corners you can purchase "Maps to Stars' Homes" for a self-tour of where the rich and famous reside. One nearly expects to encounter Matt Dillon or Cameron Diaz, live, crossing the street. No particular structure makes Beverly Hills world famous. No Taj Mahal or Eiffel Tower. Just a lot of multimillion-dollar homes on meticulously tended grounds, block after block. Raskin's address was on Cardinal Drive, one of many estate-lined streets that run between Sunset Boulevard and Santa Monica Boulevard. The house number indicated a location closer to Sunset, and, as it was an odd number, on the west side of the street.

I turned onto Cardinal and crept along until I found the right address. A circular drive looped through the front lawn, with a spur going around back for deliveries and domestic service. I parked near the front door, trusting that the Taurus would not burp any drops of black oil onto the spotless driveway.

A large brass knocker turned out to be purely decorative. I rang the doorbell. I heard sounds from within, and a few seconds later the door opened to reveal a fiftyish man in sandals, shorts, and a polo shirt, clearly not the butler. "Mr. Raskin?" I inquired. "I'm Dagny Jamison."

"I'm Bill Raskin. Please come in," he said, extending a hand. The foyer was large enough to hold a grand piano. In one corner, under a staircase, was a small botanical garden. In another corner was a curved love seat, situated perfectly for observing the art on the opposite wall.

As we entered the main part of the house, a man around Charles's age joined us. Raskin introduced him as "my son, Bill." I assumed that he was Judy's half-brother from Houston. "We can sit and talk in the lounge," said the senior Raskin. He led the way past the conservatory, the billiard room, the library, the study, and other such rooms found in your average Beverly Hills home. Here, one might have a game of Clue with real rooms, real people, and, as I glimpsed a pair of heavy brass candlesticks, real weapons.

Soft drinks had been set out, along with some snack foods, in anticipation of my visit. I was offered a chair near the refreshments, and took a Coke when asked to help myself. The others did the same and we all popped the tops of the cans at the same time and poured the contents with exaggerated deliberateness into the chilled glasses that were also provided.

Bill Senior was a handsome man—lean, energetic, and giving the impression of a coiled spring. Only streaks of gray in the hair and crinkles about the eyes suggested late rather than early fifties. Bill Junior had not inherited his father's aquiline nose, high cheekbones, or limpid brown eyes. He must have taken more after his mother.

Before our silence became awkward, Bill Senior began. "This is a hard time for us, as I'm sure you appreciate, Ms. Jamison. I don't understand why a private investigator would concern him…, uh, herself in a death that didn't interest the police. And particularly, if I may say so, one about my daughter's age who might pass more easily for a fashion model than a detective."

"Thank you for the compliment," I said, wondering how the job market was for one-breasted models; maybe not too bad, there being tens of thousands of women in a similar state. "I've had my California P.I. license for five years. I was in the military police in the service, I have a degree from UCLA, and I have my own practice in Raleigh, North Carolina. In my role today I represent Jamison and Jamison, a private investigation firm in Santa Barbara that's a respected, professional organization."

I was riding way too high on my horse and disregarding wisdom learned from my dogs: avoid biting when a simple growl will do. I was worn and weary from the events of the past two days, and this house of misery weighed heavily on me. Tactlessness was the result.

Raskin raised his hands in a mock pose of surrender. "I didn't mean to offend, and I'm not making a pass. Lucy explained her side of it, and I accept that for now. How can we help you?"

I expressed sympathy for their loss. I apologized for appearing at a time when Judy's funeral was uppermost in their minds. I asked questions that would encourage them to talk about Judy. Bill Senior did most of the talking, with Junior nodding in agreement from time to time. Both men controlled their grief, which took a great effort on the part of Senior. Junior's presence, I sensed, owed more to filial duty than to any strong affection for his dead half-sister. The second wife, Judy's mother, never came up in the conversation.

When both men had relaxed, I cut to the quick of my visit. "Who might benefit from Judy's death?" I asked. Junior stirred uneasily. Eventually, *he* would, but not soon, I judged.

In answer to my question, Bill Senior handed me some papers that had been lying on the table beside him. "Judy, Troy Stanton, and three other people took out a twenty-five-year lease on a gold mine. They formed a partnership. If a partner dies, the surviving partners inherit. It's all in these papers, signed and legal, near as I can tell."

My jaw dropped; my eyebrows rose. That's what I love about this business. You go from zero to warp speed faster than you can say Millennium Falcon. I struck gold with this gold mine, for here indeed was the missing motive, a motive universally acknowledged: greed.

Chapter 7

I had trouble believing my daughter's suicide, continued Raskin. "I don't want to air family laundry, but her mother died in a similar way. How can such a thing happen twice in a man's life? What kind of a God overlooks these hideous affairs? I'd give all this"—he swept his arms—"to the next person through my front door if it would undo the horror." He paused to regain his composure. Junior looked shocked.

He began again, more deliberately. "My conversation with Lucy fed my disbelief. Dead is dead, I suppose, but I didn't want her to have died out of misery, as her mother had. I thought she was…I wanted her to be a happy person, not one who'd take her own life. I tried to think of why anyone would want her dead. A lovers' quarrel turned violent was my first thought. I met Troy Stanton several times. How can you tell if someone's capable of violence?"

His misery was now undiluted by attempts at composure. "Now Troy's dead," he continued, his voice cracking, "and I don't know what that has to do with Judy. I thought of other relationships she'd had, whether they had ended acrimoniously. I know she dated an older man for a while when she was at UCLA. She teased me once or twice, saying she liked older men because they reminded her of me. She never brought him home. I'm not sure I ever knew his name. Did you, Bill?" he asked. He lowered his head, squeezed his eyes, and wiped them. Junior had to switch his head motions from nodding agreement to a quick shake to indicate that he didn't know the name.

The older man was probably the "gangsta." If it proved to be necessary, I felt sure I could discover his identity, if only by going through Judy's personal effects at a later, more appropriate time.

Bill Senior continued, "Then I remembered the gold mine. A couple of years ago—the exact date's on the paperwork—Judy told me she wanted to invest in a gold mine. It'd been worked to the point of unprofitability, but new technology might improve future yields. But the real reason she wanted to do it wasn't for the money, she said. One of the partners was a high-ranking Churok Indian. She felt the partnership would cement her ties with him. He was helping her with her research."

"Who were the other two?"

"A married couple. They're in Guatemala, helping poor farmers through one of those new age cultist churches. Judy knew them from school. They bought a forty percent interest and made a deal with God,

Judy told me: any money earned from the gold mine would be donated to the church."

"Do they ever come back here?" I asked.

"Not that I know of," said Bill, "but then I wouldn't have any reason to know. I never met them."

"Does the mine make any money?"

"I doubt it. When they closed the deal two years ago, the five of them went up to the Churok Reservation and camped out by the mine. There was a ceremony led by the Churok partner to coax the earth gods into giving up their treasure. I remember Judy being excited by it. She said it deepened her knowledge of the ritual language. Troy was enthusiastic for a different reason. He thought they could reopen the mine and make a killing."

I asked to borrow the papers. They'd have the location of the mine and the names and addresses of the partners. With that information, I could track down the two in Guatemala. I could also find both the gold mine and the Churok partner, who might be glad to see me when I told him he now had a third interest in a gold mine instead of a fifth. I promised to make copies right away and return the originals by registered mail. Junior put on a disapproving air but said nothing.

I had one more loose end to clear up before driving back. "Did Judy use a pharmacy down here?" I asked her father.

"Yes, the one on Little Santa Monica. Kirk's Pharmacy, it's called. Why?"

"I'd like to find out what medications she was taking, if any."

"They won't tell you. They wouldn't even tell me if I were to ask. Nobody's entitled to her medical records without a subpoena."

"That's okay. It's not important. If you think of anything, would you call me?" I handed each man a business card. They both showed me to the door. As I walked to my car I turned for a final wave goodbye. Bill Senior was looking thoughtful as he fingered my card. Bill Junior looked relieved.

I completed the semicircle back to Cardinal Drive. I turned right in the direction of what the locals called Little Santa Monica, a spur of the same Santa Monica Boulevard that takes one to Santa Monica Beach. I parked by the Exxon station at the corner of Little Santa Monica and Cardinal. A bunch of kids just out of school jostled noisily by, boys in one group, girls tagging behind in the other. The red and yellow sign of Kirk's Pharmacy was in view a block and a half away to the east. On my cell phone, I got Kirk's number from directory assistance and had it dialed automatically. I asked for the pharmacy.

Charles had given me a crash course in anabolic steroids, which are synthetic male sex hormones. Used legitimately, Nandrolex may be part of a chemotherapy treatment for breast cancer. (It wasn't part of my regimen, however.) Used illegitimately, it's favored by athletes of both sexes, because it promotes muscle growth, reduces muscle recovery time after exercise, and decreases healing time after muscle injury.

Nandrolex is a popular steroid for "pyramiding," Charles had explained. The athlete uses increasing amounts of the drug over a six-to-ten-week period. This is followed by decreasing amounts over an equal period of time, followed finally by a period of abstention called cycling. During cycling, workouts are tuned to achieve peak performance on the day of an event. Cycling also ensures that the athlete will pass any blood or urine tests.

There are also adverse reactions, or side effects. One of them, unique to Nandrolex, is the fingernail alteration that Charles had observed on Judy's corpse. More pernicious side effects in females are acne, unwanted hair growth, and irreversible clitoral enlargement. Charles had checked for these, and others, when he autopsied Judy. He had found nothing to accompany the white striations on her nails.

A female voice came on the line and said, "This is the pharmacist."

"This is Judy Raskin and I'd like to refill a prescription," I lied.

"Do you have the prescription number?" asked the pharmacist.

"I'm sorry, I don't have it with me. It's for Nandrolex. I'm sure I have several refills remaining. My oncologist suggested two more weeks of it."

"What was your name, again?" asked the voice in the telephone.

"Judy Raskin, R-a-s-k-i-n."

After a pause, "I'm sorry, Miss Raskin. I brought up your records and we don't have a prescription on file for Nandrolex. Are you sure you have the right pharmacy? This is Kirk's in Beverly Hills."

"I'm sure. I fill all my prescriptions there. My family lives just up the street on Cardinal. Would you check carefully? Could I have gotten the name of the steroid wrong?"

"Miss Raskin, I'd like to help. I don't show you ever having received Nandrolex or any of the Nandrolone anabolics. Who's your doctor? I'd be happy to call for you."

"No, it's okay. Maybe I did get the medicine elsewhere. Sometimes the drugs confuse me and I'm not feeling too well. I'll call the hospital. They'll know what to do."

I keyed off. Judy might have obtained steroids illegally, or even through some other licit channel, but why? She wasn't into bodybuilding, or athleticism of any kind, nor did she have any of the nasty conditions treated legitimately by anabolic steroids, such as anemia. There wasn't any point to a personal appearance in Kirk's so I headed back to Santa Barbara.

The fingernails remained a piece of the puzzle fitted to no other piece, but no clues were forthcoming from my interview with the Raskins. It was after six when I unlocked the front door of John's house. The one message on the machine was from John. He was still in Vegas with no immediate plans to return home. He left me a list of errands he needed done.

I felt as though I'd had a full day. I called Lucy and brought her up to date. She knew about the gold mine but didn't know about Troy's involvement. She was all for driving to the Churok reservation immediately, the previous day's exhausting trip seemingly forgotten.

I was adamant. I told her I would check out the gold mine myself and if possible, meet with the Churok partner. I also told her that Charles would assist in Troy's autopsy on Monday, so we'd find out about anything suspicious right away. I stated my unconditional refusal to spend another night in her car.

She started to argue but I interrupted her, then hesitated a moment. I don't often share the details of my private life with any but close friends, not that there'd been much to discuss lately. I was never half of a giggly twosome that went to the powder room to discuss our dates. But I'd met Charles and Lucy on the same day, met them both due to the circumstances of Judy's death. I felt enough of a bond among the three of us to tell Lucy of my plans to spend the weekend with Charles.

This took the fight out of her. She was genuinely pleased at my prospects for romance. I said I thought Charles wouldn't mind a side trip to the reservation. She made me promise to call her if anything came up, and wished me luck with Charles.

I couldn't reach Charles at home or work. I left messages on both machines. I felt like crashing but I wanted to talk to him first. I made myself a stiff gin and tonic. John keeps the gin in the freezer, making it as viscous as salad oil and perfect for mixing without ice. I decided to wile away the time until the phone rang by cooking dinner.

I brought out a skillet, sprayed it with Pam, and covered the bottom with olive oil. I threw in a couple of tablespoons of minced garlic, and while that was slowly heating, chopped an onion into small pieces, which I added to the pan, stirring slowly and basking in the aroma. That brings me to the point where I actually figure out what's for dinner.

Brother John often orders in from a nearby Chinese restaurant. The portions are huge and inevitably there are cartons of leftovers. I located one half full of kung pao chicken judging by the peanuts. It didn't have fuzz on it so I assumed it was safe to eat. Chinese food goes well in the Mediterranean base of onion, garlic, and oil. I tossed in the entire contents. For carbohydrates, I cut some leftover rice noodles into bite-sized lengths and added that to the already sizzling mélange.

I was feeling mellow, thanks to the gin, and ravenous, thanks to having forgotten to eat lunch. A B-52's CD sat on top of the stereo. I started it playing; it was music from my early teens, comfort sounds, chocolate for the ears, or maybe *rockolate* for this particular band. A half-filled bottle of a Washington State Chardonnay accompanied my meal, edging out a Merlot that remained in its holder.

I spent some time after dinner on my laptop updating the Judy Raskin case file. There was plenty to add, what with the gold mine revelation, and two new players: Bill Sr. and Bill Jr. I couldn't entirely eliminate the junior Raskin from having played some kind of role in his sister's demise. He didn't seem all that broken up about it, and eventually it would be to his benefit. I made a note about Judy's pharmacy record, and added to the "gangsta" information I already had.

That done, I turned on the tube and found a baseball game between the San Diego Padres and the Atlanta Braves. Greg Maddux had a no-hitter going and that kept me awake and interested for the two and a half innings it took for the phone to ring. I muted the game and picked up.

"Chaahles heah," said the voice at the other end.

"Daaagny heah," I mimicked.

"Dagny, I'm sorry I couldn't ring you back sooner. I just listened to your message. I worked late to clear up matters for my holiday. I hope we're going."

I recapped the day's events as quickly as I could. I finished by asking if he minded a detour to the Churok Reservation to check out the gold mine.

"I'd like that enormously," he said. "I don't feel as though I am experiencing as much American culture as I should."

"I hope this gold mine won't bore you."

"I can't think of anything I might do with you that'd be boring, Dagny."

"A fine piece of flattery, Dr. Clarke. Shall I pick you up around eight tomorrow morning?"

"Suppose I nip round to your place at eight? We ought to take my Subaru wagon. It has all-wheel drive and plenty of room for gear."

"You haven't been carting bodies in the back, have you?" I quipped.

"Just parts (paahts) of bodies, but not to worry—I'll give it a good wash. I'll see you tomorrow morning, Dagny. Have a good night."

I'd never taken a friend on an investigation. Summers, when I'm with John, we sometimes work together, but that's different. He's a P.I., too. Still, I reasoned, Charles is a medical examiner, akin in some ways to a P.I. I needed him to be at Troy's autopsy, and he might provide a lot of help at the gold mine.

I decided to pack. Right away I had a nice clothes/work clothes problem. San Francisco was a city where people dressed to the nines to go out. With my wardrobe, I couldn't dress to the ones. I'm the casual type. I did have one decent outfit that one of John's girlfriends once lent me and never took back. That would have to do. The rest—jeans, khakis, and a pair of slacks—would mix, if not match, with a couple of tops, jerseys and sweaters.

I checked my semi and placed it carefully at the bottom of my handbag. I keep it "topped off," that is, a bullet in the chamber and a full magazine, giving me one shot more than its specified capacity. That extra shot once saved my life, and took the life of Sparky's parents' killer, who had counted me out of bullets in a heart-stopping shootout. The Glock 26, or "baby Glock," has built-in features that prevent it from firing accidentally, so there's no actual safety to be set or unset. It is also light in weight—only 26 ounces when fully loaded and topped off. Part of the trip was business, and violence wasn't out of the question.

The next morning I awoke before the alarm clock went off. I had a double tingle of anticipation, one for the gold mine and one for Charles. An early morning jog energized me even more. I hummed through the post-run ablutions, rechecked my packing, and ate a light breakfast while studying a map of south central California.

By the time Charles 'nipped round,' I had planned our route. The Churok reservation lies along the Makrui River, north of Los Padres National Forest. As the crow flies, its nearest point is only fifty miles from Santa Barbara. The airborne traveler would overfly the forest with the San Rafael Wilderness on the west and the Dick Smith wilderness on the right. No such course is possible for the earthbound.

Our route was simple, but would take us three times the distance. We'd drive up the 101 to Santa Juanita where we'd pick up state highway 166 leading straight into Churok territory. I'd taken that precise route two years ago to depose a witness who was too ill to travel to court.

Charles was dressed in well-worn jeans, a baggy sweater that had also seen several tours of duty, and a pair of shit-kicker boots that were positively sexy. I threw my gear into the back seat of the Subaru and off we went. He'd brought two large Styrofoam cups of steaming coffee. Mine lasted till Las Cruces, where Charles suggested a pit stop, and in good time. Thank goodness he wasn't one of those men who assumed a woman's bladder was the size of Lake Michigan. He'd seen a few up close and personal in his daily work, I guess.

I retrieved the directions to the mine. We stayed on 166 until the reservation. Six miles past the 'Welcome to the Churok Nation' sign, we turned right on Cowslip Road. At first, the road was populated on both sides by small houses on large tracts of land, four or five to the mile. The houses became even farther apart as we drove south toward the forest. The road began to climb, and within a mile the pavement ended. We stopped where the road forked into two unpaved branches.

A metal sign pockmarked by .22 caliber potshots indicated Winchester Canyon to the right. To the left, promised the sign, we would find Whitewater Spring Canyon. That was our direction. Charles engaged the all-wheel drive as the sturdy wagon moved smoothly onto the dirt road. I noted the odometer. Precisely 4.6 miles from the fork would be a turn leading to the mine, or so said the map.

The road ascended in earnest. With the increasing steepness came the inevitable switchbacks. It took a quarter of an hour to reach the turn, which was so severely overgrown we would have missed it had we not been creeping along and counting by tenths of a mile.

Up to this point the all-wheel drive had been useful but not strictly necessary. But I doubt a conventional car would have made the last half-mile. The road degraded into little more than a streambed, with deep ruts and ominous potholes. Bare traces of wheel tracks helped guide us, and the little wagon didn't falter.

The road ended at a cleared, terraced area about 50 by 100 feet. Off to one side, the forest was slowly digesting some ancient, rusted machinery. On the other side were heaps of rocks and dirt overgrown with vegetation. Facing us was a large, square black hole in the hillside, the entrance to the mine (or *adit* for crossword puzzle fans). Above it, a sign read: Lucky U Mine, and below, in large capital letters, were the words: TRESPASSERS WILL BE PROSECUTED.

Chapter 8

The directions were right on the mark, said Charles.

"Yes," I agreed, repelled by the desolation around us and the yawning maw of the cavern. "I suppose that, as we're here, we should look around."

"No need to buy tickets," quipped Charles. "They've quite gone out of business."

He maneuvered off to the side and we got out and stretched. Forest sounds and smells abounded. Every few seconds a creature stirred unseen. The strong midday sun drew forth rich scents from the lush vegetation that covered the hillsides. On two sides of us the forest sloped off sharply. Charles examined the rusted heap of machinery without comment. Finally he said, "Let's go in. I'll get a torch."

Visions of caveman Charles holding a bundle of burning sticks flickered in my head. He opened the back of the car and brought out a large flashlight. We walked into the mine, penetrating some dozen yards before looking around. Already the temperature was markedly cooler. In contrast to the outside, inside the mine the air had a brown odor—a mixture of earth, wood, machinery, and oil.

"Ah, here we are," exclaimed Charles.

"What's that?"

"The rails. They have to get the ore out somehow. The usual way is to use gondolas on tracks, filling them up inside the mine, then winching them out. Some of that rusty machinery we were looking at had parts of the winch."

"How do you know all this?" I asked. "Not from Harvard Medical School."

"Hardly," said Charles. "I logged on to the Internet last night and put gold mine into a search engine. I wanted to be something more than extra baggage. I printed out a few pages." He pulled several folded sheets of paper from a pocket. "Everything you ever wanted to know about mining, and then some."

"How far in do you think it goes?"

"It's hard to tell. This is probably a drift mine, for working placer deposits of gold."

"Placer deposits?"

"That's what mining engineers call them. They're concentrations of minerals, gold in this case, accumulated through erosion. Water probably ran through here for millions of years, depositing the heavier gold-bearing ore in a vein. This mine taps into the vein, which is in there somewhere," he explained, waving his pages of information at the black interior.

We walked in deeper, Charles sweeping the light left and right. Every so often he stopped to examine the huge beams of timber that were holding the mountain back from crushing us. When they met with his approval, we'd move on a few dozen yards and repeat the procedure.

The adit gleamed brightly in the distance, the size of a playing card. "Ah, here we are," exclaimed Charles for the second time.

This time it was obvious what had caught his attention: a tunnel off to the right. A bit farther up, another tunnel branched off to the left.

"We're in the vein now," said Charles. He turned into the first tunnel, ducking his head. The main shaft had an eight-foot ceiling. This ceiling was much lower. "Mind the slope," warned Charles, as we entered the narrow passageway. No longer being able to see the little square of daylight spooked me. I moved closer to Charles who continued to peer curiously about.

Along both sides of this tributary were cavities where the gold-bearing ore had been excavated. A bend in the tunnel prevented us from seeing where it ended. "I'm curious to see where this goes," said Charles. "It appears to be following the vein."

We rounded the leftward bend. Another dozen feet of tunnel widened out into a cul-de-sac. Against the far wall were some old miners' tools, a couple of shovels, an immense wheelbarrow, and an assortment of pickaxes. An ancient leather jacket rested atop a wooden crate.

Charles shoved the jacket aside. Through the little dust storm raised, I could make out two words, stenciled in red letters on the crate. These were the "D" words of mining: Danger and Dynamite.

"Hmmph," muttered Charles. "Not much here, really. Shall we go back?"

I agreed unhesitatingly. I'm not ordinarily claustrophobic, but this was different. It was an oppressive kind of closeness. Who knew how far the shaft extended, or what kinds of dangers awaited the intruder? It was this acting-up of my imagination that caused me to ignore the first scuffling sound. I didn't want to spook either Charles or myself. But when I heard it a second time I grabbed Charles's arm.

"Did you hear that?"

"I heard something," he said. "Probably an animal."

"Christ, you don't think a bear lives here, do you?" My imagination was in overdrive.

"No, we'd have smelled a bear. It's probably...ouch!"

We had emerged into the main shaft, Charles ahead of me on my left. He reached up to his neck and swatted at something, tried to speak, and crumpled into a heap, pulling me down with him. Something flew past my ear. Out of the corner of my eye, I saw the figure of a man silhouetted against the square light of the entrance.

Instinct, honed by my military training, made me go flat. Shielded by Charles's body, I reverse belly-crawled into the tunnel we had just left. I reached out and grabbed Charles by the right ankle and pulled as hard as I could. His body scraped across the gravelly floor of the mine. This wasn't going to do his face any good.

I bit my lip to keep from screaming. My heart pounded in my ears, and I was beginning to hyperventilate. I began rapid shallow breathing to control my panic.

In a few seconds I regained control. I felt Charles's neck for a jugular artery. His heartbeat was strong. I pulled him farther in, rolled him over, and put my ear on his chest. He was breathing normally. What in hell was going on?

"Charles," I whispered, shaking him and slapping his cheeks the way they do in late night movies. "Charles, wake up. I think someone's trying to kill us." No response. I turned him around and grabbed his shoulders. He was easier to drag this way. We retreated to the cul-de-sac, bouncing from wall to wall in the pitch dark.

The flashlight had gone out when Charles hit the ground. There was little chance of retrieving it now. I keep a tiny penlight in my bag—but who takes their handbag into a mine? I wish I had. More than the penlight, I missed the Glock.

I felt all over Charles for blood, starting with his head. Only a bullet could drop a man that fast. I didn't remember hearing the soft pop of a silenced gunshot, but I could have missed it.

I couldn't feel blood anywhere. He was still breathing as if he were sleeping. I wondered if he had one of those disorders where you fall asleep suddenly at unexpected times. I doubted that. Since he'd been driving, he'd have warned me. Besides, I clearly saw the outline of a person. Though my imagination was aroused from being in the dark mine, I'm not prone to hallucinating.

I listened for someone approaching. A man with a gun and a bright light would find us easy prey. I thought I could hear voices whispering, but I couldn't make out the words. Only the hissing penetrated the dark. That meant we had at least two antagonists. I crouched silently, listening so hard it made my head hurt.

After some interminable minutes, I decided to creep up the passageway toward the main shaft. Maybe I'd hear something, or see something. Maybe I'd get myself killed. I felt gingerly for a weapon. I didn't want to knock something over and give away our location. My hand touched the wooden crate. I pulled it back quickly. What if there was still dynamite in there and it detonated? We'd have a cave-in. We'd be buried alive, even if we weren't killed instantly.

Charles moaned. I felt my way over to him, found his mouth, and put my hand over it. "Are you okay?" I whispered, keeping my voice low and speaking directly into his ear.

He perceived the need for silence. He swallowed, breathing quietly, deeply, as he regained composure. He felt for me, put his hands alongside my head. I tried to turn my ear toward his mouth but he used both hands to keep my head straight and pulled my mouth down on top of his. I returned his kiss, a wave of relief and passion replacing the fearful anxiety. I supposed that if I were going to die, there were worse ways to go. He stopped long enough for me to say, "Listen." Though I couldn't see him in the dark, I could feel his face become serious. I could picture Charles's serious look in my mind's eye.

"What happened to you?" I whispered.

"Tranquilizer dart. The kind they use on wild animals. I felt it in my neck, and then I was gone. How long have I been out?"

"Ten minutes, maybe twelve."

"Gawr, what great stuff. Takes down a thirteen stone animal instantly. Total unconsciousness, complete recovery. I feel fine, no headache, no nausea. I'd love to know what it is."

"Charles," I pleaded, "get real. Someone's trying to harm us, or kill us. Are you going to walk out there and discuss pharmaceuticals with them? They may be back with guns any minute."

"You said I've been out ten minutes. If they intended to shoot us, what stopped them?"

"I don't know. They may have been surprised when I pulled you back out of the main shaft. I think they thought we were cornered, sitting ducks in a shooting gallery. They may not know about these other tunnels. If they know I'm a P.I., they may think I'm armed. That'll make them cautious."

"Are you?" asked Charles.

"No, dammit. I left everything in my handbag in the front seat. If they find my gun, they'll know we're unarmed."

We sat in silence for a few seconds. A flicker of light glanced off the wall accompanied by faint shuffling sounds. Again, a flicker, a little brighter. Someone was coming down the main shaft, sweeping a light from side to side, just as we had done.

I whispered, "Shit. We need to do something. Can we find one of those picks? We need some kind of weapon. I refuse to make this easy for them."

I started feeling around again. "Oh, damn, I keep bumping that box of dynamite."

"The dynamite!" exclaimed Charles. "Where? Put my hand on the box."

"Here, it's here," I said, guiding his hand. "What the fuck are you going to do with dynamite?" I whispered throatily. "Are you crazy?"

The hinges on the old crate squeaked loudly as Charles lifted the top. "Capital, capital," Charles muttered under his breath. "They left some."

The creaking hinges gave away our location. A flickering of two lights grew brighter from around the bend. Gravel crunched underfoot as they approached our tunnel.

"Good of them to provide light," said Charles. "Stay here!"

"Charles, please, I'd rather be shot than trapped in a cave-in. What are you doing with the dynamite?"

"Stay here! Turn around. Cover your ears. Trust me." He gave my arm a squeeze and moved off. I had only a moment to contemplate how many times a man had said, "Trust me," and I'd later wished I hadn't. But here in this mine, trapped in the dark, what choice did I have?

Charles's silhouette was barely visible. He was bent forward, his left arm swung back, grasping the stick of dynamite by its middle. He moved forward rapidly, in a crouch, as if bowling. He gave a sharp plosive grunt, like the kind weight lifters make. I turned, covered my ears, and closed my eyes tightly.

Just before the loud crack, Charles scurried back. The flash of the explosion penetrated my closed eyelids. The echo of the detonation reverberated throughout the tunnel and throughout my head. I listened breathlessly for the sound of falling rock, partially deafened though I was. What I heard was loud cursing and rapidly retreating footfalls.

Then Charles was holding me. "You okay?"

I was shaking so hard it took me a moment to get my voice.

"Dagny, talk to me," pleaded Charles.

"I'm okay," I murmured. "I'm having a real blast. And you?"

"Very funny," he said, giving me a crushing hug. "I'm okay. My ears are ringing, but I spun round the corner in time to avoid the direct shock wave. I think our friends will have trouble hearing for a while. I doubt they'll bother us anymore."

He hugged me harder. For an instant we lost our balance. I staggered a couple of steps backwards, kicking the box of dynamite with my heel, and nearly falling backwards into the open crate.

"Jesus, I'm gonna blow my ass away," I blurted out, as Charles steadied me.

"Don't worry. Dynamite isn't that sensitive to shock." He kicked the crate to emphasize his point, and my heart jumped into my mouth. "My main fear when I bowled that stick into the wall of the main shaft was that it wouldn't detonate."

"I didn't know you were a bowler."

"Oh, I am, but not in American ten pins. I bowled for East Surrey, a cricket team. It's like pitching in your baseball. A good cricket bowler can hurl a ball as fast as a pitcher. I wasn't bad for an amateur. I rolled the dynamite off my finger tips so it'd hit flat on."

"Weren't you worried about cave-ins?"

"I'd examined the shoring and it was solid. The dynamite exploded in an open place, so most of its force dissipated into the air. Mines are built to withstand blasting. I'm going to have a peek into the main shaft. I think we discouraged them. They probably think we have a bazooka," he chuckled.

I followed Charles. Before reaching the main shaft we stopped to listen. An engine cranked. We stepped out into the main shaft and gazed into the square of light. I couldn't see a thing, but I heard a vehicle retreating.

In the faint twilight of the shaft, we peered around for the flashlight. Charles spotted it a few feet from where he had fallen. The top had jarred loose, but it was easily fixed and we had light again. Charles scanned the wall with the light.

"There's where the dynamite detonated." He shined the light on a charred patch of wall about two feet from the ground. "I bowled a low ball for fear of hitting the lintel over our tunnel entrance. But it had to be high enough and fast enough to strike the wall. I don't think bouncing on the ground would've detonated it."

I had to laugh. About his considerable medical abilities, Charles was quite modest. But when it came to his cricket skills, he couldn't keep himself from bragging.

We began to walk toward the entrance, Charles idly swinging the flashlight. A metallic glint caught my eye. "What's that?" I cried.

"What's what?"

"Something shiny. Let me have the light." I searched the floor in front of us. "It's my baby, my baby Glock." I squealed with delight.

"Some bastard was going to shoot me with my own gun. It was blown right out of his hand. It looks none the worse." I blew the dust off it and tucked it in the waistband at the small of my back.

I squinted at Charles. The light revealed the damage done to his face. "I'm afraid the side of your face got a bit messed up when I dragged you. I'm sorry. I'll clean you up as soon as we're out of here. Maybe this will help." I moved my lips over his scrapes, touching them lightly, ending up on his lips.

"Quite better already," he said after a long, searching kiss.

We were nearly out of the mine when I heard a car's engine laboring up the hill. We moved back into the dimness of the shaft off to one side. I palmed the Glock. I stared toward the road, narrowing my eyes against the brightness. The surrounding vegetation shimmered from green to blue to green. I blinked hard to help my eyes adjust. A moment later the grille of a large car bounced into view.

Chapter 9

The black and orange car advanced purposefully into the clearing, turned and pulled up behind the Subaru. On the driver's door was the logo of the Churok Tribal Police. On the roof, the blue lights were flashing.

I tucked the semi back in my waistband and prayed silently that our would-be assassins hadn't stolen my P.I. license and gun permit. "Keep your hands in front of you," I warned Charles. We exited squinting into the sunlight.

"Good afternoon," I shouted. The two policemen, who'd been examining the Subaru, turned toward us, hands resting on holsters. We approached slowly. "I'm Dagny Jamison. I'm a private investigator. This is Dr. Charles Clarke. I represent a client who is a part owner of this mine. She asked me to check it out for her."

We approached closer. "I have a pistol tucked in the small of my back," I called out. "I have a permit to carry it, but I'm going to let you remove it." I turned around and held my arms out to the side. To their credit, they didn't draw their weapons. One of them came over and removed the semi. He stared at it for a moment, and then decocked the hammer, released the magazine, and removed the remaining, chambered bullet. He asked Charles if he had any firearms, and accepted the denial at face value.

"My license and permit are in the car, if you'll allow me." They did. I opened the passenger door of the Subaru, composing lies as fast as I could in case my wallet was missing. The contents of my bag had been dumped on the passenger's seat. To my relief the wallet was present and untouched. On the other hand, the men who attacked us were not thieves; this was all the more scary. One cop took my P.I. license and gun permit, asked Charles for his driver's license, and retired to the squad car for a computer check. I repacked my handbag.

The three of us waited in silence. The Churok cops didn't waste words. The one who'd been back to the squad car returned after ten long minutes. He looked me over carefully, checking height, weight, and complexion. Satisfied, he returned my license, permit, and pistol. "You check out," he said. "Technically, your permit's invalid on the Churok reservation, but we try to get along with the State of California. If you wouldn't mind, lock your firearm in the glove compartment when you're on the reservation."

I promised I would, thanked him, and waited for them to leave. No such luck.

"We came up here to investigate a report of an explosion." He waited expressionlessly.

Charles opened his mouth to explain, but I cut him off. "My client, Miss Judy Raskin, asked me to find out whether this mine has any potential value. I asked Dr. Clarke, who's trained as a geologist, to help me. We set off a small charge to test the vein." I was hoping either that this lie was reasonable, or the cops knew less about mining than I did. It must have been one or the other because they bought it.

"What about your face?" he asked Charles.

"I'm afraid in retreating from the detonation I stumbled and collided with the wall," lied Charles.

Oh, this is wonderful, I thought: we are lying together.

"Do you have any papers giving you permission to be on this property?" asked the second cop, who up to now had been silent.

"Yes sir, I do." I fetched out the leasing agreement I got from Bill Raskin and handed it to him. "You can see that Miss Raskin, Mr. Stanton, Mr. and Mrs. Blair, and Mr. Greatoak, who is a Churok, are all partners."

The two cops looked at each other. They exchanged a few words in Churok. Then the second cop said, "We know Mr. Greatoak as Towippa, one of the elders of the Churok Nation. Perhaps, since you're setting off explosives in his mine, you would care to meet him."

I took this as a quid pro quo request. They knew they had cut us some slack. Now we needed to cooperate, which was easy enough since I had intended all along to find Mr. Tommy Greatoak and fill him in on the deaths of two of his partners.

They allowed us to drive our vehicle. We followed the police car down the rutted trail. When we reached Whitewater Spring Canyon Road, with its less demanding surface, Charles felt able to talk. "Why didn't we tell them we were attacked, Dagny? They might be able to radio ahead for a road block."

"For one thing, those thugs would be long gone. For another, we don't have a description of them or their vehicle. For a third, I'd prefer to leave them in the dark as to what happened to us. For all they know, we blew ourselves up. Or maybe they think they did something to cause the explosion. I'm sure they hauled ass out of there. I doubt they wanted to answer questions from those two," I said, nodding at the police car in front of us.

"I've never had anyone try to kill me," replied Charles. "I guess I don't know what to do."

"I *have* had people try to kill me," I said grimly. "My brother's given me pointers on how to avoid such a fate, and my military police training helps a lot. I'll try to keep us alive. Anyway, I think it's me they're after. I'm not sure why. If I've learned something that threatens anyone, I sure as hell don't know what it is."

"We're in this together, Dagny. I'm not going to leave you to face this alone."

"Brave, sweet, sexy Charles," I said, squeezing his hand. "You've already saved us. That was a helluva gutsy performance inside the mine. If this keeps up, I'm gonna have to start wearing a pacemaker. I about had a heart attack."

We reached the bottom of the canyon. The cop car signaled for a right turn on Moorland Boulevard We followed. To our left was the Makrui valley, arid and flat, where most of the Churoks lived. The canyons of the national forest were on the right. Every half-mile or so would be a sign for such-and-such canyon: Guevara Canyon, Badde Canyon, Shelby Canyon, Cecelia Canyon, Blue Canyon, and so on.

We crossed the Makrui River. Just over the bridge was a sign for the hamlet of Horse Potrero, population 452. We slowed to a respectful 25 miles per hour as we drove down Main Street. People were out in numbers, milling about. Some were patronizing the few small businesses along the road—a hardware and feed store, the Henny-Penny five-and-dime, a mini-supermarket whose unabashed green sign read 7-EVEN.

The local hangout was Fosters Freeze, a burger and ice cream joint with half a dozen concrete picnic tables for outside seating. The town's liquor store was next door to it. A number of people were sitting on the tables, feet on seat benches, enjoying their favorite beverage. A woman was playing a guitar. Several dogs roamed the premises, looking for someone who actually had food.

The road rose and crested, offering a view of the Makrui River, a shimmering multi-colored ribbon winding through the sun-soaked valley. At the bottom of the hill, the cops signaled for a right turn. We followed them onto Chaparral Canyon Road. The houses, as everywhere on this part of the reservation, were of the small clapboard variety, set well back from the road. A couple of miles into the canyon, the patrol car signaled, slowed, and made a left turn onto a gravel driveway.

As we crept along, dogs of various sizes, shapes and colors materialized to run alongside the two vehicles. They escorted our little convoy with enthusiastic barking until we stopped a respectful distance from the house at the driveway's end. The cops made no move to leave their car, nor did they honk. They waited, we waited, the dogs circled, baying and barking.

Suddenly a particularly large specimen put his front paws on the driver's side window and leered at Charles, mouth agape. Charles grinned and lowered his window. The moving window spooked the dog and he disappeared. Charles clucked for it to come back and the large black head was suddenly inside the car. This was a very good sign; Charles liked dogs. I couldn't imagine a lover who didn't. The whole scene reminded me of how much I missed my two greyhounds at home in North Carolina, though I knew they were being shamelessly spoiled by my dog/house-sitter.

"That's a nice boy, good boy. What's your name?" said Charles, as he scratched behind the dog's ears and rubbed the top of its head. A bit of slaver dripped on Charles's bare arm. "He's just a big old loopy Lab," said Charles. I reached over and scratched the massive head. He was the biggest Labrador retriever I'd ever seen. I stroked his ears, silky as fine velvet.

The jaws opened and moved to encompass my wrist, a typical Lab gesture of friendship. Charles apparently thought I'd be afraid and reassured me. "He likes you, Dagny. When Labs like something, they want to hold it in their mouth. He won't hurt you. He wouldn't hurt a fly. He's a big, friendly baby boy, aren't you?" The last few words had dissolved into baby-doggy talk, and were directed at the animal.

"Why are the cops just sitting there?" I wondered aloud, my hand now stroking the creature's muzzle, which he apparently liked because when I stopped he craned his neck to nose my hand.

"Maybe they called this Mr. Greatoak and they're waiting for him to come out. I gathered he was an important person. American cops, they'd just walk up and bang on the ruddy door. They don't know if that person's eating, sleeping, or making love. Maybe these Churoks are more attuned to others. Remember how they waited without talking back at the mine. They're comfortable with silence, and patient. They leave a person space to think and consider."

"Yeah, and time to make up stories if they're in a pinch, thank goodness," I added gratefully.

A deep voice boomed the single word "Quiet," which had an immediate effect. I had relegated the barking and snuffling to background noise, so the silence was even more striking. The Lab jumped down. The other dogs stopped in mid-bark and looked toward the house.

Standing on the front porch was a colossus of a man—a veritable Paul Bunyan—with a long, black ponytail secured by a red and turquoise band. He wore overalls and a plaid work shirt with rolled-up sleeves. The only place this man wouldn't stand out would be in the defensive line of a pro football team. Whether because of his size or his gigantic voice, he commanded respect from the pack, which seemed to await his orders.

At last the cops got out of their car. They walked toward the house as Mr. Greatoak, for that was who it was, descended from his front porch to meet them. There was no handshaking, but a conversation had already begun. In a moment one of the cops beckoned to us.

We exited the Subaru and made our way over to the three men. The big Lab accompanied us, his tail swishing back and forth. The other dogs were watchful, deferential.

One of the cops introduced us. "This is Dr. Clarke and Miss Jamison. Dr. Clarke works for the coroner's office in Santa Barbara; Miss Jamison is a private investigator."

Turning to us, he said, "This is Mr. Greatoak, one of the leaders of the Churok Nation." Ordinarily I would have offered my hand, but handshaking didn't seem to be customary, and Charles had picked up on that, too.

"I'm pleased to meet you both. People call me Tommy." The colossus said something to the two police officers in Churok. They nodded to us and left. "I hope Rikka and Nostawwa were polite to you. I've known them since they were children. They're good boys."

Greatoak's voice was deep and resonant, mellow as old bourbon aged in oak. He looked down on us benevolently. Despite his daunting size—he was nearly a foot taller than Charles—I didn't feel threatened by him, though I wouldn't have minded if the cops had remained.

"They did their job," I said. "We have no complaints."

"Good, good. Please come in. I want to hear everything about my little sister Judy."

We followed him to the front door. The Labrador escorted us inside, the only dog so privileged. "I see you've met Izzie," he said, reaching down to stroke the big head.

"That wouldn't be short for Isidore by any chance?" said Charles, using the dog's name to help break the ice.

"It's short for Izupimma," the big man said, and in answer to Charles's questioning look continued in a friendly tone, "I named him as I was named. When I was born, I weighed nearly fourteen pounds. My parents named me Towippa for my size. 'To' is Churok for 'oak,' 'wip' means 'large' and 'pa' means 'very.'"

"But what's that to do with Izzie?" asked Charles, genuinely interested.

"Oh, like me, he was a giant of a newborn. The name that I gave him means great dog. 'Izu' is our word for 'dog' and 'pim' means 'large' and the 'ma' makes him very large."

"I thought 'wip' meant large," said Charles.

"Oh, we have many words for 'large' in Churok," said Greatoak, "because in our eyes, there are many kinds of largeness."

"Well, in any case Izzie's a great name for a great dog," replied Charles. He made some clucky smoochie sounds to get the Lab's attention. Izzie moved within stroking range of the hand Charles proffered. "And if I may, Greatoak's your Anglo name, is that right?" continued Charles.

"Yes, and since Anglos require first names, I ended up with Tommy, which isn't short for Thomas. It's Churok 'to-mi' meaning 'wise oak.' 'Mi' means wise."

"Then is wise dog 'izumi'?" asked Charles.

"Yes, indeed," beamed Tommy. "You and Judy should be friends. She loves to analyze Churok."

The linguistic chatter gave me a chance to gather my thoughts. The "little sister" pet name that Tommy used for Judy told me that breaking the news of her death was going to be distressing.

The two men were silent. I was about to speak when Tommy shifted his gaze to me. "Forgive me, Miss Jamison. I've been extraordinarily rude, babbling on, ignoring you like this. I'm afraid the Churok language is one of my weaknesses. Please forgive me."

"Not at all, Mr. Greatoak."

"Tommy, please."

"Uh, Tommy. Please call me Dagny."

"And Chaahles" said Charles r-lessly, raising his hand like a schoolboy.

"Tommy," I started over. "I'm afraid I have some terrible news."

Chapter 10

Tommy's smile vanished. We were standing in the living room, into which the front door opened directly: an architectural feature of low-cost housing from the nineteen-forties. On the wall opposite the front door was a fireplace. Over the fireplace was a simply framed print of an oil painting. Its violent brush strokes portrayed fiery yellow stars and comets against a sky-blue background. Next to the fireplace was a floor-to-ceiling picture window looking out on a rear patio. The kitchen was in the front of the house—another feature of the forties' design—adjacent to the living room, and separated from it by a wall.

Against this wall stood a sofa, on which Tommy invited Charles and me to sit. Tommy settled into a large easy chair next to the fireplace. Sundry artifacts of Churok culture covered nearly all the available wall space, reminding me of Professor Akrich's office, though without the academic clutter. The furniture coverings contained patterns I'd have guessed as being southwest Indian—Navaho, Hopi, Zuni—but my knowledge of Native American styles is limited. The only decorative concession to any idiom remotely modern or Anglo was a Tiffany lamp on an end table by the sofa.

"I was hired to investigate Judy Raskin's death," I said. "That's why I'm here." I paused to let the news sink in. From talking to the Churok cops, I'd learned that stretches of non-talking were important. Tommy appreciated the silence. He didn't respond immediately.

Then he said, "Judy's dead? How? When?"

I told him of the events that had culminated in Judy's death. I related how Lucy had hired me, how we had met Charles, our mad dash in pursuit of Troy, and his tragic end. I concluded with a summary of my visit to Judy's father and the revelation about the gold mine. I omitted our recent skirmish inside the mine.

Tommy listened carefully, drawing in his breath sharply when he learned of Troy's fate. During my narrative, tears spilled from his eyes and trickled slowly down his cheeks.

"This day compares in woe to a day long ago when she, night-born beneath a thousand points of light, returned to the eternal mother," he said, when I'd finished.

We waited through the gloomy silence that followed this cryptic remark. Tommy attempted to compose himself several times, reaching out to stroke Izzie, who placed his huge head on Tommy's knee.

"Judy loved Izzie, and Izzie loved Judy. I'm glad he cannot understand, though he senses my grief." Tommy gently removed the dog's head and sat up straight in his chair, once again an imposing presence. "I don't understand Professor Akrich's actions. I find it hard to believe Judy killed herself. I'd like to help you discover the truth. But those who seek the truth must tell the truth. Why did you lie to the police?"

I wasn't buying the truth-seeker, truth-teller business. Tommy had motive enough to be rid of both Judy and Troy if the gold mine was valuable. For all I knew, he was behind the late subterranean unpleasantness.

"I needed to protect my client's interests, and our own, for that matter. I don't think it's always wise to tell the cops everything. For all we knew, they were going to bust us."

"Dagny," he said, looking me straight in the eye, "you come onto the Churok reservation, trespass, and set off explosives. The cops did their job with restraint, don't you agree?"

I nodded.

Tommy leaned toward us. "These boys, these cops, I've known them since they were children. I know their families. I know their extended families. They're good boys and they're good cops, but they're young and inexperienced. They don't know how ridiculous your dynamite story is. How about telling me what really happened?"

While Tommy talked, I reasoned. If he was one of the bad guys, he already knew anything I could tell him. He also could reach over and throttle us each in one huge hand, claiming later we attacked him. But if he wasn't involved, he'd make a good ally. Judy's death, in one way or another, was linked to her association with the Churoks. Tommy could tell us about that.

I decided to be candid. I told Tommy what happened from the moment we entered the mine to the arrival on the scene of the two police officers. When I had finished, he leaned back in his chair, rubbed his chin, pursed his lips, and was lost in thought for some moments.

"You had a close call," he said at last. "You acted bravely. Do you think your attackers had anything to do with the two deaths?"

"Perhaps," I said. "Or perhaps they were protecting the mine. There aren't any hidden partners, are there?"

"No. Originally there were the five of us. Now there are three. There are no hidden partners, as you say. The only reason I'm a partner is due to a legality. Churok law requires Churok participation in any land project. When Troy and Judy wanted to lease the mine, they needed a

Churok in the partnership. I agreed to help them. I was even willing to put up my one-fifth share of the leasing cost, though I believe the mine to be exhausted. Modern technology may be wonderful, but it isn't alchemy. It cannot turn dirt into gold."

"How did you come to know Judy and Troy?"

"It's a long story," answered Tommy. "Do you want to hear all of it?"

"I'd like to know everything you can tell me." I wriggled deeper into the comfortable sofa, crossed my legs, folded my arms, and prepared to listen.

"First, let me give you a little background. Until recently we Churoks, like most Native Americans, didn't have a way to write our language. We passed our knowledge on through word of mouth, and taught it to our children so that they'd remember and teach their children. Within our nation, the best rememberers are chosen through contests of memory. They're like the scholars and professors of your society."

I realized I wasn't going to remember all of this in detail. I reached into my bag and retrieved a pen and a steno pad. Tommy didn't object.

"One person becomes the leader of the memorizers. He's called Huruku in the Churok language. Huruku remembers the stories of the Churok gods, and how the Churoks came to earth—for this is our most precious knowledge. Others, under Huruku's guidance, remember knowledge of our earthly history, of the law, of plants and animals, of medicine, and so on."

I was scribbling as quickly as I could, spelling words phonetically when I had to. Tommy saw me and slowed his speech down a little.

"When I was a young man, almost thirty-five years ago, I was apprenticed to one of the greatest Hurukus who ever lived. She was the first female Huruku in our history. In Churok, her name was Himma Lilina Wonna Kara-tae-plu. Word for word, it means *night birth thousand light-points-beneath*. She was born late at night under a clear, moonless sky. When she learned English, she called herself Starry Night, and by that name was she known to white people."

His eyes flicked up toward the mantel, and it dawned on me that the print was of the Van Gogh oil painting of the same name.

"For ten years Starry Night taught me. She showed me how to expand the vessel that was my memory, and when I had learnt how to do this, she filled it with the knowledge that I'd need to become Huruku one day. She showed me how to expand my soul, and when I had done this, she filled it with the spirituality required of a Churok elder. She was as close to me as my own parents, who considered her one of our family. Those were my happiest days. I shall not look upon their like again in this world."

Tommy was a riveting speaker. My cynical side kept running a sincerity check, but if Tommy was faking his earnestness, then I was in the presence of a most accomplished actor, and probably in mortal danger. There was intensity in the man that I both admired and feared.

"One day, a brash young student from UCLA appeared at Starry Night's door. He was a charming, compelling, self-possessed youth. He spoke Churok in a rudimentary way, but even that was astonishing—a considerable accomplishment for a foreigner. He said he wanted to learn everything he could about the Churok people and their history. He said he'd spare no effort to reach his goal, but that he needed the help of Starry Night. His name was Julius David Akrich."

"Professor Akrich!" I exclaimed.

"Yes," nodded Tommy. "Starry Night took a liking to young Akrich. His dedication to learning about all things Churok was deeply appealing to Huruku, whose life's mission was to foster such learning. The fact that he was an orthodox Jew also attracted Starry Night to this young scholar. Although we Churoks do not believe in one supreme male god figure, we revere all spiritual belief."

Charles was nodding in rapt admiration and Tommy paused to let him say something if he felt like it, but Charles leaned forward to listen even more attentively and remained silent.

"For two years Akrich came to the reservation weekends, school holidays, and summers. He taught us to transcribe Churok using the letters of the English alphabet in special ways, so we were able to write our language if we chose. He perfected his knowledge of both modern Churok and, most impressively, of ancient Churok, the ritual language. He sat with me and other rememberers when Starry Night instructed us. She wouldn't permit the use of a tape recorder, nor the taking of notes. She told him, 'If you want to learn about the Churoks, you must learn in the way of the Churoks, which is to remember.'"

Interesting, I thought, that that which we originally did as a matter of necessity becomes obligatory in the name of tradition, even after the need is gone.

"The third year I knew Julius he came to live with Starry Night. He no longer needed to take classes at UCLA and could devote all his time to research. He'd accompany her every day as she carried out her duties as Huruku. At night they'd sit in front of her fireplace. She would repeat the myths and rituals until he knew them perfectly. He'd tell her stories from the Jewish bible, which the Christian missionaries didn't teach us."

"Ah, tales from the Old Testament," interjected Charles. "Some good stories there—ones that are more multicultural than the writings of the Apostles."

"Yes," said Tommy. "We Churoks, too, tell of floods and plagues in our early history. Starry Night was deeply interested in comparing the two theologies. It is one of the obligations of Huruku to know about other religions...but to continue. One morning, about six months after he took up residence with Starry Night, I received a terrible phone call from Julius. He was beside himself. It was Starry Night's habit to greet the rising sun with the prayers of her ancestors. Julius, too, arose early for the morning rituals of orthodox Jews. On this day, Starry Night hadn't appeared by the time Julius was done praying. Out of concern, he entered her bedroom. He approached the bedside, fearful of offending her, but dismayed at her stillness. She had died in her sleep."

Tommy stood up and walked past the mantel, hands in his pockets, then reversed his direction and stopped and faced the Van Gogh print called Starry Night.

He said, "I am a big man, a strong man. But that day, I was weaker from grief than a sick child, and fearful of the responsibilities I would have to assume, but wasn't prepared for."

He turned to face us, his expression doleful as he recalled that period of his life. Even as he spoke, the room grew darker, shaded by passing clouds.

"Starry Night was dressed and buried in the manner our laws prescribe for Huruku. For seven days and nights all Churoks put aside their differences to unite in a single body of woe. With the help of others, I, the new Huruku, and one of the youngest ever, led our people in prayers of mourning. Julius made his own prayers. His mourning would last for one year, as decreed in the Jewish religion."

Izzie got up from his place beside Tommy's chair, walked over and plopped himself down at Tommy's feet.

"Though he was grief-stricken, Julius carefully observed the burial rituals reserved for Huruku, which became a part of his research. He was a great comfort to me. He knew so much about Churok traditions—in many ways more than I did—and he was able to help me become Huruku. I'll always be in his debt."

Tommy stepped over Izzie and switched on the Tiffany lamp on the table close to which Charles and I were sitting. The light cut the gloom, and revealed even more clearly the sadness in Tommy's eyes.

"Eventually Julius went away. He had his own life and career to think about. He became a professor and wrote books about the Churoks. At first, he visited us once or twice a year to brush up on his knowledge. Later, he sent his students in his place. They were assigned to study aspects of Churok life that he hadn't had time to delve into."

"And one of them was Judy Raskin, is that right?" I interrupted.

"Yes, I'm coming to that. I would do almost anything for Julius, but I wouldn't allow him or his students to record our rituals. In this I was faithful to the strictures of Starry Night. Then Judy came. Unlike the students before her, who took their visits like class assignments, to be written up, turned in, graded and forgotten, Judy was more concerned with making friends and helping people. She wanted to learn the Churok language, both ancient and modern, and to make herself more Churok-like. She ate and dressed as a Churok, and wore her hair like a Churok."

Tommy paused to gather wisps of his own hair and to retie his ponytail.

"Of course, I knew Judy was observing us. She had to. She was working for, and being paid by, Professor Akrich. She stayed up late every night compiling notes, studying, practicing. She wasn't nearly as good a memorizer as Julius had been, but she succeeded through hard work."

Tommy returned to his chair, sat down, and immediately rose again, too agitated, I presumed, to remain seated. He was remarkably agile for a man his size—and age, for I deduced he must be nearing sixty. He walked again over to the mantel and gazed at the Starry Night print for a full thirty seconds. Finally, he turned to face us, leaning gently against the mantelshelf and mindful not to disturb the now sleeping Labrador.

"One day Judy took me aside. 'Tommy,' she said, 'you must let me record the rituals. The transcriptions don't do them justice. It's impossible to capture the nuances of ancient Churok by listening, remembering, and transcribing.' Your professor did, I countered, but she was adamant. 'Dr. Akrich made a lot of mistakes,' she said. 'We students thrive on correcting them. You know that.'"

He pulled a wry face and shook his huge head. He walked over to the windows that looked out onto the front yard of his house and stared out them, speaking with his back to us.

"Judy was right. Professor Akrich's efforts were prodigious, but in works of such magnitude, errors are bound to occur. I finally told Judy I would discuss it with other tribal elders. I might have anticipated the result. Nobody could say no to Judy, so universally did the Churoks who knew her, love her. Thus she had the honor of making the first electronic recordings of our rituals."

He turned away from the windows to face us once again. The wry expression had turned mournful. His eyes shone moist and black as he continued, "I can't believe she's dead. She was so young, so vital, so spiritual. Though she was not outwardly religious like Julius, she had the strong spirit of religion in her. And it's that spirit that makes me believe that she wouldn't take her own life."

During the silence that followed, Tommy resumed his original seat.

Finally, I asked, "What was the cause of Starry Night's death? Was she very old?"

"Not so old," said Tommy. "Around sixty. She just died in her sleep."

"But of what?" I pressed. "Did she have a heart attack, a stroke?"

"I don't know."

"Wasn't there a death certificate?"

"We Churoks have our own way. She died in her sleep. What does it matter what she died of, in technical terms? We mourned her for seven days. We returned her spirit to the earth mother, who will guide it to the next world. That's all that's important."

Charles, the medical examiner, was about to quote the gospel according to the laws of the State of California. Before he could speak, I linked his arm in mine to distract him and looked up and caught Tommy's eye.

"One last question, if you don't mind," I said. "Is there anyone among the Churok people who might bear Judy ill will, or benefit from her death?"

"As I told you, Dagny, Judy was well loved by everybody. She had no enemies, and nobody profits from her passing."

"If you'll forgive me, the way the contract is written, the death of any partner benefits the others."

Tommy sighed. "Yes, I understand your suspicion. But I tell you, Dagny, if the mine were full of gold, I'd give it all for the two lives. The point is moot, however. The mine's worthless, and one-third of nothing is no more than one-fifth of nothing."

"I didn't mean to imply anything," I said. "I just want to clarify my thoughts. Thank you for telling us what you did."

I was about to make excuses for leaving, when Tommy stood up again. Something about the way he stood this time told me that excuses were unnecessary. He said, "I'm sad and confused; sad about Judy, and confused about Julius's role in these awful happenings. I hope what I've told you is helpful. We Churoks are a peace-loving people. Amongst us there's little violent crime. Yet if I were to encounter a person who had harmed Judy Raskin, I couldn't be responsible for my actions."

He escorted us to the door. "You should probably leave the reservation before the cops tell their story to someone who knows you don't test mines by exploding dynamite in them, especially when you're also in the mine." He guffawed at the thought, and then he turned serious again. "I don't fathom where the bottom of these mysteries lies. If I can help, please call on me."

He walked us out to the car, the dogs swarming around us. None had the dignity of Izzie, who walked at his master's side, head high, eyes alert. "By the way," added Tommy, "if you want a real tour of the gold mine, let me know. I'll take you there myself."

He waved us down the driveway to the road.

Chapter 11

The approach to San Francisco on U.S. 101 runs alongside a bay named for the city. Cool, damp, salty breezes greet you well before the city's skyline comes into view. Soon you are entering the city. Twin Peaks is visible off to the left, Candlestick Park to the right. The skyline looms ahead.

If you stay on the 101 to the end, it disgorges you in a dreary, urban setting in a tourist-free nook of San Francisco. One navigates simply by aiming for the skyline and its bright lights. This strategy will inevitably get you to Market Street, the main drag, as many San Franciscans call it, where cheap shoes and clothes are the principal retail commodities. Tourists, drunks, druggies, transvestites, and prostitutes of both sexes make up much of the pedestrian traffic on Market's wide, well-lit sidewalks.

I had made reservations for us at a hotel on Geary Street called the Tawdelta Fielding. I had booked one room with two double beds, leaving my options open regarding the sleeping arrangements. The directions from the hotel staff member were "Market to Geary, two blocks up Geary." I found an inset map of downtown San Francisco on our big map of California and tracked our progress along Market Street.

I spotted the Tawdelta Fielding as we turned up Geary toward Union Square. It was on the left side of the street, but Geary is one way, and Charles, good English driver that he was, did not find it unnatural to drive in the "wrong" lane.

The marquee on the overhang in front of the hotel actually read Tawd l F l ing, owing to burnt-out bulbs. At first glance, I thought it was Tawdry Fling. My imagination was working the night shift when it should have been asleep.

Charles parked the Subaru in front of the hotel by the white-painted curb, where signs proclaimed all the punishments of hell to anyone parking there who wasn't checking in.

Tawdry Fling was an accurate description of the hotel's lobby. Faded velour reds dominated the entire décor: furnishings, walls, rugs. The reservation desk was an island of brightness in the large, dimly lit room whose shadows barely hid the threadbare state of the upholstered sofas and plump chairs. Age had overcome elegance.

It was after midnight. It had been an incredibly long and event-filled day. I was tired and dirty beyond caring about elegance. I was hoping foremost that the clerk with whom I'd made the reservation hadn't flubbed it, but I needn't have worried. A room was awaiting us. I redirected my hopes to a wish for cleanliness, too tired to be concerned that I had brashly chosen not to book two rooms.

The night clerk checked us in as if midnight arrivals were commonplace. Then I saw it. A discreetly placed sign behind the counter announcing rooms available by the hour. Charles saw it at about the same time. His eyebrows rose but he filled out the required check-in without missing a beat. The clerk handed us keys to room 404, gave us directions to the elevator, and instructions on where to park the car.

A bell tinkled. Out of the shadows appeared a bellhop old enough to be my grandfather. No matter. He could handle what little luggage we had. I accompanied him to the room while Charles saw to the car. I tipped the old guy a dollar. He looked unhappy at this, so I found four quarters in my change purse and handed those over. Seeing the futility of more looks, he murmured something under his breath and left.

I locked the door and looked around. The room was small, the result of an earlier subdivision of a larger room. The furnishings were shabby but appeared clean enough. Two double beds occupied half of the floor space. A chair, chest of drawers and a table with a sixteen-inch TV set occupied half of what was left. The original walls were thick and solid, built to withstand earthquakes. The newer, dividing wall was so flimsy that even sign language might be overheard in the adjoining room, I thought goofily, for the rhythmic creaking of the bedsprings behind the thin partition, along with the periodic moans, might as well have been inside our own room.

I began to unpack. I finished with my stuff in three minutes and was mulling over the propriety of unpacking for Charles when he rapped on the door. I opened it and was shocked. Exhaustion contorted his handsome face. The abrasions on his cheek flushed angrily, redder now than at Tommy's, and were oozing again.

"Will we be staying one hour or two? I forget how much I paid you."

"You idiot," I giggled. "You're so out of it you don't realize you're half dead."

"You're wrong, Dagny. I do. I walked into the loo instead of the lift and my first thought was, 'What's a commode doing in a lift?'"

Charles's suitcase was on one bed. I led him over to the other.

"Sit!" I ordered. "Stay!" He did. I thought I'd try *heel* and *rollover* a little later.

I wet a small towel and used it to cool and clean Charles's face. As I did this, he put his arms around my waist and gently rested the uninjured side of his face on my breast. "This is wonderful, Dagny. We'll have a great time together. I just need a short lie-down."

He let go of me and slid into a recumbent position, his feet still on the floor. I grabbed his legs and got him fully onto the bed. I removed his shoes, and as the room was chilly, covered him with the half of the bedspread that he wasn't lying on. I brushed my teeth, stripped, and crawled into bed under the blankets. I squirmed as close to Charles as the intervening bedclothes would allow. He was already dead to the world.

My sleep was slower to come. I wasn't as exhausted as Charles. He was surely suffering the aftereffects of the tranquilizer. And I'd dozed for the first hour after leaving the reservation, and when I'd done my share of the driving I'd talked to keep myself alert, which had prevented poor Charles from sleeping.

I'd wanted to talk about the case as we drove. Putting words to thoughts deepens my thinking, and Charles was a good listener and a good reasoner. We had agreed in our impression that Tommy had been forthright. Everything he'd said about Judy was consistent with what I'd learned from Lucy, so I'd felt I could assume that the things he'd said that I didn't have knowledge of were also true. I'd had a nagging suspicion, though, that he may have discovered the gold mine to be valuable. The elimination of two of the partners would increase his share from a fifth to a third. People do kill for less.

Charles had ventured the opinion that Tommy didn't seem to covet wealth. "Tommy strikes me as a person who's figured out that while poverty alone may create unhappiness, wealth alone doesn't create happiness."

"Perhaps he believes that," I'd countered, "but he may want the gold for his people. I'd bet many Churoks live close to poverty. I think we can agree that Tommy's idealistic, and might act on behalf of the tribe."

"I suppose he might do, but premeditated murder isn't as highly practiced among Native Americans as among other Americans."

"Maybe that doesn't extend to killing Anglos."

"Maybe. And maybe Tommy's the exception."

We'd driven in silence for a while, and just as Charles had been about to nod off I'd picked up a thread of the conversation.

"I wish I knew more about the damn gold mine. How can you tell if a gold mine's worth anything?"

Charles had yawned and sat up in his seat. "You'd need to have samples assayed. As mining technology improves, lower assay results become acceptable. Could be a P.I. type job, finding out if an assayer's been consulted recently."

With Charles once again at the wheel, I had run through possible reasons for the deaths of Judy and Troy: a double suicide; two murders; murder-suicide or suicide-murder.

Charles had found them all plausible. Judy commits suicide and Troy copycats out of grief. Or some unknown party kills Troy, blaming him for causing Judy's suicide. Or someone kills Judy and a distraught Troy dies by his own hand. Finally, Troy knows something about the murder of Judy and is murdered himself before he can act on it.

We had some reasons for not believing that Judy had committed suicide, but I still wasn't sure. If she hadn't, the possibilities were halved. I had even less to go on with Troy. Charles's suggestion that we wait for Troy's autopsy was sensible. I needed more data.

In detective work, common threads and generalities often lead to solutions and truth. Akrich was a common thread. He knew Tommy. He was Judy's and Troy's mentor. He'd played a significant role in events on the day of Judy's death. I put another interview with him on my mental to-do list.

Charles had been alert then, speaking animatedly, scanning the California landscape as he pushed the speed limit—very different from the exhausted man I was now curled up against. The warmth of his body and his rhythmic breathing, combined with a cessation of the amorous activities behind the porous wall, lulled me into a deep sleep.

The first glow of dawn and a resumption of traffic noises outside half wakened me. I saw Charles lying on his back, his mouth half open; he was snoring lightly. Sometime during the night he'd removed his clothes, for I saw them in an unruly pile on the room's sole chair. I rolled over into a fetal position with my butt pressed against his hip. As often happens with morning sleep, I dreamed. My dreams are often vivid and violent, perhaps because I've seen more violence than has the average girl not quite thirty.

I was at the Alamo. The battle was lost and I was hiding in a room with Tommy, who was sick in bed. Soldiers burst through the door and I tried to conceal myself behind his bulk. They were dragging Lucy with them; she was screaming and cursing at them in Spanish.

I tried to negotiate with the soldiers. I explained to them (in Spanish, so I dreamed) that if they let us go the sick man would take them to a hidden gold mine. Then Lucy broke away and we were running for our lives. Lucy was trying to find her grandmother's room. She was Mexican and would convince the soldiers not to harm us.

We spotted an elevator. "Let's take it," said Lucy. "These soldiers don't understand elevators." I jumped in but the door closed in Lucy's face. I pushed buttons like crazy hoping to hit the one for *open door*. The elevator began to move, but it didn't go up or down—it moved sideways. This freaked me out. I tried to keep it from moving by pushing against the wall. I pushed hard, hard, and then the wall gave way. I fell through it and landed atop Charles.

We were on the floor next to the bed. Charles was on his back, cocooned in the bedspread. I was lying stark naked on top of him. He was remarkably composed under the circumstances.

"These are peculiar mating habits, Dagny. Do you prefer the floor?"

"I don't prefer anything," I said, somewhat embarrassed. "I had a weird dream. I must've pushed you out of bed. I'm sorry."

"Not at all, not at all. This is a terribly nice way to wake up," he said, craning his neck for a better view while struggling to free his arms.

I slid up his body so that we were face to face. "Leave your arms in there," I said, sliding my arms down to pin his in place and putting the full weight of my body flat on him. "I'm too grungy to make love. And besides, I have something to tell you, something important."

Charles became still and pulled a serious face, the one I'd imagined in the mine.

I nestled my head against his cheek and spoke to the little cranny between his collarbone and his neck, the muffling effect making it somehow easier to talk. "I was sick once when I was in the army. They found cancer at my yearly physical. It was real bad and it had spread. They needed to do a mastectomy. Just a single; to save my life. So I'm not whole. I mean my body isn't whole. I'm okay with it now, I mean my head is, but I didn't want you to be surprised or put off."

"Oh, baby," he cried. "Let my arms out so I can hug you. You can't know how crackers I am about you. Don't ever imagine I care about a thing like that. No, what am I saying! Of course I care about it…I mean, Oh, you know what I mean."

That was the first time since I'd met Charles that he'd ever been flustered, and it struck me first as touching, then as funny. I rose up to let him see me, and at the same time released his arms, and simultaneously with that, I began to giggle. He drank me in with so loving a look that my emotions short-circuited and I began to sob between giggles.

Charles reached out his arms to pull me gently, ever so gently, down upon him. He held me tightly and rolled us both over, pulling away the remaining bedclothes. He laid his mouth softly over my mouth. His body slowly sank to merge with mine.

I had been fluttering with anticipation, my heart a whirligig, when suddenly I froze. Someone had turned the doorknob, sprang the latch, and entered the room.

Chapter 12

On two past occasions I had thought I was going to die. My life didn't flash before my eyes. I didn't, in that instant, forgive those who'd trespassed against me. I certainly didn't have a sneak preview of heaven or hell. Mostly I was trying not to wet my pants and end up the brunt of cruel jokes.

It therefore amazed me how much thought whirled through my mind when I heard the door open. I remembered that twenty-four hours ago two men had tried to kill us. I saw no reason they couldn't have followed us to the hotel and gotten a key to our room; if the first shot hit me in the head I wouldn't even hear the dull pop from the suppressed pistol.

Simultaneously, I reran the dream. The Alamo, the escape, the errant elevator. It all suggested imminent danger.

My sense of humor hadn't left me because also in that moment I thought how surprised our killers must be to have caught us in the act. What were those law school words? In *flagrante delicto*. I even had time to regret that, well, we hadn't quite finished.

Charles's voice interrupted these musings with, "Get the bloody hell out of here. What do you think you're doing!"

"Lo siento mucho, bot thee dor wass not lock-ed," came the reply. "I knock but you deedn't hear me."

The maid exited quickly, leaving us deflated. "For a moment, I thought those thugs from the cave had followed us," said Charles.

"God, me, too. We have to start being more careful." I wriggled out from under and rose to my feet, standing over Charles. I reached for his hands, leaned back with all my weight and pulled him to his feet, and then into a body clench. "Let's take a shower."

It was well after noon when we ventured outside. I was famished. Sex has that effect on me. The day clerk told us where to get coffee and donuts. We took our breakfast to Union Square and found an unoccupied bench in the hazy San Francisco sun. In the daylight Charles's face was looking better. Each sip of coffee and bite of donut energized us a little more. We planned a walking trip that would take us the length of Market Street to the pier.

As we walked, I shared my dream with Charles. The dream agitated me in a way different from an ordinary nightmare. Something about it jibed with something that had been bothering me. Charles helped put it together.

"Do you think Lucy's in any danger?" he asked. "If someone thinks you know too much, maybe they think she does, too."

"Of course!" I pounded my fist into my hand. "I need to call the Worthingtons." In my haste I nearly withdrew the pistol from my handbag instead of the cellular.

Doris answered. Lucy had taken off Friday to visit some friends in La Jolla and wasn't expected back until Monday night. She hadn't left a number where she could be reached, nor any names. "So there's no way to get in touch with her?" I asked Doris.

"Not that I can think of. I'll ask Ernie when he gets back, but you know, college kids, they don't worry about that sort of thing. Is she in some kind of danger?"

"Naw, not at all, just wanted to touch base." To make my nonchalance even less convincing, I asked Doris "to watch for anything unusual, just in case."

"Aieee, sometimes I'm such an idiot," I said to Charles after I'd clicked off. "Now I got them worried and I don't know what good that does."

"Oh, it can't hurt. Something's up, and the more eyes and ears alert, the better. Anyway, Lucy was on her way to La Jolla at the same time those blokes were harassing us in the mine. She'll be safe from those two, anyway."

"Unless a third person's watching her."

"If you're worried, we can drive back."

"Charles, you're sweet, you're sensitive." I kissed him lightly. "I'm being paranoid. This whole business has me spooked. I'll call Monday on our way down to Santa Cruz. Let's enjoy San Francisco. Let's enjoy us."

Hand-in-hand, we walked to the end of Market Street. We strolled along the Embarcadero, which lines the bay along the Port of San Francisco, and soaked up the sights, smells, and sounds. The terminus of the Embarcadero is the famous Fisherman's Wharf. It sports more tourists per square foot than any other site in the city. We joined right in, walking out on the quay where seals begged and barked in the water below.

At the end of the quay is an excellent view of Alcatraz Island, the former federal prison known as The Rock, and now open to the public for tours. The Golden Gate Bridge was barely visible through the thin fog that lay on the waters of the bay.

Touristing, too, is hungry business. Alioto's on the Wharf looked enticing and soon we were peeling shrimp, tearing sourdough, and quaffing Anchor Steam, San Francisco's own brew.

Still tourists, we made the rounds of Ghirardelli Square. Built above what were once fish canneries, the Square is a collection of upscale shops including galleries, boutiques, cafés and my favorite, a chocolatier. The air in this shop makes you feel as though you're afloat in a sea of chocolate. We'd thought we were full when we left Alioto's, but for Ghirardelli chocolate, there's always room.

We ducked in and out of shops, amazed at their variety, eccentricity, and sometimes out-and-out kitsch. A shop of old photographs, a shop of nothing but clocks, a shop selling candles in every imaginable shape, including famous sculptures like "The Kiss." There were shops of bangles, baubles and bright shining beads, shops of weird clothes, shops of very weird clothes and shops of very, very weird clothes.

One specialty store was full of mirrors. I like mirrors because they allow me to observe others furtively, one of my favorite pastimes, a real stereotypical P.I. pastime. In a small, hand-held mirror I watched Charles watch me in a wall mirror with a look of such loving lust that my heart lurched in my rib cage. I grabbed his hand and pulled him out the door. "Charles, I'm shopped out. I could use a nap if we're going to stay out late. Let's catch a cable car back."

He found that idea "most agreeable." We caught the Powell Street cable car, a direct ride to Union Square. The two tacky blocks down Geary to the Tawdelta Fielding seemed like two miles. I let my left arm slither around Charles's waist. His right arm encircled my shoulders. We took it "hip-to-hip, rockin' through the wilderness," as the B-52's song goes.

That evening Charles made reservations at a French restaurant overlooking the bay. The Rock was lit up, a galaxy of light amid a universe of ominous waters. Ships were entering and leaving the harbor, drifting past the once-dreaded prison, their lights commingling.

Charles ordered a Pouilly Fuissé which he described as "a chardonnay with a pedigree" in place of cocktails. We sipped the wine, held hands across the table, and tried to decode the hand-written menu. It was a two-person job. My expertise was writing. In teaching myself to read upside down, I had gotten good at deciphering handwriting from any angle. Charles's job was to interpret the French words I spelled out to him. "Food always tastes better when the menu's in French," deadpanned Charles.

Whether that old chestnut of a joke had any truth to it or not, the food *was* delicious, the wine was delicious, and Charles was delicious. We did have some kind of fun that night.

Sunday we decided to walk across the Golden Gate Bridge. We shopped for a picnic lunch and bought a bottle of the same wine we'd had the night before. The lolling is reputedly superb on the other side of the bridge, with views of the harbor, the city, the bridge itself and the open sea. Lolling with Charles seemed more enticing to me than any other imaginable diversion.

I always thought the Golden Gate Bridge was something you admired if you were happy, and jumped from if you were unhappy. I never knew that the Bridge was such a melting pot of San Francisco society. Rich and poor, adult and child, yuppie and hippie, cops and drug dealers, even a cowboy and an American Indian, trekked along the mile-long walkways. Below, hardy souls windsurfed in the bay, challenged by the stiff breezes, the choppy sea, and the changing currents. Further off, The Rock, bereft of its nighttime sparkle, hunkered glum and gray in the morning light.

On the opposite side were several partially wooded grassy knolls. We ambled toward these until we found a private little copse. We spread the blanket we'd borrowed from the hotel. Charles got out his Swiss army knife corkscrew, extracted the cork from the bottle, and decanted some wine into a tumbler with the Tawdelta Fielding logo, a T inside a triangle.

We sat cross-legged facing each other, the wine between us. Charles reached out and gently clasped his hands behind my head. I put my hands on his thighs for balance. He pulled me toward him with a light but relentless pressure until our lips met. We remained this way, with intermittent wine-sipping breaks.

During one such break, Charles pointed a thumb and forefinger gun at me. "Hands up, Dagny." I raised my hands in mock surrender. With a cat-like quickness, Charles stripped me naked to the waist. There was a time when this was not easy for me. My surgery had left angry red scars and welts, which had taken more than a year to subside. One potential lover, on seeing the scars and asymmetry, had been too repulsed to make love, and it left me painfully self-conscious. With Charles, I was already relaxed. He looked at me lovingly and analytically. Charles could do this seemingly contradictory thing.

"They did a nice job, Dagny, if I may say so as a medical doctor. The scarring is minimal, and you have a beautiful breast, a most attractive lovely…" and he moved his head down to kiss me gently.

"Under the blanket," I said, my voice husky with desire.

No trip to San Francisco is complete without a visit to, and a meal in, Chinatown. We took the Powell Street cable car to Jackson Street. From there, Chinatown is an easy walk downhill. As we descended, delicious food odors rose to meet us, whetting our already eager appetites.

It was dumb luck that we ended up in Quang Phuc Dong's. The inside was brash to the point of camp, what with the décor of statues, fountains, statues in fountains, fountains in statues, jade figurines in elaborately carved niches, and walls adorned with red velvet dragons. The Chinese waiter had grown up in England, and when he heard Charles speak he humbly suggested that we allow him to bring the best dishes of the house. "If you don't like it, you don't have to pay," he said. When the feast ended we paid willingly and tipped handsomely.

The human being is never fully happy. Though I was sated in all ways imaginable, my thoughts turned to Lucy, and they were dark thoughts indeed. I checked my phone messages and there was nothing from her. I called the Worthingtons again. This time Ernie answered. He said Lucy had called earlier and was planning to stay a few more days in La Jolla since classes were over. "Did she leave a number?" I asked.

"She said her friends had just moved in and the phone wasn't hooked up yet."

"Did she say where she was?" I persisted.

"The Covenant Apartments," said Ernie. "The only name she mentioned was David Balfour. I wrote it down because I knew you'd want to know."

"Did she leave me a message? No, of course not, you'd tell me. Did she say anything about calling me?"

"I'm sorry, Dagny. I've told you everything. I didn't want to be pushy with Lucy. You know how independent she is. Besides, a lot of kids head for Newport or Laguna or La Jolla after finals. It's a big party scene."

I thanked him and asked him to have her call me immediately if he heard from her again. I called La Jolla information for the rental office of the Covenant Apartments. They didn't have a listing. Nor did they have a listing for a David Balfour. Lost in thought, I was holding the phone, trying to decide what to do next when Charles began massaging my neck.

"What did you find out?" he asked. I told him. He made me repeat the names.

"What is it?" I asked.

"Nothing I can put my finger on. Balfour is a good British name."

We were silent while Charles's wonderful fingers worked magic on my neck. Some of the tension drained from me.

"Maybe they don't have a rental office. Or maybe their listing's under a different name, like the company that owns them, or the agency that handles the rentals," offered Charles.

"Maybe," I conceded, but misgivings hung darkly over me.

In bed, I found comfort in the shelter of Charles's arms. The memory of lovemaking under the trees pushed worries aside and soothed my soul.

Chapter 13

We rose early. The autopsy was scheduled for 10:00 a.m. in Santa Cruz, a good two hours' drive from the hotel. We drove west across the peninsula to the coast, where we had breakfast in a diner overlooking the Pacific Ocean and with a view of the famous Cliff House restaurant.

I was on Route 1 again, this time approaching Santa Cruz from the north, and with Charles at the wheel instead of Lucy. Halfway between San Francisco and Santa Cruz is Half Moon Bay, an exotically named place that suggests the South Seas and romance. As we passed through, I snuggled closer to Charles despite the bucket seats of his Subaru.

An hour later we entered the city of Santa Cruz. Some of the buildings of the university were visible high up in the hills, those same hills amongst which was the dale of death where Troy's life had come to an ambiguous end. I hoped this visit to the city would shed light on the mystery of his death and resolve the ambiguity of suicide or murder.

Charles consulted his neatly printed instructions. "This is straightforward," he muttered. We got off at Route 9, and drove past the Historical Museum directly to the hospital, a gray, six-story concrete building. Unobtrusively tucked behind it was the entrance to the Santa Cruz County Morgue. The driveway behind the entrance descended steeply into an underground parking garage.

Once inside the facility, Charles identified himself to the waiting-room receptionist, who immediately paged Dr. Peters. She invited us to sit in some blue Naugahyde chairs by a squat, square table on which lay several out-of-date magazines.

"How well do you know Dr. Peters?" I asked.

"I sat next to him at a luncheon during a medical examiners' conference last year and we hit it off over our shared interest in steroid activity. He's keen on investigating the Nandrolex striations at the nail root. That's why he agreed to delay Troy's refrigeration for three days. He finds the striations suspicious, just as we do."

"I'm kind of nervous," I confessed. "The way you are when you're waiting for the results of a blood test. God knows I've experienced that plenty."

"I'll let you know what's happening as soon as I can. They won't let you watch, you know."

I knew. I once attended an autopsy as part of my Military Police training in the army. It's grisly business, cutting open a body and removing its organs one by one for examination. Even the brain comes out. A surgical saw cuts off the top of the head much as one would open a pumpkin to make a jack-o-lantern. The brain is removed and carved up like a roast beef. Each slice is studied for any abnormality that might relate to the cause of death.

I had watched the entire procedure without ill effects. I remember feeling smug when two of the big guys, sergeants, had to excuse themselves. Military cops in training learn to have strong stomachs. It's required for the job. Nor blood, nor guts, nor shit, nor puke should make a copper, or a P.I. for that matter, unable to perform his duty.

All cops have close encounters of the noxious kind with one or more of these substances. We were taught to treat them clinically, in effect, to intellectualize the malodor. But just in case my intellect failed, I also learned to breathe entirely through my mouth, not permitting a single stinking molecule to touch the smell receptors in my nose.

No amount of readiness or willingness on my part would be able to get me in to watch Troy's autopsy. The law is clear about who may and who may not attend. As a registered medical examiner in the state of California, Charles could attend. As a spectator, which is all I would be despite my high fallutin' P.I.'s license, I could not.

Bob Peters burst through a pair of metallic double doors, spotted us immediately, and charged up to Charles, right hand extended. He was a wiry little man about two inches shorter than me. His quick, bird-like movements made him appear brusque.

Charles introduced me. We shook hands and exchanged the usual banter, but he couldn't disguise a look of consternation. Charles understood right away. "Dagny knows she can't attend the autopsy," he told Peters, who brightened at not having to turn down a request from Charles, whom he obviously respected.

"Yes, well then, Dagny—quite an unusual name—you're welcome to wait in my office. The magazines are more current, or perhaps you like medical books."

"Thanks, but I need to make a long distance phone call. My cell phone isn't getting a signal in this building. Is there a pho—"

"Please, feel free to make calls from my office. No problem. Dial 9 to get out." He was pleased to be able to help.

We followed him back through the double doors, ignoring the Employees Only sign. Two right turns put us in his office, which was not unlike Charles's, which I remembered vividly since it was where we had first met. He pulled the telephone across his desk close by a chair where he invited me to sit. The two of them left, Peters nodding and smiling goodbye, and Charles rounding his lips into a fleeting kiss.

I tried the Worthingtons. No one answered. I punched in directory assistance for the San Diego metro area. Maybe this Balfour person had lived near La Jolla before moving there. If I could get his previous number, I might find someone who knew him. A computer answered and asked me for city and listing. I asked to speak to an operator instead. A male human came on the line. I tried my pathetic little girl voice, the one with just the barest hint of a sob. "I'm trying to locate my father, who left us when I was a teenager. His name is David Balfour—B-a-l-f-o-u-r. I heard he was in southeastern California."

"Ma'am, there are two area codes covering territory larger than the state of West Virginia. Don't you have a city?"

I ratcheted up the sob a notch. "Is there any way you could try?"

Lucky for me there are male operators. I doubt a female would have fallen for this. "I'll see what the computer dredges up for us," he said sympathetically. I could hear the key-clicks in the background. "I have three David Balfours, and three Initial-D Balfours."

"Could you tell me what cities?" He gave me four numbers in San Diego, one in Needles, and one in Stovepipe Wells, which is in Death Valley. I pressed my luck: "Could you also check under the spellings B-a-l-f-o-r and B-a-l-f-o-r-e."

"I thought he was your father. Don't you know how your name is spelled?" retorted the now skeptical operator.

"He may be using a different spelling," I countered.

"He may be using a different name…but I'll check for you."

"Thanks."

"No Davids or Initial-Ds under those spellings."

I thanked him again and hung up.

I began with the Davids. I dialed the number in Needles. A woman with a shrill voice—like Chef Julia Child's—picked up. I asked for David Balfour and she told me he was at work. She had some kind of a British Isles accent, but not like Charles's. She offered me his number, which I pretended to write down. That wasn't the right one.

I tried one of the San Diego Balfours. "This is David," said a voice. I waited to see if it was a person or a recording. "Hello?" inquired the voice.

"Hello, my name is Susan Radford and I'm a friend of Lucy Navarro's, and she said you'd give me some information about living in La Jolla, because I'm thinking of taking a job there and I want to have some idea what it might be like to live there and how much an apartment costs and, you know, stuff like that." Susan is the chatty one of my multiple personalities.

"Lucy who?"

"Lucy Navarro," I said, rolling the r's like Lucy did. "She's a friend of yours, isn't she?"

"I don't know no Lucy Navarro, but you sound kinda cute. What did you say your name is?"

I hung up. I let the second San Diego David's phone ring fifteen times, one full minute. No answer. I'd have to try that one later.

Peters's phone bill was mounting, but hey, he had offered. I tried the Initial-D Balfours and got two non-Davids and a no-answer. So much for the Balfours. A similar effort to get a fix on the Covenant Apartments amounted to zilch. I returned the phone to its cradle and idly scanned the bookshelves for something interesting to read.

I stopped at the title *Anabolic Steroids: Facts and Comparisons*. It was a thin book compared to some of the fat ones on anatomy, diseases of the skin, blood chemistry, and reproduction. I withdrew it, pulling the book on its left half way out to mark its place on the shelf. The copyright was current. I sat down to read about Nandrolex, to which the book devoted a chapter.

The first thing I learned surprised me. Nandrolex is manufactured by Wellex Corporation, a pharmaceutical company headquartered in Santa Barbara. I skipped the chemical formulation and methods of synthesis. All anabolic steroids are synthetic derivatives of testosterone, the male sex hormone. The actions are simple enough: Nandrolex promotes body tissue-building processes. Its legitimate use is for treating certain kinds of cancer and some rare blood and kidney disorders. Much of the chapter described contraindications, warnings, precautions, and adverse reactions.

These health hazards included leukemia, diabetes, seizures, vomiting, diarrhea, jaundice, and death, to name a few. Death as a health hazard! I guess that's one way to look at it.

I was thankful that my own cancer hadn't required so powerful a drug. Nandrolex isn't good for us girls. It makes us grow hair where we don't want it, lose it where we want it, and enlarges our clitorises. In short, it turns us into men. We could end up wearing comfortable shoes and have cravings for Monday night football.

The drug tweaks male sexuality, too. In mature males Nandrolex is associated with testicular atrophy, chronic priapism, and impotence. Now I understood the lugubrious air of those Soviet Olympic weightlifters of the 1980s.

Toward the end of the chapter I found information on the white lines on the fingernails. The cause is a damaged nail root in which the new nail tissue is formed with calcium deposits that impart the white color. The precise role of Nandrolex in this process isn't understood, but it is supposed that "…the drug inhibits or enhances the activity of any of several enzymes critical to the process of nail growth."

I spent the next hour reading about other anabolic steroids. Most had the nasty side effects of Nandrolex, but nowhere else could I find a mention of the white striations.

A voice asked, "Would you like some coffee?" I'd nodded off just moments before Charles and Dr. Peters returned. The book I was reading lacked plot. "Ah, I'll bet you've been reading about Nandrolex," said Peters, glancing down at the book, not waiting for my reply to the coffee question. "A good idea, Dagny, because Troy Stanton has the telltale striations. Barely visible, mind you, but Dr. Clarke and myself agree that that's what they are. We removed a couple of fingernails for analysis."

"Could Nandrolex be the cause?" I asked.

"Possibly, but not for sure," answered Peters. "I've asked a friend of mine, Jeanette Briggs, to come down for a couple of minutes. She's a pharmacologist and she may have some insights to share with us."

The intercom buzzed. Peters flicked a switch. The receptionist announced the arrival of Dr. Briggs. "Send her in, please."

In a moment, a head of blond curls peered around the door. "You in here, Bob? Jesus, this place gives me the creeps!"

"Come in, Jeanette. The bodies are all put away," said Peters.

The rest of Dr. Jeanette Briggs came through the door. Thick glasses with heavy rims gave an otherwise handsome face a studious appearance. A starched white lab coat hid most of the rest of her from view, though I could tell she was wearing a blouse and skirt underneath. Her calves were thick, not from exercise, but because some women are built that way— *piano legs* is the unkind term for it. Her hands had a powdery look; the unpolished nails were cut short and she wore no jewelry: clues that she was a frequent wearer of disposable gloves.

Peters made brief introductions. We shook hands, Briggs holding Charles's a moment longer than I thought necessary. I couldn't blame her.

Peters summarized events succinctly, starting with Judy's death and autopsy. I was impressed. He told Briggs nothing irrelevant, wasted not a single word, and yet was comprehensive. When I mentioned it later to

Charles, he said it comes from long years of reporting medical results to a tape recorder, a practice in which conciseness is at a premium.

"Did you look for signs of steroid abuse?" asked Briggs.

"No signs of abuse, eh, Charles," said Peters, "but we're relying on your lab to test for Nandrolex."

"The effects aren't always obvious," noted Briggs. She rubbed her chin with the back of her wrist. "What mystifies me is why in both cases the striations appear to have originated close to the time of death. I know of nothing toxic that'd both kill and leave the white lines. Besides, both died as a result of hanging?" She looked to the doctors for confirmation. Both nodded.

"We didn't find any toxicity in any event," added Charles. "Liver, pancreas, adrenals, kidneys, spleen, brain, all appeared normal. Of course we'll have to wait for the rest of the lab results."

Now Peters was chin-rubbing.

"Maybe we should talk to someone at Wellex," I chimed in. They all looked at me. "Isn't Nandrolex manufactured by Wellex?" It was a rhetorical question. "Maybe they have some ideas about what else might cause the changes to fingernails."

"Yes, of course," said Briggs, as much to herself as to us. "I forgot that Nandrolex is a Wellex product. It's a little out of their specialty."

"What is their specialty?" I asked.

"Deriving drugs from natural sources. Their scientists spend as much time in Angeles National Forest as they do in their labs. Nature's drug store is as impressive as man's, and Wellex has exploited its bounty."

"And Nandrolex is a synthetic, non-natural drug, is that the point?" I asked, rhetorically, again, since I'd just read up on it.

"That's right," said Briggs, "though they may have learned to modify a naturally occurring chemical to make it. However it's made, it's company-confidential. You can count on that. Pharmaceutical companies are very proprietary, very protective of their sources and manufacturing methods."

"Couldn't we ask them for help?" I persisted, though I'd already added a visit to Wellex to my ever-growing list of things to do.

Briggs answered, "As I said, they're secretive. Their scientists wouldn't discuss their products with me. They'd get fired if they did. You might be able to approach the management."

Nobody else seemed able to shed light on the matter. All agreed the coincidence of the striations was remarkable; no one had an explanation.

The conversation changed to medical small talk and hospital chitchat. Before leaving, Charles had to sign some documents regarding

Troy's autopsy. Dr. Peters promised to send him a complete report including lab results.

I gave out business cards with the usual request. Dr. Briggs promised to call if she thought of anything significant.

We got back to Santa Barbara around dinnertime. I didn't want to say goodbye to Charles quite yet, though my mind was swimming with worries about Lucy and ideas about Judy and Troy.

We opted for a seaside restaurant called The Beach House for dinner. At a secluded table, we were reminiscing about the weekend and Charles was saying some very sweet things. I took his hand, to put it to my cheek. As it passed under the light of our table lamp, I cried out in surprise. "Charles, your fingernails!" White striations were starting to form at the roots of the nails of the thumb and index finger of his right hand.

Chapter 14

Charles was calm. He asked for my pocket "torch." I got it out of my purse and handed it to him. He examined each of his nails carefully under its light. He furrowed his brow a little deeper each time he found the beginnings of a white line. In all, five nails showed the signs.

My first thought was that Charles was going to die. My brain reversed the temporal order I'd observed of death followed by striations, to striations followed by death. Aloud I wondered, "How can this be?" Our minds converged instantly on Charles's whereabouts three days ago, and on what he could possibly have in common with the two dead students. At the same time I looked at Charles's face. His abrasions were healing but they were still visible even in the dim light. And then it hit me. With a heavy thud, one ugly piece of the puzzle fell in place.

Judy and Troy were murdered. They were knocked out by a dart from a tranquilizer gun, as Charles had been in the goldmine. Knowing how instantly Charles went down, I would guess neither victim felt a thing. They were hanged while unconscious, thus leaving no traces of a struggle.

But not no traces at all. Thanks to a power outage and a meticulous medical examiner, the singular effect of the fingernail striations came to light.

Realization struck us both at the same time. I retrieved my phone and called the Worthingtons again, full of a sickening fear for Lucy, and hoping beyond hope that she had called again. She hadn't. I handed the phone to Charles so he could call Peters at home to fill him in.

While he talked, I sipped on my gin and tonic and tried to deduce what Peters was saying, based on Charles's half of the conversation. That was difficult because Charles was mostly listening and nodding every few seconds. Peters had a lot to say and by the end of the call, a good ten minutes later, I was squirming with curiosity.

"What's up with Peters? He talked a long time."

"He thinks he knows what happened. The lab, with Dr. Briggs's help, found the metabolic remains of a thio-pentobarbital compound."

I raised my eyebrows questioningly.

"Something akin to sodium pentothal," explained Charles. "You know, the stuff they call truth serum in old movies. It's a potent anesthetic that produces rapid unconsciousness for short periods. It's used in hospitals because it puts the patient under instantly and comfortably, after which the longer-lasting gaseous anesthetics can be administered."

"Did they find any Nandrolex?"

"Oh yes, indeed. Even though they left Troy off the ice, they took bodily fluids while they were fresh. He was full of the bloody stuff."

"But why both drugs? I don't get the steroid part of the formula."

"Ah, that's what Peters was going on about. He and Briggs put their heads together and have a hypothesis. The Nandrolex retards the metabolization of the anesthetic, thus extending the period of unconsciousness long enough for the victim to be hanged and asphyxiated."

"Then that does it. We know Troy's a homicide. We can go to the cops."

"Not so easy. The coroner isn't convinced there's a link. She says the metabolic traces could've been left over from some thio-pental he took as a downer. The poor fool also had heavy traces of tetrahydrocannabinol in his bloodstream—you know, the active ingredient of marijuana, often called THC. It makes him look like a druggie."

"But what about the Nandrolex?" I protested.

"Peters pressed that point with the coroner, but Troy could've been using it for bodybuilding, and it's common knowledge that you can buy steroids on the Internet. There isn't actually any direct evidence that the Nandrolex does indeed interact with the anesthetic. It's a bit hypothetical."

Charles paused in thought, wrinkling his brow, and then continued, with tension in his voice, "The damning thing is that if we had similar results for Judy, then once both coroners saw the identical pattern, they'd jump on it. As it is, they're not going to stick their necks out. Damn, if I'd only looked sooner for the Nandrolex in Judy! As it is, the striations alone aren't sufficiently convincing. What a carve up!" He massaged more wrinkles into his forehead.

"Charles, darling." I took his hand in both of mine. "Don't lay a guilt trip on yourself. If you hadn't noticed Judy's fingernails we'd be totally clueless."

"We *are* totally clueless."

"No, we're not. We know that two deaths that were supposed to look like suicides were actually homicides. We know the MO. We know there's a Churok connection, either through the gold mine or in some other way. We know that they, whoever *they* are, know we know something."

"Which reminds me," Charles interrupted, "that you must be very careful. I'm not so sure that you weren't the target in the mine."

"I'm not sure, either. I think we both need to stay alert. Can you shoot?"

"Actually, yes. My father thought a gentleman should know how to shoot a shotgun and a pistol—the one for grouse, the other for other gentlemen."

"I'm going to lend you John's Smith & Wesson .357 magnum. It's a heavy, ugly brute, 20 years old, but it'll do the job. Even if you miss, the bang will scare most people away." Charles looked at me narrowly but didn't go into a big macho act and refuse.

"Funny," he said, "but I have the right to carry a concealed weapon. I guess they consider medical examiners auxiliary law enforcement. Thanks for the offer."

"Great, I'm breathing easier already. Look, here's what I want to do. First, I'm going to make myself believe Lucy's okay and is having a good time shacked up somewhere with Captain Wonderful. I'm not going to worry about her for twenty-four hours. In that time, I want to find out whether that friggin' gold mine's worth killing over. You mentioned something about assayers when we were driving up to San Fran. Do you have any ideas as to what I can do?"

"I hadn't thought of it before, but there's a bloke named Dave MacAllen who works in our lab. He's an avid rock collector and amateur geologist. He loves geology, but makes a better living as a biochemist. Let's put your question to him."

He looked at his watch. It wasn't very late. Out came the cell phone. Charles placed the call and used a conversational style that I call the small talk sandwich. Charles first made some small talk with MacAllen: weather, sports, wife'n'kids. Then he got to the meat of the call. He hand-signaled me for a pen and took some notes on a paper napkin. Some further small talk completed the sandwich and he was finished.

"Dave says to check with the State Bureau of Mines. Since Santa Barbara's the county seat, they have an office in town. It's an address on State Street." He gave me the napkin. I folded it and put it in my bag with the intention of going there first thing in the morning.

After dinner I suggested we drive to John's office. He kept the .357 in a desk drawer and I wanted to give it to Charles that night. I'd learned a lot from John about how to move safely from building to car and car to building, and how to detect a tail while navigating around the city. Our adversary was unwilling to commit out-and-out murder, at least so far, and the tranquilize-and-kill approach, with the ambiguity of suicide, was less effective in public or against two people.

The parking lot outside the Beach House looked harmless enough. Charles drove, bemused at my directions that spiraled us toward downtown. It made spotting a tail easy, but there was nothing suspicious.

There were several phone messages on the office's answering machine, but none from Lucy or the Worthingtons. I didn't even listen to a message once I knew it wasn't about her.

I unlocked the drawer with the .357 and got it out for Charles, along with a couple of dozen rounds. "Have you ever fired one of these?"

"This particular model, no."

"This sucker kicks like a mule with the .357 cartridges. The two or three times I used it, I loaded it with .38 specials. They're far easier on the hand and they'll stop a person as quickly as the .357s. Of course the .357s will also stop an elephant, but I for one am in favor of avoiding elephants, not shooting them."

I handed him the weapon. He hefted it and turned it over a few times, releasing, spinning, and reseating the cylinder, cocking and decocking the hammer. Finally he flipped open the cylinder again and filled it with six of the mini-dynamite .357 rounds. I hoped fervently he would not be obliged to shoot anything.

I had Charles drive me home. We circled the block carefully. Over his mild protest I made him drop me off. I needed an evening alone to think, and a good night's sleep. Before exiting the car, I reached in my bag and withdrew my semi and cocked it. I promised Charles I'd call him in the morning. I bootlegged the baby Glock on my hip like a quarterback on an end-run, and scurried to the front door and safety of John's house.

The light on the answering machine was blinking. I was hoping one of the messages would be from Lucy. No such luck, but when I played the last message, Tommy's basso boomed out of the tiny speaker.

"Dagny, this is Tommy. I don't remember if I told you that Starry Night has a daughter. She joined the Peace Corps a year before her mother died. She came by the house Sunday. She said she didn't know why, but she had an urge to see me. I told her about your visit and she'd like to talk to you."

There was a pause, as if he were collecting his thoughts, or wondering how much he should tell me over the phone.

"She's a lot like her mother. Very intuitive, very tuned-in. She wanted to...oh, never mind, this is too long for the machine. I think you should come back up and meet her. Call me as soon as you can. Call any time."

I tried to get everyone's ages into perspective. Starry Night died twenty or so years ago. Kids went into the Peace Corps when they were in their late teens or early twenties. The daughter must be in her forties. I wondered why she hadn't followed in her mother's footsteps, or how she felt about Tommy, or whether she knew Akrich—no, how well she knew him. And who was the girl's father? I was thinking of her, older than me, as a girl because I was thinking of her as she was back in the '60s.

I called Tommy. He had related the entire course of events that brought me to the Churok reservation to Melanie—that was the daughter's name. "She wants to talk about this very much," said Tommy. "If you can't drive up, maybe you can call."

I'm not high on telephone interviews if I can avoid them. I prefer to read the face, the eyes, and the body as I listen. I wanted to speak with Melanie in person.

"I'd like to drive up," I told Tommy. "I'm not sure when, exactly. Let me get back to you."

At nine o'clock sharp the next morning, I was at the door of the California State Bureau of Mines. A wiry, tanned man in gray slacks and a short-sleeved white shirt unlocked the door for me. A network of milky blue veins crisscrossed the browned sphere of his bald head, which was dotted with aging spots. He spoke with the gravelly voice of a long-time smoker.

"I'm Harry Wagner. How can I help you, uh, miss?" His eyes darted to my left hand, then back to my face.

I introduced myself, showed my P.I. license, and began to fib a little. "I represent the family of Judy Raskin. She's the young woman who committed suicide last week. You may have read about it."

"Yes, I remember. Terrible thing. Made me think of my own three daughters. C'mon back here and sit down."

He was talking as he ushered me down a corridor toward his office. "The youngest would be about your age. She was depressed once and tried to kill herself. It was a hard time to get through."

"Is she okay now?"

"She's fine. Got two boys herself—go ahead and sit right there—one just graduated junior high school, one just graduated elementary school. Sounds kind of funny, graduating elementary school, but they had a ceremony, gave him a diploma, the whole she-bang."

He took a chair behind a government-issue oak desk. I let him wind down on how bright, clever, handsome and devilishly charming his grandsons were, inserting clucks, smiles, and nods where appropriate.

"Well, you didn't come to the Bureau of Mines to hear about me, now, did you?"

I got right to the point. "Miss Raskin's father gave me these papers. They say she owned a one-fifth interest in the Lucky U gold mine. The family would like to know its worth." I handed him the papers across the desk. He took them, retrieved a pair of glasses from his shirt pocket, and began reading.

"Your friend doesn't own anything. This is a lease agreement for mineral rights."

"Yes," I agreed, "that's right. She was entitled to one fifth of any profits earned by the mine."

"Have you shown this to a lawyer?"

"The family has their own attorney. I was hired to find out what her share's worth."

"Well now, miss, it ain't worth anything to her heirs. This agreement says plain as day that if one of them dies, the others divvy up."

"My client may dispute the validity of this contract, depending on whether it's worth disputing. Can you tell me anything at all about this mine?"

"Please wait here a moment." He disappeared down the hall. I looked around for something to read. The office was barren except for a large, detailed geological map of the local area on one wall. I walked over and perused it.

He returned about five minutes later with a sheaf of ancient-looking papers. "Here's your mine, miss, your Lucky U mine." He got behind his desk and spread out the papers. "Registered in 1870. It was part of a mineral survey by the Bureau of Land Management. It had some gold in it that the Churoks extracted over the years. Looks like it turned unprofitable around the end of the war."

"Vietnam?"

"No," he chuckled, "World War II. That's what we oldies mean by 'The War.'"

"Oh, it always meant Vietnam when I was a soldier. But anyway, you're talking about, what, fifty some years ago. How can you tell when it stopped producing?"

"The Churoks quit paying their fees in '48, which means they quit working it, and if they quit working it, it must've been unprofitable. They're not dumb."

"Could today's technology make it profitable?"

"Possibly. Companies get more out of low-grade ore than they used to, but there has to be something there to begin with. Can't make a silk shirt from a pig's rump," he said, smiling and showing me his gold bridgework.

"Can you tell from the mineral survey whether it's likely to have any worth today?"

"Nope. Don't know what they took out."

"Suppose one of the five wanted to assess the mine's worth. What would they do?"

"They wouldn't come here, miss. They'd hire an assayer, up there,"—he gestured north—"probably Mojave Analytical Geochemistry Laboratory out o' Makrui, assuming they're still in business. They'd grind up some tailings and analyze them. That'd give a pretty good idea of what's left."

"Tailings?"

"Leftovers from the last time the mine was worked. They're easy to find, easy to assay."

"If there was an assay recently, you wouldn't know?"

"That's right. Why should I know? Now if the government does a mineral survey, that's public record. But you pay for an assay, it's business between you and the lab. People are secretive about gold. Always have been."

I rose to leave. "Thank you, Mr. Wagner." I reached over to shake hands with him. "I can find my way out." I started to leave.

"Miss, don't waste your time with the lab. They'll clam up, won't tell you a thing. Best to find a neighbor. Find someone living near the mine. They'll know. 'Specially the Indians. Find some old coot like me, and give him a pretty smile."

He said this matter-of-factly, not lecherously. I practiced a pretty smile on him, thanked him again, and left.

I could kill two birds with one trip. I called Tommy back and asked if I could come round and meet Melanie that afternoon. He invited me to do so.

Makrui is the largest "city" on the Churok reservation, population 9,818. The man from Texaco directed me to the assayer's place of business. It was a small, clapboarded house with peeling white paint, two blocks off the main road. A hand-stenciled lawn sign identified the Mojave Analytical Geochemistry Laboratories. At the front door, a placard frayed at the edges invited me to enter without knocking. As I did, a bell chimed and a waft of chemical smells assailed my nostrils. A middle-aged man in a stain-covered white lab coat emerged from the back. I got the distinct impression this was a one-person operation, and I was looking at that person.

For this scene the script called for me to be in the employ of Troy Stanton's family. I put the question simply. "Did Mr. Stanton ask the lab to do an assay of ore from the Lucky U mine?" I thought he would go through the motions of searching a file drawer but he just stood there, expressionless.

"I can't answer that. We have the same kind of relation with our clients as a doctor or lawyer—veerrrry confidential."

"Please," I said, "Mr. Stanton is dead. His death is suspicious but the cops aren't helping because they don't see a motive. His family is distraught. They hired me out of desperation. I need to know if his share of the mine is worth killing for, that's all. If we wait for a court order, the trail, if there is a trail, will be ice-cold. Couldn't you just tell me whether he hired you? No one will ever know I was here. Look, you just have to say. Nothing in writing. You can search me for a wire if you'd like." I accompanied my offer by raising my T-shirt to just below my breast and turning in a circle, exposing three hundred and sixty degrees of bare, wireless midriff.

He was struggling with himself. For the coup de grâce I reached into my purse and pulled out two new one-hundred-dollar bills, the ones with Franklin off-center, and laid them on the counter between us, smoothing them flat with my fingers. I went outside, put my handbag in the car, and returned empty-handed. The money was gone.

"I'll deny I ever said this. He was here. We did an assay. The results were impressive, to say the least. I suspect men have been killed for a lot less than a fifth of the Lucky U."

Chapter 15

Mind you, I'm assuming the ore he brought in was from the Lucky U, like he said. I don't verify where the samples come from. I just do the analysis. New extraction processes could squeeze a worthwhile amount of gold out of a mine with those tailings.

"Like how much?"

"Could be fifty, sixty thousand, maybe more."

"What's so great about that? Who would risk a murder charge for an increased share of fifty thousand dollars?" Actually, I knew of people murdered for the change in their pocket, but my murders were not that kind.

He gave me a funny look. "Ounces." There must have been a lull because he repeated the word more emphatically. "Ounces!"

I was trying to get my brain around the numbers. Gold was around $300 an ounce, and I supposed 50,000 ounces. I counted six zeros on my fingers, in front of which I put three times five and came up with fifteen million dollars. It sounded like the Lucky U owners were into some real money.

"I've known scams in my day," he said, talking as I calculated. "Person'll seed a worthless mine with good ore. If they're clever about it, and if the buyer is simple or too cheap to hire a consultant..." He paused to let me draw my own conclusions.

"Let me get this straight. Troy Stanton brought you *good* samples."

He nodded.

"And said they were from his mine, the Lucky U."

"Right."

"And maybe they were, and maybe they weren't."

"Right again."

"And you have no way of knowing."

"Three rights and you're out." He pointed an umpire's fist 'n' thumb at the door.

"One more question."

He shook his head.

"I'll ask it anyway. How come you remember him? You didn't have time to look it up."

This evoked a smile. "It's the name, miss, it's his name. Adios!"

I pondered that as I walked back to my car. Stanton, Stanton. Was it Stanton's Mill near Sacramento that touched off the '49 gold rush? No, that was Sutter's Mill. A moment later it hit. Duh. It's the Troy part. Gold is measured in troy weight. A guy named Troy with a gold mine would stick in the memory of an assayer.

I had a couple of hours to kill before meeting Melanie at Tommy's place. I used the time to update the files on my laptop. My abbreviated interview with the crabby assayer left one important question unanswered: when did he meet Troy? I had the impression it had been recently, surely in the past year. His recollection was too effortless for it to have been longer ago.

I thought about the legitimacy of the samples. If they were phony, what could be the point? The partners were all too poor to buy Troy out at some exorbitant cost. The notion that the five of them, two students, two religious zealots and a Churok priest would conspire to sell a phony mine was beyond the pale.

Assuming the assay was legit, a number of possibilities opened up. Someone wanted the mine and had no qualms about murdering its owners. I wondered frivolously who inherited the mine if all the owners hanged themselves. Not so frivolous was the thought that one of the owners was the killer. Back to the inscrutable Tommy, again. Good Tommy or bad Tommy? Had I been lured up here to be eliminated for knowing too much? Tommy had only suggested I talk to Melanie. Would he figure that I'd want a face-to-face talk? Was Melanie truly there? Did she even exist?

I considered returning to Santa Barbara. I could make up any number of excuses and talk to Melanie, if there was a Melanie, over the phone. Then I thought of the danger Lucy might be in, then of Charles. Surely if they—the anonymous ominous *they*—had it in for me, they'd have to get Charles, too. There was no turning back.

I backed up my files to a diskette and hand-wrote a letter to Charles explaining the latest turn of events. I wanted my investigation documented in case something happened to me. I drove to the post office where I purchased a mailing envelope into which I stuffed both diskette and letter. I sent it to him care of the medical examiner's office, noting wryly that I didn't know the home address of the man I'd been sleeping with for the past few days.

I slid my hand into my bag and hefted the semi, drawing comfort from the baby Glock's perfect fit to my hand. I didn't intend to lock my gun in the glove compartment, on or off the reservation.

I found Tommy's place easily. An oak tree painted on the mailbox at the foot of his driveway was apropos of his name, and distinguished his property from his neighbor's. A green Chevette parked by the house next to Tommy's pickup truck lent credence to Melanie's presence. As I pulled forward in the driveway the canine chorus assailed my ears. The big black Lab, Izzie, was absent, probably in the house with Tommy and his guest, presumably Melanie. I drew near the house, and remembering my lesson from the visit of the previous week, stayed in my car.

Tommy appeared on the porch almost immediately, smiling and beckoning. He ordered the dogs to hush and they went silent and let me pass unmolested save for a few furtive sniffs. Tommy greeted me with his characteristic dignity, shaking my hand gently and asking after Charles. Izzie nosed my crotch familiarly, and I hoped he wouldn't sniff my handbag with as much enthusiasm, and thus draw attention to the loaded gun. I felt foolish about the semi, anyway. Tommy might just as easily tear my head off as shake my hand.

When we entered the house a woman stood up and came forward. "I'm Melanie," she said, extending a small right hand and gripping mine firmly. I took the moment to fix her in my memory. She was shorter than me by several inches, small-boned, fine-featured, with penetrating, ebony eyes. Hair so black it shone was pulled back in a ponytail and smelled faintly of a minty shampoo. She was dressed in jeans, a plaid shirt, and cowboy boots. Her fingers had rings of various sizes, colors, and shapes, most of them of Native American design. Her ears were multiply pierced with more Indian jewelry.

"I'm Dagny Jamison. Nice to meet you." I smiled and remained silent. I liked this style of communication where one didn't plunge pell-mell into a jumble of words. It gave a person time to observe, to organize one's thoughts. We sat, Melanie and I on the long sofa, Tommy in his usual easy chair.

"Tommy told me about Judy," Melanie took up after a few seconds. "It's unspeakably tragic."

I nodded and said, "Tommy said you had a premonition that something was wrong."

"Mmm, premonition might be too strong a word. I go through phases of having dark thoughts and horrid dreams. Often they correspond to something bad in my life. It started when I was a child with the assassination of President Kennedy. For weeks after his death I'd dream of him. Always he was pursued by wild animals or evil spirits, and he was always defenseless, always defeated."

"That seems natural enough," I said. "I had a few weird days and nights myself after the calamity of my generation, the Challenger disaster one terrible January day. I was sixteen. I couldn't stop thinking about the woman on board, the schoolteacher, and how she could be anyone: me, my mother, one of my own teachers. But anyway, I didn't mean to interrupt."

"When I was in the Peace Corps," continued Melanie, "I had a nightmare about owls—a Churok symbol of death—disemboweling a lamb and eating the viscera. It depressed me all the next day. We were in a small Indian village in the Yucatan, pretty much cut off. That's when the news of my mother's passing reached me."

"Do you have these spells often?" I asked.

"That's the thing. I rarely do. Maybe once every two or three years. Half the time something bad's happened. An aunt dies; a friend's crippled in an accident. It's always after the fact, though. That's why I don't think of them as premonitions. I call Tommy when I have these feelings. He helps me find the source if he can, and shows me how to soothe my spirit."

"Would you mind telling me why you called him this time?"

"I'd been feeling bad for a week. My dreams were similar to those when my mother died. I finally called Tommy and he told me something dreadful had happened. He told me about your investigation. I'd like to share some thoughts I've kept to myself for a long time, except for Tommy." She looked into his face as she said this.

Tommy walked over to Melanie, knelt, and engulfed her little hand in both of his. "Are you still sure, Mulakaniya-mo, or should you let this matter rest? What can be gained, opening this old wound?"

"It's connected, somehow. The forbidden writing, my mother's passing, now the deaths of a young woman and a young man. We Churoks, we could not, cannot, look into this matter. It's too close to us. In the forest you see only the individual trees, but the forest itself is a whole, living organism."

Tommy looked glum. I was thinking to myself, *Excuse me, but would someone please tell me what we're talking about here?* But if I'd learned anything from my dealings with the Churoks, it was to keep my mouth shut and wait.

Melanie continued, in an aside to Tommy, "And I like this woman, this Dagny and her strange name. She has rauki haranttia. The Anglos call it street smarts. I trust her, even though I don't believe she trusts us entirely."

I tried to remain expressionless and not think of my loaded weapon.

"I trust Dagny, too," Tommy said. "Tell her. Tell her everything you remember."

I couldn't restrain myself any longer. "Please tell me anything you think may bear on the deaths of these two students. I promise you, if it doesn't have to do with laws being broken, you can trust my discretion."

Melanie said, "There are broken laws, but not your laws. We Churoks believe in our oral tradition. We don't want certain things written down, even though Professor Akrich taught us to write our language. That's because we believe this knowledge was spoken to our ancestors by our gods, who instructed them to remember, and to teach their children as they'd been taught."

"Tommy explained some of this to me when I was here last week."

"My mother, Starry Night, the Huruku before Tommy, believed the time had come to record our knowledge in a more permanent way than the human memory. Of course she could read and write English, but the English alphabet doesn't fit the Churok language. Professor Akrich taught her to write Churok using a special phonetic alphabet that he devised. He then encouraged her to write down what she knew. He had a great influence on her and much opportunity to persuade her, because he more or less lived with us for the years that he was a student."

Melanie withdrew her hand from Tommy's and he returned to his chair. She leaned forward, speaking even more earnestly.

"Starting when I was about twelve, my mother wrote every night. She wanted to write an encyclopedia of Churok knowledge. She swore me to secrecy when she told me what she was doing. She wrote about plants, animals, medicine, history, art, literature, and engineering. All was word-for-word from our sacred oral rituals. Never had they been written down in an orderly, systematic way, though the students like Judy would hear, memorize, and write down pieces of them. We didn't always like that, but we tolerated it."

"Engineering?" I asked, when Melanie paused to take a breath.

"Of course that's not what we call it. It's how to take down a large tree, or build a house or canoe. Anyway, she wrote a page every night in her careful, neat script, using the new alphabet she learned from Professor Akrich. I wasn't that interested in reading it. You know how teenagers are. But the stacks of paper grew as I grew. She kept them in notebooks in a bookcase in the back of her bedroom closet—seven notebooks for the seven subjects, each appropriately labeled."

"I wish I had known," interjected Tommy, his glumness unabated.

"You couldn't be allowed to know. You, and the others, were committed to memorizing the rituals. It was the Churok way. My mother wanted to preserve our culture unchanged, and at the same time she prophesied its change. Saturated by the materialism of America, how much longer would the youths of our tribe dedicate themselves to years of learning with little reward? For less effort they could become accountants or lawyers."

"They could do both," threw in Tommy. "Many religious leaders hold other jobs."

"Perhaps," said Melanie. "But in any case my mother was highly conflicted. As Huruku, she was sworn to defend the sacred oral traditions. But as a thoughtful person aware of the modern world, she wanted to save the wisdom, lore, and science of our people in a more accessible form. I believe Professor Akrich encouraged her and told her it was her right as Huruku to do this."

"But see how it turned out, Mulakaniya-mo. Aren't we like the Americans in Vietnam who 'destroyed the village to save the village'? Did our gods not make their will known?"

"You know I don't believe our gods, or anybody's gods, intervene in our lives on earth," retorted Melanie. "Not any more. Not since last contact. We control our own destiny. Even the ancient ones believed that."

"We must agree to disagree on this matter," said Tommy.

"When I got news of my mother," continued Melanie, "I naturally came home. It took a couple of days. I hitched a ride on a mail plane to get to where I could fly back on commercial airliners. I arrived barely in time for the funeral."

She stood up and walked to the mantel over which hung the painting that bore her mother's name, a night scene with a dozen bright splotches of starry yellow. She looked into the painting as she spoke.

"My mother had few possessions apart from the house and furniture. She valued knowledge, not wealth; beauty over riches. When I went to our house, I was in a sorry state. The sudden loss of her, so young, relatively, was a terrible shock. I could barely put one foot in front of the other. I couldn't bring myself to go into her bedroom, where she kept her personal things. I thought I'd ask someone to help me. Then I remembered her writing. If it was discovered that my mother, of all people, had blasphemed in this way, her memory would be stained."

Izzie had risen and was nuzzling Melanie's hand, copping some head rubs and ear strokes. Melanie turned away from the mantel and obliged the big dog, cuddling a silky ear in her little hand and bending down to kiss the black muzzle.

"Before retrieving the notebooks, before even entering that dread room, while my head was relatively clear, I had to decide what I would do. I considered burning them outright. If I'd done that, I could never have prayed to my mother's spirit with a full heart. I knew such an act would be against her wishes. I thought about turning them over to Tommy, the new Huruku. But Tommy had enough burdens and enough doubts. The revelation of my mother's tradition-breaking writing would weigh too heavily on him."

Tommy stirred as if he were about to protest, but remained silent. Melanie returned to the sofa to sit next to me, coaxing the compliant Labrador to put his head in her lap.

"In the end, I decided not to decide. I'd lock up the notebooks, and when my grieving was over, take up the question afresh. After the burial I went home, emptied a small suitcase, found the key to its locks, and proceeded to carry out my plan. I brushed past my mother's clothes and found the bookcase. The notebooks weren't there. I didn't panic. I thought she had a better hiding place. I searched the closet and her room thoroughly, ignoring the grief that her personal belongings aroused in me. I couldn't find the books in the bedroom, so I continued through the rest of the house. I grew up in that house, and apart from my mother's room, I knew every nook and cranny. It was easier than looking for money or jewelry. Seven notebooks take up a lot of space. I would've found them if they were there."

She turned to look at Tommy.

"Then I thought of you. You had taken charge of the death rituals, and of removing her body. Maybe you'd stumbled across the notebooks and taken them. I had to confide in you, and I must say you were a bit shocked when I did."

"To put it mildly!" exclaimed Tommy. "I swore by your mother's sacred soul that I knew nothing about them."

"Oh yes," said Melanie, "and I believed you. And wasn't it amazing! As we wondered about their disappearance, we both had the same thought at the same time, and the same word formed on our lips."

Chapter 16

Akrich, they both said in unison.

"Professor Akrich often stayed in my mother's house when he was on the reservation," continued Melanie. "He was like family. I guess you know he discovered her body after she passed."

I nodded.

"My mother wasn't open about her writing. She did it in the privacy of her bedroom, which doubled as a study. No one was allowed in that part of the house, not even me. My father died when I was very young. As a child, if my mother was in her room and I needed her, I'd call her and she'd come to me. When I had nightmares she would comfort me and sleep with me in my bed, never me in her bed. Still, Akrich may well have known of her writing and taken the notebooks to protect her. He would understand the impact of their discovery by someone like Tommy."

Melanie paused and Tommy took the opportunity to offer us something to drink. Melanie had been talking non-stop. She asked for tea. Tommy and I had diet Cokes. Izzie got a XXXL dog biscuit and resettled himself by Tommy, munching contentedly.

Tommy picked up the story's thread. "Julius moved out of Starry Night's house after she died, into the house where students usually lived. He asked for, and received, permission to attend the funeral rites. Starry was much beloved by our people, and it's our custom to give everyone a chance to express their feelings. Julius, too, spoke briefly in Churok. He was the first non-Churok ever to do so."

"I still remember how amazed I was to hear an Anglo speaking Churok nearly flawlessly," added Melanie. "And his words were sweet and sincere, and people were moved."

"On the final day," continued Tommy, "there was a funeral procession to the Churok burial grounds. It was miles long. I didn't get home until well after the final prayers because of my new responsibilities. I hadn't been home half an hour when Melanie called. She asked me to come to Starry's house, her house now. Her voice had an edge that urged me to go immediately. When I got there she told me about the notebooks, and we knew we had to take Julius into our confidence."

Melanie interrupted. "This was a tough decision, because even though we agreed that Julius was the logical suspect, if he didn't know, and there was something else happening—maybe they were in a bank vault or something, who knew—then another person would be in on it. A Churok proverb goes: A secret known to three is like water in a sieve. It rhymes in Churok, by the way."

She smiled, now, finally, a bit more relaxed.

"We had little choice," resumed Tommy. "I called him and he came right over. When he saw that we were alone, he went out to his car and returned with the notebooks. The look of relief on our faces was mirrored in his own when he saw that we knew what they were. He explained that Starry had confided in him because she needed his help in writing everything correctly."

It was my turn to interrupt. "But if he took them to keep Tommy from finding them, and then was relieved later that Tommy knew—" I was thinking aloud—"then something still doesn't add up."

Melanie said, "I suppose he couldn't be sure who might find them, and what the consequences would be. I think he was afraid both of their being discovered, and his being blamed for encouraging my mother; and of them not being discovered, and him bearing the knowledge of them and not knowing what to do."

"We may never know what made Julius act," said Tommy. "At the time, I thanked him for being forthright and returning the notebooks. He was very concerned about their fate. He said he'd reconsidered the wisdom of writing down the sacred words, and was no longer in favor of it."

"Which surprised me, I have to say," injected Melanie, "given that he had been a prime motivator in having my mother create them."

"Nonetheless, he was very persuasive," said Tommy. "He said that his professor at UCLA, William Gribith, who is a renowned anthropologist and friend of the Churoks, favored the oral tradition."

"But it wasn't clear that Professor Gribith was advocating the destruction of the notebooks. It was vague, and I wasn't about to give in to that," said Melanie.

"Spell the professor's name for me, please," I asked.

"G-r-i-b-i-t-h," said Tommy. I jotted it down; it was another thread in the weave of this mystery.

Tommy went on. "For the sake of preserving the Churok oral tradition, Julius begged me to destroy the notebooks. I was inclined to do so but Melanie wouldn't hear of it. In the end, I promised to defer my decision for a year, and to pray to our gods for guidance."

"When the year was up, then what?" I ventured.

"I postponed my decision for another year, then another and another. I couldn't bring myself to destroy the work. I couldn't bring myself to add to it, or condone it. It's not our way. My life's ambition is to preserve the Churok Nation. In America, which I love as I do my own people, it's possible to be both Churok and American. Many groups do it. Part of what I liked about Julius is that he manages to be both an orthodox Jew and an American."

"Do you still agonize over these notes?" I asked.

This time Melanie answered, her brow furrowing. "They disappeared. They're gone. It happened—what would you say, Tommy?—sometime in the past six months."

Tommy nodded agreement.

"You see why," continued Melanie, "even apart from my dreams, there's a logical reason for concern."

"Do the notebooks have any actual value?" I asked, and immediately regretted my choice of words. Before I could correct myself, Tommy answered.

"Dollar-value, no. No self-respecting institution would traffic in such goods. Their true value is cultural."

"Do you have any idea who might steal them?"

"If their existence were known, any number of Churoks might seek to destroy them," answered Tommy.

"But nobody knew about them," I said.

"Three of us knew, originally. It's possible that Julius confided in one or more of his students, who've been coming to the reservation for years. Perhaps they let something slip. I'd almost rather see the notebooks destroyed than turn up in the wrong hands to embarrass us."

Melanie winced but didn't say anything.

"Could a student have stolen them?"

"They weren't in a bank vault," said Tommy. "Technically, they belong to Melanie."

"I kept them in the same closet where my mother kept them. It never occurred to me that I needed to protect them because I didn't think anyone but us knew about them. My house would be easy enough to burgle. Heck, we Churoks don't lock up much, do we, Tommy? We don't steal from each other, and we don't have enough to make it worth an outsider's trouble."

"Has there been any trace of the notebooks since? Any hint of who might have them?" I asked.

"None at all," answered Tommy.

"When did you last see them?" I asked Melanie.

"I remember seeing the suitcase in December because that's where I stashed holiday presents after I wrapped them."

"Holiday presents?" I asked.

"We Churoks celebrate the Winter Solstice. It hasn't always been an important day in our history, but it gives us an excuse to join in the festivities of the season. A bit like the Jewish holiday Hanukkah. Julius once explained to me that it isn't a high holiday in Judaism, but its nearness to Christmas makes it more widely celebrated."

It was late afternoon. The sun already was approaching the tops of the mountains, and even though there were hours of daylight remaining, we would soon be in shadows. I asked to use the bathroom. I washed my hands and rooted around in my handbag a bit to kill time. I thought I'd give Tommy and Melanie a few moments alone to confer. When I returned, I asked if they could add anything more. Both shook their heads.

It took about five minutes of good-byeing to get away. Both Tommy and Melanie expressed a sincere desire to help. I gave a business card to Melanie with the usual request. I started to leave but Izzie had planted himself squarely across the front door and I wasn't sure how to act. My greyhounds don't do that sort of thing.

"Move, Izzie," growled Tommy. The big dog lifted his head toward me.

"He wants to say goodbye," said Melanie.

I put my hand on his head, which he maneuvered so that my fingers were behind his left ear. I gave him some scratches and said, "Bye-bye, Izzie." This seemed to satisfy him and he moved out of the way as if to say, "Permission to leave granted."

I drove to town and stopped at a Quickie Mart gas station. I filled up and asked for my change in quarters when I paid. A decrepit phone booth, soon to be a relic of the twentieth century, found only in history museums, stood sadly askew outside the door of the little convenience store. The phone still worked, however. I needed to make some calls and there wasn't any cellular service. A call to directory assistance got me UCLA's main number and connected me to it. The operator at the central switchboard transferred me to Professor Gribith's office.

"This is Anna. How may I help you?"

She helped me by making a 10:00 appointment with Dr. Gribith for the next morning.

I called John's phone at home. The machine answered and I keyed in the code that causes it to playback messages. There was one from Charles, a terse "Please call me ASAP." Nothing from Lucy, or the Worthingtons regarding her. John's office phone had no messages.

I tried Charles at work and the secretary told me he was in a meeting. I explained that I was outside of the cellular area and would call back when I could, and to please ask Charles to wait for my call.

I wanted to update my files before I forgot any details, but I didn't want to take the time. I figured I could review everything in my head while I drove. That would keep my mind off the tedious drive between Makrui and the 101.

I had a trove of new information. I began my rumination with the Lucky-U gold mine. Suppose it was worth a fortune and only Troy knew? That gave him motivation to murder Judy. Who murdered Troy? Another owner, Tommy, who might easily be privy to Mojave Analytical's results? Or could Tommy commit both murders? He was strong enough, probably clever enough, but I was having trouble imagining him a murderer. I decided to trust my instincts about Tommy, ignoring the lamentable occasions when my instincts had been all wrong—I was hoping they'd improved.

Suppose the mine was worthless and Troy had salted it, maybe conspiring with Judy, or even Tommy, to bilk some hapless buyer. It wouldn't be a first, but unless the sale actually happened or was pending, the motive for murder was weak. I didn't know for sure that a sale hadn't taken place, but it would be difficult with two owners out of the country. I put that one in a do-not-open-until-all-else-fails file.

I considered the possibility that someone else knew the mine was valuable and thought only Judy and Troy knew. With them eliminated, they could persuade the other three partners to sell cheaply. I considered variations of these ideas. None appealed to me. None rose above the threshold of plausibility. It made my head throb. I lowered the driver side window and let the late afternoon breezes sweeping down the Sierra wash over me.

My head cleared within a few minutes, and in a few more minutes, it was too cold in the mountain air. I raised the window and moved mentally on to the entanglements created by Starry's notebooks. Judy steals 'em, and someone steals 'em back, leaving Judy dancing in the breeze. Troy finds out and he dances, too. Or Troy steals 'em from Judy but he gets caught and pays the ultimate price. Who were those assholes in the mine, anyway? Hell, maybe the notebooks were stashed there. It's dry, and not a likely place to look. That might account for the assault on Charles and me.

But notebooks? People kill for strange reasons, but why notebooks? It would be helpful to know what was worth killing for in those pages. The true location of the Garden of Eden? Directions to the Fountain of

Youth? Maps to buried treasure? Something about the Lucky U? That's a thought. So Judy and Troy steal and translate the notes about the gold mine. Based on what they learn, they lease the mine. They bring Tommy in because they need a Churok. The other two I wasn't sure about. Maybe they thought it would dilute suspicion when the mine yielded its fortune.

A fine theory, but the timing of events was at odds with the facts. They leased the mine before the notebooks had disappeared. It could be that they stole enough peeks into the writing to know the mine held some kind of secret. They leased the mine and then found they needed to study the notebooks in detail. That's when they stole them outright. Or maybe they hid or destroyed the notebooks because they didn't want others making the discovery.

So intent was I on these thoughts that I took a curve too fast and found myself staring at the left front headlight of a Mack truck. I swerved out of the way just as a blast from its horn reached me. I needed to let matters simmer in my subconscious and think of something more pleasant and less distracting. I opted for Charles.

It was a good choice because I realized that I'd forgotten to call him. I powered up my flip phone and the *roam* light came on. I stopped well off the road to make the call. The near head-on had made me a bit more cautious than usual. This time I caught Charles in his office.

"I miss you already," he said. "San Francisco spoiled me."

"Sorry I didn't get back to you sooner. There isn't much in the way of telephones or cellular service out here."

"Yes, I remember that. Pretty drive through the mountains, though. Are you all right? I've been jittery since last night."

"I'm fine," I said. "How about you? Found any gentlemen to shoot?"

He laughed. "Not yet, but I'm looking." He paused a moment. "I think I have some news."

"Lucy," I cried, and felt my knees go rubbery.

"It's about Lucy, but she may be okay."

"Is this bad news or good news?"

"I'm not sure. Do you remember the message she left?"

"How could I forget? I spent a couple of hours on the phone looking for the Covenant Apartments and David Balfour."

"Dagny, have you ever read Robert Louis Stevenson?"

"Charles, for Chrissake! Can we talk about my reading habits another time?"

"No, seriously. There's a point here."

"Okay, let's see. I once read *Treasure Island*."

"I see," said Charles evenly. "Did you ever happen to read *Kidnapped?*"

"No, I don't think so. But wait. I think my parents rented the video for me when I was a teenager, still living in Turkey. I remember the Turkish subtitles."

"Keep remembering, love. What was it about?"

"A boy on a ship. The boy was cute, I remember that."

"Can you remember his name, Dagny?"

"Sure it was David...oh no, it couldn't be."

"His name is David Balfour," filled in Charles, "and the ship is the Covenant."

Chapter 17

I broke the silence with a moan. My worst fears were realized. Nausea gripped my stomach and a zincky corrosiveness rose to my throat, leaving me speechless. Charles was speaking my name and asking if I was okay.

I got my tongue back. "I'm okay. It's a shock to know my client's been abducted by people who kill so readily."

"I'm sorry. I wish I'd seen the connection sooner. The names churned around in my head until I saw a billboard that advertised Cutty Sark scotch. The schooner in the picture jogged my memory and it all came clear at once. Terribly clever of Lucy, don't you think?"

"Very clever," I agreed weakly. I tried to imagine the course of events. Lucy must have been snatched sometime between Thursday night, when I last spoke with her, and Sunday, the day she called the Worthingtons. They probably forced her to call to forestall suspicion at her absence. Most likely she was killed immediately. With the body well hidden, the killers would have days for their trail to cool.

"Are you there, Dagny? Say something, love."

"I'm here. I'm just wondering if Lucy's even alive now."

"Why let her call if they planned on killing her? Why not just do it?"

"I'm not sure. Maybe they wanted to buy time to fake another suicide. Imagine the newspaper headline: Student despondent over friends' suicides takes own life."

"She may be alive, Dagny. They don't know we know about these murders. They think they've got away with it. They may not want to risk killing again. Maybe they're just trying to scare Lucy, or keep her out of the way for other reasons. I think there's hope. How can I help?"

"Several things. Try to convince your boss that there's been a murder, and try to get Peters to do the same."

"Right. I'll have another go at the coroner."

"It'd help if we knew the connection between the Nandrolex and the anesthetic effect. Maybe you could give Jeanette Briggs a call and see if she's had any more thoughts."

"I'll ring her up right away. Good idea."

"And one more thing. I've been planning to visit Wellex. If I can convince them that one of their drugs is being abused, they might help. I wish I knew someone there."

"The lab here uses some of their products. There must be a sales person. Maybe I can get you a name. What'll you do now?"

I briefed Charles on what I'd learned from Melanie and told him of my appointment with Gribith. I decided on the spur of the moment that I'd drive straight through to L.A. and stay the night. I needed time to think, and the drive would provide it. I gave Charles the number of Hilda's "modeling studio"—I had a standing invitation to crash there when need be. I promised I'd call around ten the next morning.

The westering sun was a bloodshot eye behind a misty veil of clouds, toward which I was now driving. I met U.S. 101 where it runs past the Santa Maria raceway and turned south. I had nearly three hours of cruising and cogitating ahead of me. I sped past Santa Barbara, barely noticing my temporary hometown. At Oxnard my head was again achy from sorting facts and weighing probabilities, and dejection covered me in a dark mantle, for the knots that tied up the riddle of the mysterious murders refused to unravel.

There are two routes from Oxnard to Los Angeles: one inland, the other along the Pacific coast. I opted for Route 1, putting the ocean on my right, and the coastal range on my left. I lowered the passenger side window to admit the ocean's flavor. The sights and scents of the water were soothing, and by the time I reached Interstate 10 in Santa Monica, my head had cleared once more and my despair had abated. I needed to focus on my interview with Professor Gribith. All I could do for Lucy was to try to learn more about the events and people that constituted this terrible mystery.

I was at the western terminus of Interstate 10, less than a mile from the Pacific Ocean. From here, amazingly enough, you could drive straight through to Jacksonville, Florida, without a traffic signal, stop sign or dangerous intersection. I had little desire to visit Florida, however. Though my home is in North Carolina, when summer comes I prefer the Pacific to the Atlantic, and the variable breezes of California's west coast to the steady, sodden sunshine of the South.

I stayed on the I10 a mere two miles, quitting the freeway at Bundy Drive, a street name that became nationally known during the murder trial of O.J. Simpson. I took Bundy to Montana Avenue and followed that street to where it abuts a V.A. Hospital. Hilda's modeling studio is actually a twelve-unit apartment house with a recreation room serving as the studio. The "models" work and sometimes live in the units, coming down to the studio to re-enact several times every day the charade that they are models and not girls for hire.

Hilda is an intelligent, warmly wonderful woman who believes in the value of a dollar, and takes friendship to be the most serious relationship a person can enter into. I have known her since my college days at UCLA. There are always one or two vacant apartments and my earlier call to Hilda had gotten me one in the back of the building where it was least likely to be noisy.

I arrived as dusk was giving way to darkness. The modeling business was in hiatus, it being too late for the day-timers, and too early for the evening clientele. One model held down the fort, leaning on her elbows behind the rec-room bar, naked from the waist up. Hilda wore a flowered muumuu and was ensconced in an overstuffed, oversized easy chair in an inconspicuous corner of the room. She's always sincerely happy to see me, and I her.

"Come sit by me and give me your news. Pull that chair over. How are you getting along? Are you whipping that disease? How is your brother? You don't need to go out. I put a bottle of white pinot and some pasta salad in the fridge for you."

"You're a dear, Hilda." I bent down to kiss her cheek "I'll just be here for one night and I have to leave early. Thanks for letting me stay."

"You have to pay with news, darling, so start talking. Begin with your health."

We chatted amiably for an hour. When business revved up, and one too many men leered in my direction, I said my goodnight. I took a short stroll to enjoy some fresh, salt-tinged air before retiring. I longed to jog on the grassy center divider of San Vicente Boulevard, about a quarter mile away. I could run to the ocean and back, about three miles, but only a crazy or suicidal woman jogs alone in the dark. Anyway, I didn't have my running gear.

I found my unit stocked with wine and food as promised. Hilda had even remembered to leave a corkscrew. Better still, she'd found an old gym bag of mine that I used to keep at the apartments. The contents were freshly washed. Now I could run in the morning.

I removed the cork from the bottle and the plastic wrap from the pasta, and that took care of dinner preparations. I retrieved the laptop. Though it was only nine hours ago that I was bringing my files up to date, I had lots more to add. I sipped and chewed and typed for an hour and a half. I made a few tentative notes on questions for Professor Gribith. I stripped, showered, and crawled into bed naked. I set the alarm clock for 6:30.

My internal alarm beat the clock by ten minutes, as it so often does. It was still dark out, but by the time I dressed and walked over to San Vicente, it would be light enough and safe enough to run.

I was amazed at the number of people already out jogging. They mostly knew each other, an informal San Vicente grassy-median jogging club. I got mostly smiles from runners going the opposite way. A big fellow came up from behind and ran next to me for a moment, matching my pace.

"Can I hit on you?" he asked pleasantly, breathing no harder than if he was sitting on a park bench.

"I guess you have already," I replied, trying to control my breathing.

"I'm not the pushy type. If it feels right, call me."

He handed me a business card—interesting line—and pulled ahead effortlessly. "What's your name?" he called over his shoulder. I half-smiled and shook my head. He held up his watch and pointed to it. I understood. If I called him, I'd be the one he met at 6:45. He probably names his girl friends Miss Seven Thirty or Mrs. (why not) Quarter After Eight. His name was Leon and he was employed by the St. Louis Rams football team. I wonder if he hit as hard in the stadium as on the jogging path. He was a smooth dude, and attractive if you go for the thick-necked Nordic type.

No matter what they say, most women don't mind being hit on if it's done tastefully and sincerely. It took my mind off business, briefly, and I was better off for it. I picked up the pace a bit in a fanciful pursuit of Leon, but despite my additional efforts he slowly pulled away. At Ocean Avenue I did an 180º and began the grueling uphill part of the run. I broke a sweat and pushed myself hard. My legs and lungs felt good. I was in the "zone," where physical exercise fills my whole being, and my mind enters a meditative state. By the end of the run the tension of the previous day had relinquished its grip.

Back in the room, I showered and put on yesterday's clothes. UCLA was only a mile away as the crow flies, but on the traffic-laden streets of west L.A. the trip may take twenty minutes. The sprawling campus is a labyrinth of roads and cul-de-sacs, none of which permit parking. Tow trucks respond to illegally parked cars faster than ambulances to heart attacks. People joke that UCLA has three passions: football, basketball, and parking.

At a kiosk I exchanged three dollars for a parking token and a one-day parking permit to be attached to the inside of my windshield. I declined a map of the campus. "Follow the blue lines, please," instructed the attendant.

As a student I rarely parked on campus, preferring bus transportation. I was surprised to find that I needed to follow the colored line painted on the pavement to avoid confusion at forks in the road. This might be a good method for helping freshmen find their classrooms. Blue for Math, red for History, yellow for English, green for Biology.

The blue line took me to the entrance of a parking deck, access to which was barred by an orange and white striped gate. Outside the driver's window was a box with a slot and a weatherworn sign that said, "Deposit token to lift gate." I did so and the gate rose out of my way. Inside, unoccupied stalls were numerous since it was early in the day.

I'd left myself some extra time. I was meandering in the general direction of central campus, remembering my college days, when an idea struck me. UCLA had a business library, and I had time to visit it.

The business library was wholly contained in the much larger University Research Library. It was nearly empty when I got there, most students preferring to work late and sleep late. I asked the librarian for help finding information about Wellex Pharmaceuticals. She tapped away on her computer for about a minute. A printer came to life and spewed out a page, which she tore off and handed to me along with a guide to the library.

I sat down at a table and looked over the printout. *A History of the American Pharmaceutical Industry* was one of several references that caught my eye. It turned out to be a government publication available only on microfilm. My helpful librarian found it for me and came out from behind her counter to show me how to operate the reader. The entire work fit onto a spool of microfilm slightly larger than a roll of Kodacolor. I unraveled the first few inches of film and held it up to the light. It contained dozens of pages, each compressed to the size of a Lilliputian postage stamp.

I threaded the spool in the reader as instructed and forwarded the film to the first page, which contained a table of contents. The material on Wellex began on page 193. I fast forwarded to that page and began reading. Wellex had been founded in the early 1960s by Richard Maas, a brilliant young biochemist, and financier Gerald Wolfe, a scion of the Wolfe family.

I knew about the Wolfe family. They had adopted Santa Barbara as their hometown after World War II, and owned at least two large estates. Gerald was a prominent member and generous benefactor of the community.

The company's initial successes had been in products for blood testing. Blood is full of stuff I've never heard of. Clotting factors, lipids of all kinds, proteins with unpronounceable names, bodies, and antibodies. Doctors like to know how much of what is in the blood, and those measurements require the use of other complex substances, some of which Wellex invented and manufactured.

By the late sixties, Wellex had focused on the synthesis of bio-chemicals ordinarily found in nature. These drugs became the financial mainstays of the company when the blood products business became too competitive. They were used for treating symptoms ranging from nausea and diarrhea to insomnia and impotence, and included some blockbusters—products that are practically household names.

A list of drug patents owned by Wellex was given at the end of the article, along with a synopsis of the principal effects of each of the drugs. Nandrolex was on the list, the only mention of that drug in the article. The synopsis didn't tell me anything I didn't already know. I had begun to rewind the spool when I thought I saw some intriguing letters at the top of my field of vision. I refocused the machine and searched for them deliberately: *anesth* is what had flashed subliminally in my mind. I found the word. Wellex had patented a drug in 1964 that they had called Welnarkothal. It was an anesthetic.

Chapter 18

It was nearly nine-thirty. I needed to call Charles and head over to Professor Gribith's office. I could return later and read the patents. I jotted down the patent numbers. Heck, I could probably get the patent info off the Internet from the comfort of my home or office.

I descended in an elevator with half its light bulbs burnt out. Graffiti had been washed off, reapplied, rescrubbed away. Writers intent on permanence, leastwise until the next paint job, scratched their messages into the paint. Most of it was of a prurient nature, but the science nerds had gotten in their licks: "186,000 mps—it's THE law," proved that someone was thinking about something other than sex.

Downstairs near the door I got a strong cellular signal. I put through my call to Charles's office. He answered on the first ring. I told him what I had learned. "Give me those patent numbers," he said. "I'll have Jeanette Briggs look into them. You won't have time, anyway. You have a 2:00 appointment with a Dr. Maas at Wellex, over on Yorktown Avenue. That's spelled M-a-a-s, Richard. He's the—"

"Vice president in charge of research and one of the founders," I finished.

"Ah, you *have* been doing your homework."

"I got lucky. Anything from Lucy?"

"Nil. Incidentally, you'll have to pass through a metal detector at Wellex. They keep tight security because of the daft blokes that try to break in and liberate their animals. You'll have to stow your heat."

"'Stow my heat'? Surely English gentlemen are taught not to speak American movie slang."

"I heard Humphrey Bogart say it once in a film. I've waited ten years for the right moment to say it myself, and I wasn't about to give it up on behalf of English gentlemen," he said, with pretended grumpiness.

"Seriously, thanks for the warning. I'll let you know if anything comes up."

Outside the library, sunlight was streaming between the buildings and trees, casting sharp, black shadows. There was a refreshment stand near the library with a few sparsely populated benches in front of it. I had time for a cup of coffee and a blueberry muffin. I reviewed my notes on Wellex, sipping coffee and breaking off pieces of muffin to stuff in my mouth. Behind some jacaranda trees, the rear entrance of Haines Hall was a one-minute walk away. At five to ten I washed the last of the muffin down with the last of the coffee and went to keep my appointment.

Professor Gribith's office was in the northeast corner of the second floor of the two-story building. The door was open. Behind a desk just to the right inside the doorway, a woman was working intently on a computer. She was middle-aged, thin, and her long, dark hair was tied back. She turned to face me, removing a pair of glasses with heavy plastic frames and thick lenses that had created excavation sites on either side of her nose.

"You must be Anna." I said.

"And you're Miss Jamison, right?" she replied pleasantly. "I'll tell Bill you're here."

She disappeared into an inner office for a moment, then reappeared and motioned to me. As I approached the inner sanctum, she slipped past me and returned to her desk. Professor William Gribith met me in the doorway. "I'm Bill Gribith," he said, extending his hand.

We shook hands. "I'm Dagny Jamison, Dr. Gribith. Thank you for seeing me."

"Let's sit over there," he said, nodding toward a couple of padded wooden chairs, "and please call me Bill. We're much less formal than you might think."

I knew that, having been a student at UCLA. It wasn't unusual even for undergraduates to address certain professors by their given name. Older people outside academia still imagine a distinguished professor as wearing a suit, maybe a frumpy suit, but a suit nonetheless. This stereotype would also peg him as portly, balding, soft-handed, myopic, and short. That image is sometimes correct. Julius Akrich fit it well. But the lanky figure before me wore shorts, sandals and a T-shirt. Bill Gribith had a firm handshake; his palms were calloused. He had a full head of wavy, gray-streaked hair, and clear, penetrating, gray eyes that looked me up and down. His ring fingers were unadorned. I'd bet half his female students wanted to go out with him.

He slid down a little in the chair, clasped his hands behind his head, and fixed his eyes on mine. He invited me to begin. I had already decided to trust his discretion and tell him everything I had learned. In return, I hoped that he might then provide some shred of knowledge that would help me find Lucy. While he had already heard about the deaths of Judy and Troy, my reasoning that they were murdered left him visibly moved.

"I find it hard to believe." He ran his hand through his hair and massaged the back of his neck. "Not you, Dagny," he added quickly, "but that these kids were killed. There's never been anything like this in my thirty-five years of teaching. If everything you've told me is accurate, I have to agree with your conclusion, unlikely as it seems."

His support was welcome. I had been over the facts many times—organizing, arranging and interpreting them—and had hoped I would be able to present my deductions with the same logical certainty they had for me.

"But I interrupted you," he said. "I take it there's more."

I related what Melanie told me the previous day and finished with Lucy's kidnapping. This agitated him so much he rose from his chair and walked across the room, stuck his hands in his pockets, pulled them out, ran one through his hair again, came back and sat down. I explained to him why I didn't think going to the police would help yet.

"Why come to me?" he asked, after a long silence.

"Because the Churoks are the common thread that tie Lucy, Judy, and Troy together, and I want to find Lucy very badly. I want to learn everything I can about the people and events in the lives of the three students."

"And they're all students of Julius Akrich, my former student, right?"

"That's right, Professor, I mean Bill."

"So that's another thread, isn't it?"

"Yes, but I consider it part of the Churok thread."

"And the gold mine," he went on, "is another Churok thread."

"Yes, sir, that's my interpretation."

"So it's more like the Churok sewing circle." He smiled at his own joke. "Are there any non-Churok commonalities? Maybe they patronize the same dry cleaner, shop in the same super, bank at the same bank?"

I smiled politely and went on, "I haven't had time to find out any more about the three, and time is of the essence. The Churok connection is the best lead I have, so that's the one I'm following."

"I think you're right," he finally said, after gazing at me for a minute. "How can I help you?" He leaned forward in his chair, his knees nearly touching mine.

"I'd like to know more about this person they call Starry Night. I'd like to know more about Tommy. And I'd like to know more about Professor Akrich."

"You're not recording this conversation?" he asked, nodding at my handbag.

"No, sir, I wouldn't do that."

"How privileged is our conversation?"

"I'm not a priest, doctor, or lawyer. If I ever had to give sworn testimony, I'd have to be truthful. But let me add that private investigators with big mouths don't last long. My livelihood depends on my discretion. I'd go to great lengths to maintain the privacy of our meeting."

"And your client, isn't that Lucy Navarro? Is she entitled to know everything? She's paying you, I presume."

"She hired me specifically to investigate Judy Raskin's death. Anything I discover regarding it I'd have to tell Lucy, assuming she'll be around to be told."

"And other stuff?"

"What are you getting at, Bill? I'm not a tabloid reporter, for crying out loud."

"Hmm, paparazzi. I never thought of that." He grinned broadly. "They bothered me once. I think I'd know one if I saw one. You don't fit the description." His look turned serious. "I can tell you a few things that may help you. If they have relevancy to these horrid crimes, then I'm glad to do it. If these students have tangled with the Mafia or some such, and the Churoks and the university are not common threads, then I'd want confidence respected. The effectiveness of my own research into Native American cultures relies fairly heavily on my discretion. Matters are often confided in me with the assurance that they won't go any further."

"Yes, sir. I can only stand on what I said."

"I appreciate your being frank. What I have to say isn't earth shattering. I'm not Perry Mason. I can't point to the murderer. I knew Starry Night for years. She was a great leader, but she also felt that the grandiosity of her ideas and the nobility of her motives, together with her high office, gave her certain rights. That's why I wasn't surprised when you told me about the notebooks. I'm not so sure her efforts were as secret as Melanie and Tommy seem to think. And she had political enemies within the tribe—politics is universal. They wouldn't have hesitated to use the notebooks against her."

"What about Melanie?" I asked. "Could she have been caught up in the politics? Does she have an agenda of some kind?"

"Good question. I don't think so. Like teenage girls everywhere, Melanie didn't get along that well with her mother. I believe she welcomed the opportunity to leave the reservation. She spent some time in the Peace Corps, I think. She didn't care for tribal politics and she didn't share her mother's passion for preserving Churok culture."

"Whoa, I'm confused. I thought Starry was the one who was breaking tradition."

"Starry felt that the change in the oral tradition was necessary to preserve the larger body of culture. It's perhaps like amending a constitution to adjust to changing times."

"How does Tommy fit into the picture?"

"Tommy's passionate about the Churok culture and very much the traditionalist. I'm surprised he tolerated the existence of the notebooks. He's worked hard to preserve the Churok way of life. I don't think he'd put up with any attempts to compromise it."

"Could he have destroyed the notebooks, or lied that they were stolen?"

"Maybe. But he could destroy them openly, and even claim credit for it. If he left them alone all those years, he probably had a reason."

"You used the word *passionate*. Is he passionate enough to kill someone he thought was betraying him or undermining his philosophy?"

Gribith's forehead wrinkled while he pondered an answer. "The Churoks aren't a violent people. They believe deeply in the harmony of nature. Killing disturbs that harmony. For a Huruku to use violence in the name of promoting harmony would be the ultimate contradiction. On the other hand, religious wars have always been contradictory. What religion lacks 'Thou shalt not kill' in its doctrine? What religion fails to kill in defense of that doctrine? We cannot conceive what evil deeds may be committed in the name of goodness."

"In other words, 'maybe.'"

He smiled at that. "Yeah, I guess so."

"Professor Akrich is a common link among the three students, and he was your student once, like you said"

"Yes, indeed. My bright shining star of a student scholar. Julius could wring facts out of data, and theories out of facts, like no other scholar I've known. He's made a brilliant career out of his Churok studies. When he was a young professor his publications were controversial. He made unconventional and unsupported statements. For a while I thought his career was in jeopardy, but time proved him right. Nothing promotes a career like being both controversial and right."

"Have there ever been any difficulties with students? Lucy said that Akrich came down pretty hard on Judy."

"Julius has had many students over the years, though few as promising as Judy Raskin. There've never been difficulties, apart from the common ones."

"What are the 'common ones'?"

"Oh, students drop out or don't fulfill their scholarship commitments. There are disagreements among us professors and our students regarding methodology, theory, style, and what have you. These disagreements can be acrimonious. We're not one big happy academic family. Good scholarship requires tension and disagreement."

"Does anyone ever get violent?"

"Actually, yes. Physical scuffles occur. But really, Dagny, we don't kill each other, much as we'd like to sometimes."

"Did you know Judy personally?"

"Somewhat. She was an undergraduate here. She took two classes from me and earned an A both times. She was a lovely person, too. I wrote a recommendation to graduate school for her. I also saw her at conferences. When she was on campus, she'd poke her head in to say hello. She is, or would've been, my academic grandchild, a student of my student. I can't tell you how badly I feel about what has happened."

"After the blowup at her defense, where she was denounced and humiliated by Professor Akrich, was there a danger that she might implicate another person, a collaborator, who might also have their career jeopardized? Would that someone want to kill her, making it look like suicide in circumstances where suicide was plausible?"

"It's unlikely but not impossible. Of course, I don't fully understand the circumstances, but I'll say this: if Judy had gone and shot Julius, I'd be less surprised. She was the injured party, after all. It seems to me he could've found a more tactful way to handle the matter."

"Have you spoken with Professor Akrich since?"

"Yes. He called to tell me about Judy, how sick he felt about the way he'd dealt with the situation. I think he wanted my understanding—my forgiveness, as it were."

"Did you give it to him?" I asked.

Gribith shrugged. "Julius is a reputed professor in his own right. He doesn't need my approval or forgiveness. He must've been under tremendous pressure. I wasn't sympathetic. I told him I thought he should've called the whole thing off, either without explanation, or by inventing some harmless lie. Then the matter could have been settled in private."

"How did he respond to that?"

"He agreed. He explained the circumstances of the plagiarism to me, and how shocked and betrayed he'd felt. He's a religious, moral person, and cheating's an anathema to him. He wanted to excuse himself on the basis that, had it been caught later, it would've reflected poorly on the university, and, of course, on him. I still couldn't condone what he did, but I think his regret at how events transpired is genuine."

I couldn't think of any further questions. I asked Gribith to keep my visit a secret. Particularly, I wanted his promise that he wouldn't discuss the fact that these suicides were homicides. I felt a bit guilty telling him. I thought anyone who knew might be in danger. Since arriving in L.A., I had been taking precautions to make sure nobody was following me. I was as positive as I could be that no one was. John had trained me well. Gribith promised his discretion and agreed to ask Anna to do the same.

I handed him my card with my well-rehearsed "If anything occurs to you, please call."

His response surprised me. "I'm going to think hard about this," he said. "There's something nagging deep in the back of my mind. Do you ever get that?"

"Do I ever! It's common in my business. And when I retrieve whatever it is, it's generally useful."

"I'll do my best to dig it out. It gets tougher as you get older. Maybe it's nothing. I'm especially concerned about Lucy. I wish I could help more. I promise I'll call if I have any ideas."

I exited the building into a dazzle of light. Half a dozen students were sprawled on the grassy square in the quad soaking up rays. One boy had stripped down to his boxer shorts; his clothes were folded under his head for a pillow. The female next to him had hiked her skirt to just beneath her crotch to expose her discreetly open thighs to the streaming ultraviolet. It was nearly noon and I needed to get a move on if I wanted to be on time for my appointment with Richard Maas. I trekked back to my car, planning the return route to Santa Barbara as I walked. At this time of day I'd do best to take the interstates. It's about 90 miles and I could make it easily in 90 minutes.

I drove up to Sunset and turned left, then north on the 405 to the 101. From there, I could run on autopilot and digest what I had learned from Bill Gribith. I, too, had an unfocused mental itch, a feeling that something wasn't kosher. This was good. Often it presaged a breakthrough. Scratch, itch, rich, Akrich—I free-associated. I think I'd known all along that I'd have to speak again with Professor Julius Akrich.

Chapter 19

But first things first, and first was my interview with Dr. Maas. Yet another doctor. What was this, six? Charles and Bob Peters were medical doctors. Professors Akrich and Gribith, Jeanette Briggs and Richard Maas were doctors of philosophy. I was running in a rarefied crowd. If only I could harness all that brainpower to my cause, I might get somewhere. But then, they'd all have to pull together, and I wasn't sure they all would.

I was clueless as to what to expect from my interview at Wellex. Pharmaceutical companies are among the most proprietary businesses in the world. Everything is patented, trademarked, and ultra-secret. There is always pending litigation involving pharmaceuticals on some court calendar. It isn't hard to see why. A cure for AIDS would be worth billions. Hell, a cure for the common cold would be worth billions. Who wouldn't pay fifty or a hundred bucks to cure a damn cold?

My ploy was to appeal to the company's civic-mindedness. While they aren't legally responsible for what people do with their products, they might take an interest if something they manufactured was being used in a novel way to commit murder. I hoped to get a fix on how Nandrolex might get into the tranquilizer darts that had immobilized Judy, Troy, and Charles.

Traffic thinned as I climbed out of the San Fernando Valley. I kept my mile-a-minute average despite a five-minute stop near Thousand Oaks for gas, a snack, and a quick visit to the restroom.

I turned onto Yorktown Avenue at a quarter to the hour. It winds through an industrial complex of so-called clean industries such as computer software and telecommunications. Private roads that lead to parking facilities branch off the main artery. The various company names and street numbers are proclaimed in white letters stenciled vertically onto redwood posts at each corner.

I turned right at the road whose signpost read Wellex, Inc. and found myself in a parking lot separated from the main building by a large, rectangular, reflecting pool. Near the pool was an area reserved for visitor parking. I pulled into the nearest available space. I removed the Glock from my handbag and locked it in the glove compartment. I took one of the several wide footpaths that crisscrossed the water. A huge glass door—bullet proof, no doubt, and perfectly balanced to open at the lightest touch—gave entrance into a reception area protected by two armed guards. One of them, a black man with biceps the size of cantaloupes, stood at the far end of the lobby by the entrance to the building proper. The other stood behind a counter where non-employees had to register.

I identified myself and told the guard I had a two o'clock appointment with Dr. Richard Maas. He picked up a phone, dialed some numbers, and after a moment hung up. "Dr. Maas's secretary will escort you," he said. "Please print your name and company on the sign-in roster and on the badge." He handed me a clipboard and a blank nametag. I signed in as Dagny Taggart Jamison of Jamison & Jamison, Private Investigators.

I took a seat in one of the chairs by a table on which lay several issues of in-house glossy magazines about wonder drugs and the wonderful scientists who had discovered them. Many of the scientists portrayed were women, including a Nobel Prize winner. Times they are a-changin'.

A male voice interrupted my thoughts: "Miss Jamison, I'm Greg, Dr. Maas's secretary." Jesus, times really are changing.

I followed Greg into the building. The big guard opened the door for us, and when we walked through I heard singing. The sounds came from a theater large enough to hold a couple of hundred people. Singers were on the stage belting out a lively rendition of "She's a Grand Ol' Flag." A small man in a dark suit, wearing horn-rimmed glasses and brandishing a baton, gesticulated frantically in front of the group, jabbing first one way, then the other, as he attempted to balance the voices and keep them in synch.

"That's our company's little choral group," explained Greg. "They're rehearsing for the Fourth of July party."

"Do they get paid for singing?" I asked.

"They give up their lunch hour to rehearse," Greg answered. "You'd be surprised at the number of people who do music. The conductor is our chief research chemist. Do you see the gray-haired lady in the red sweater? She's secretary to Mr. Wolfe, the company president. She has a great voice. And the guy playing the bassoon—corporate finance director. The pianist—you can barely see her across the stage—is the VP of I.T. That's information technology, of course."

We continued down the hall past a door signed To Animal Facility. "What's with the animals?" I asked.

"We raise our own special breeds for drug testing. Dogs, rabbits, mice, even monkeys. The biologists guarantee their genetic uniformity. That helps us isolate the effects of the drugs we test."

I grimaced mentally at the idea, but I certainly owed my life to cancer-fighting drugs that had attacked my disease without overwhelming and killing my body. They had had to be tested and I could only hope it had been done without inflicting cruelty or unnecessary suffering on animals.

Dr. Maas occupied a large corner office in the back of the building. As I was ushered in, he stepped out from behind an executive desk to greet me with a strong handshake. He was short, not even up to my height, with the solid build of a man who gets more exercise than golf on Sundays. His mottled skin, large, crooked nose, and thick ears gave him the appearance of an ex-fighter. He was well groomed, however, and his neatly combed hair made no attempt to conceal his half-bald head.

"How can I help you, Miss Jamison?"

I obviously didn't need to introduce myself. Dr. Richard Maas was a man who made sure he knew whom he was speaking with and why. I'd resolved on the drive up to be frank. I'm naturally secretive, never giving anything away without a purpose or a price. In the case of these murders, I felt I endangered the people I told, and increased the danger to myself. But I badly needed this man's cooperation. I was gambling that he'd be candid when he understood the urgency.

"Thank you very much for meeting with me. I'll try not to take up too much of your time. Would you give me ten minutes to tell you why I'm here?"

He agreed, and invited me to sit in a comfortable, leather-bound chair; he returned to his own seat behind the huge desk.

For the second time that day, I related the events as concisely as I could. I omitted only my piece of research into Wellex itself.

On first mention of the white striations I watched him closely for a reaction. There was none. He heard me out more or less expressionlessly, making small tsk-ing sounds and headshakes when I described the deaths. I appealed for his immediate aid because of Lucy and the off-chance that she was still alive.

"I'm not sure what you want from me," he said.

"Do you have any idea why Nandrolex would be in a tranquilizer dart?"

"None at all. It may not be Nandrolex. Other substances might cause the striations."

"Do you know of any?"

"No, but they may exist nonetheless."

"I don't suppose you'd be willing to give me a list of buyers of Nandrolex?"

He made a harumphing sound. "I can't do that, Miss Jamison. Such information is proprietary."

"Can you give me any idea of how widespread the drug is? Do you sell a lot of it, or a little?"

He shook his head. "Confidential information. No can do."

"In a police investigation there'll be a search warrant."

"Legal can deal with it."

I was fed up with his laconic replies. I know when I'm being stonewalled. Later, I might appeal to Mr. Wolfe, the president. He'd be more attuned to the public relations issue. I gave Maas one more chance.

"Dr. Maas, Wellex manufactures and holds the patent on Nandrolex. They also hold patents for various anesthetics. An anesthetic was used to commit two murders. A third person's in mortal danger, if she's even still alive. Nandrolex's signature side effect was present in the bodies of the murder victims. There's a logical connection here. Are you sure there isn't a way you can give me something to go on?"

"I'm sorry. We're a highly competitive industry. There's no way I can share sales information with you or anybody who walks in here. Frankly, Miss Jamison, I think you ought to turn the matter over to the police. Murder, if murder it is, is their purview. So's missing persons, for that matter."

I bit my tongue. Technically, he was right. What ticked me off was that I'd explained carefully why the police weren't yet involved. It was an hour wasted. Only in retrospect did I realize that not having to conduct a tedious investigation of Nandrolex buyers was a disguised blessing.

His tone of voice had essentially dismissed me. Maintaining my cool, I said goodbye. Maas was the gentleman, escorting me to the door and handing me over to Greg, with another patently insincere apology.

I turned in my badge and signed out. Outside, I called U.C. Isla Vista on my mobile. I asked for Dr. Akrich and got his secretary. "He's on the board of his temple and they meet every Wednesday from three to five. Can I make you an appointment for tomorrow? He doesn't usually come back to the office."

"Could I catch him there, at the temple, do you think, after he's done? Would that offend him?"

"You wouldn't be the first person to do that. It's not a religious thing on Wednesday, just business. The synagogue's on Church Street, where it crosses Roman Road."

I knew exactly where that was. I had some time to kill, so called the Worthingtons. They hadn't heard anything from or about Lucy. Nor were there any relevant phone messages at the office or at home.

As I powered off the flip-phone it occurred to me that I might learn something if I could poke around the office of Julius Akrich in his absence. Pangs of guilt about the illegality of such an action were allayed by my gut feeling that he had information that would help me to unravel the tangled threads of the two murders and of Lucy's kidnapping.

Breaking and entering is a useful skill for the private investigator, and my training under the tutelage of my brother John included a short course in picking locks. This particular job wouldn't be easy. Akrich's office was in a main corridor on the third floor of a busy building. I doubted I could pick the lock without attracting attention. On the other hand, maybe I'd find the door unlocked. Or maybe a cooperative secretary would give me a key to fetch my, uh, backpack, which I remembered leaving in his office. Or maybe I'd win the lottery. I was grasping at straws, but it gave me something to do with the time.

Once more I was on a university campus. It was like being back in school again. I dug my lock picks and a pair of thin, tight-fitting gloves out of my handbag and slipped them in the pockets of my jeans. I locked handbag and pistol in the trunk and, feigning the air of a student, trekked across campus to Akrich's building. I climbed the two flights of stairs to his floor and walked over to his office. He wasn't supposed to be there, but just in case, I knocked, waited, and knocked again. I tried the door. No way. The hall was empty for the moment. I knelt down to examine the lock. Lock-picking has an element of luck. Sometimes you can do the job in a minute; sometimes it takes half an hour. I was reaching into my pocket for the picks when I heard someone coming up the stairs. I resumed knocking.

It turned out to be the person who occupied the office two doors down. When he saw me knocking, he told me that Dr. Akrich took Wednesday afternoons off. I thanked him and tried out the "I left my backpack in there" story. He said that one of the secretaries would probably let me in. They had master keys. He directed me to the main office on the first floor. I thanked him and started to walk back to the stairwell. I took the stairs slowly, trying to formulate a story that would end with something like "I could just nip up there with the key, you needn't bother." A simple handover of the key seemed improbable, though.

I was about to enter the main office when the fire alarm on the opposite wall caught my eye. Inspiration struck. I returned to the stairs. I climbed to the fourth floor and located the women's restroom. It was unlocked and unoccupied. I walked back up the hall so that I was standing three floors above the main office entrance. There was a fire alarm here, too, same wall, same place. Engineers, bless them, are so regular in their designs. I scanned in both directions. No one. Quickly I donned the gloves. I took a deep breath, held it, and broke the glass.

A shrill tone filled the air. Light bulbs in wire cages blinked on and red lights flashed up and down the hallway. I darted into the restroom, disappearing from view just as office doors began to open. I locked myself in a stall, sat down on the commode, ready to pull my legs up if anyone entered.

People were walking to the stairs at a clip, some shouting to others: "Is this a drill?" and "Hey, is this the real thing?" I stayed in the stall until I no longer heard footsteps, plus one full, measured minute. I had a narrow window of time in which to work and I needed to balance the risk of discovery with immediacy of action.

I left the stall and opened the door to the hallway a smidgen. I listened intently. A few sounds floated up the stairwells from below but they quickly faded.

I wasn't sure how much time I had before the fire department and cops showed up. They'd go directly to the alarm that I'd pulled. If I hadn't picked my way into Akrich's office by the time I heard them coming up the stairs, I would duck into the third-floor ladies' room.

I moved quickly down to the third floor and over to Akrich's office door. Sirens wailed in the distance. I took a few shallow breaths to slow the adrenaline. My heart flip-flopped like a freshly caught mackerel on a wooden deck.

It was a Best lock, commonly found at institutions because they could be keyed for various levels of mastering. It's not a particularly difficult lock to pick, unless your hand is shaking.

My piano teacher, when I was a kid, had a relaxation technique that she'd taught her students for those scary days that we had to play in recital. It was a combination of breathing, and subtracting backwards by sevens, and, surprisingly, it got the shakes out.

I started at Akrich's office number, 305: breathe, 298; breathe, 291; breathe, 284. At 256, I'd become calm and I inserted the pick into the keyhole, much as I might have played the opening notes of a piano piece. I no longer heard sirens. The voices threatening revocation of my P.I. license were silent. There was only the lock and me, connected by the coercing shiv of stainless steel.

I was unaware of the passage of time when the music I was making came to its final measure: jiggle, jiggle, jiggle, click. The knob turned just as boots scraped up the stairwell. I slipped inside, silently shutting and locking the door. Outside, sirens sang a descending scale. I became aware of driblets of perspiration trickling from my armpits down my rib cage. I sat down and took stock.

The office was as I remembered it, full of artifacts both freestanding and hanging, piles of books and papers spread about the floor, tightly packed bookshelves, several filing cabinets, a desk, and a credenza. I needed a search strategy. I decided to assume that anything vital would be locked up. I was so pleased with my success at the door that I was itching to pick another lock.

My eye caught the telephone answering machine. It was an archaic tape machine that keeps old messages until overwritten by new ones. The message tape was about one-quarter used. I punched the rewind button. When the tape was rewound I punched play, turned down the volume, and pressed my ear against the speaker. The first message, a lunch invitation, conveniently mentioned the day of the call. It was Wednesday, exactly a week ago. There were several messages from Mrs. Akrich, and several from students, judging by the deference in their voices. About a dozen messages into the tape was a voice with which I was familiar.

Chapter 20

Dr. Akrich. This is Lucy. It's Friday morning. I just wanted to tell you, I'll be going to La Jolla until Monday, late. I'll be back on campus Tuesday. I'll see you then. Thanks. Bye. Oh, it's Friday morning—Oh, I already said that. Okay, bye.

There was nothing else of interest on the tape. Lucy's message gave me hope that Akrich might be able to help me find her. I needed to speak with him today, as soon as I was done here. I could hear me now: "Hi, Professor Akrich. This is Dagny Jamison. I just finished breaking into your office. I wonder if you could answer a few questions."

I looked around, trying to decide which lock to pick first. All but one of the filing cabinets was unlocked. The locked one should be simple. In five minutes I had it open. Aha! Two drawers were full of hanging files of student records. I removed one labeled 'Judy Raskin.' It contained forms announcing academic milestones such as 'Preliminary Examination for the Degree of Doctor of Philosophy.' In a separate folder within the file were grade transcripts dating back to her first semester at UCIV. She had straight A's. There were also expense reports for trips to the Churok reservation, and several letters of commendation for her services to the Churok community. Nothing seemed related to her fate, except a memorandum announcing the date of her dissertation defense—which would turn out to be the last day of her life.

Troy Stanton's file wasn't as thick. His grades were spotty and he didn't have any complimentary letters. What was there looked normal to me. I pulled Lucy's file just for comparison purposes. It contained the same kinds of paper work. Other files checked at random were similar.

The bottom two drawers contained stacks of exams, some dating back twenty years. I pulled the drawers out as far as they'd go and slid my fingers around and under the piles. Nothing.

I looked around for my next task. Akrich's office was a veritable junkyard, at least to my eye. On top of the credenza, between two piles, was a familiar-looking object. During my first visit I'd thought it was a typewriter under a dust cover. Uncovered, it turned out to be a microfilm spool reader. Some of Akrich's research material must be on microfilm, but another thought occurred to me.

I tried the sliding doors of the credenza but he kept them locked. Credenzas are designed to keep out the casual snooper, not the professional. I could have jimmied the doors in less than five seconds but that would leave traces. I didn't want to raise suspicion. The lock, as it turned out, was easy pickin's.

I parted the doors. On the top shelf were canisters of microfilm as I'd expected. I picked one up. It had an official-looking label bearing the title and author: *On the Practice of Cranial Surgery among the Native American Tribes of Central California*, by Jason Philip Brainard, Ph.D. The next few I picked up were similarly labeled. Finally, I found what I was looking for—one without a label.

The reader was similar to the one I had used earlier that day in the library. I turned it on. The motor that drove the spools hummed softly and the backlight illuminated the screen. I removed the microfilm from the unlabeled canister and threaded it into the projector. I pressed the forward button until something appeared on the screen. I adjusted the focus.

The page contained lines of carefully hand-scripted words in a foreign language written in English letters. The lines of writing were straight and uniform, written between the rules from a page of notebook paper. I fast forwarded a bit and refocused. Same writing. I repeated the process until I was sure I was looking at copies of Starry Night's notebooks.

I continued to fast forward until the film went blank. There was still about a fifth of the spool left. He had got the contents of all seven notebooks onto a single reel. That added up. A reel this size would hold two weeks' worth of the Los Angeles Times, including advertisements. That would be a thousand-plus pages.

I wondered why he hadn't photocopied the notebooks. The answer was simple. In the mid-seventies xerography was not as widespread as it is nowadays. There probably wasn't a Xerox machine within a hundred miles of the reservation. It would have been cheaper and more convenient to photograph each page with a special camera. The microfilm format was easier and safer to hide and to store.

I rewound to the first page. Starry Night had been no dummy. The little 'c' with a circle around it had been drawn in, followed by what I remembered to be her actual Churok name. Now there was no doubting the source. Duplication of the material was a copyright infringement, apart from the ethical lapse it represented. I returned the empty canister to the shelf and pocketed the spool. I wasn't sure what Akrich's role was in Lucy's kidnapping, if any, but the microfilm was a worthy bargaining chip, never mind my own ethical lapses.

Footsteps came from outside. The 'All Clear' had been given and people were returning to the building. I had to hope that Akrich wouldn't find some reason to return to his office, and that none of the secretaries needed to get in. Fortunately it was late in the afternoon. I knew the janitorial crew was done for the day. My guess was most of the staff went home rather than hang around waiting for the authorities to declare the building safe. Anyway, I was 'in for a penny, in for a pound,' as I once heard Charles say.

I turned my attention to the desk. On top was a computer surrounded by stacks of papers, books, magazines, and a week's worth of mail. As I was looking through this detritus, I inadvertently bumped the computer's mouse. The pattern of lights that had been moving lazily around the computer screen disappeared, revealing a message. "You have new mail: Press <ESC> to read it now." Here was an unforeseen opportunity. I could be reading Akrich's electronic mail. I tapped the <ESC> key. The date and some other stuff spilled onto the screen, followed by the instruction to press <space> to read the mail. I tapped on the space bar. The other stuff went away leaving the message body:

sltovj.

yjrtr od s [tobsyr ombrdyohsypt mpdomh stpimf/ esyvj upitdr;g/ jrt ms,r od fshmu ks,odpm/

=,ssd

I'd carelessly let the header slide by. It would contain information about the sender. There was probably an easy way to bring it back, but I wasn't familiar with this particular e-mail system, and I didn't have time to hack. The message itself was encoded in some way, presumably by the sender's computer. All I could do was copy it carefully and try to figure it out later—it might well be a simple substitution code, like the Jumble puzzle in the daily newspaper.

This was the only new mail. Akrich had most likely checked his e-mail just before leaving his office. It wasn't immediately clear how to read his old, saved mail, but I assumed that anything incriminating would have been deleted. I thought at the time, with the twenty-first century just a few months away, that I'd have to add hacking skills to my repertoire as a P.I.—or at the very least learn the ins and outs of all commonly used e-mail systems.

I didn't want Akrich to know someone had been tampering with his computer. There was no way to make old mail new again, but I could at least obscure my tracks. I unplugged the computer as if the electricity had cut off. That probably happens from time to time, and the confusion of the fire alarm would make it plausible. The computer's drone ceased and when I looked up the screen was black. I waited a couple of seconds and plugged it back in. The whirring started up again, joined by an assortment of beeps, clicks, and chattering sounds. After half a minute it quieted down and the screen displayed Akrich's desktop. In a few minutes the screen saver would kick in and the computer would appear normal to the unsuspecting eye.

I returned to my search of the desk, moving gingerly, unwilling to disturb the computer another time. The shallow middle drawer had an accumulation of years-old office junk: pencils, pens, paper clips of every variety, coins, some chopsticks, a pair of glasses, old roll books, and a box of toothpicks. The large filing drawer on the left contained a rusty coffee maker, a couple of mugs, some Styrofoam cups, several partially filled jars of instant coffee, tea bags, packets of sugar and non-dairy creamer. There was a drawer full of stationery and envelopes. Another had stacks of notebooks. I found nothing of interest.

It was 4:30 and I wanted to meet Akrich at the synagogue. There was the small problem of leaving the office. If someone saw me who knew Akrich was away, I could be in trouble. Of course, I could wait until after hours, when the hallway was sure to be empty, but time was critical. I took the bold approach. I removed my left glove and opened the door a crack with my right hand. I caught the door with my foot and removed the other glove at the same time, careful not to touch anything. I turned and said to the empty room, "Thank you for your help, Dr. Akrich. I think I understand the questions much better now. Shall I pull the door closed?" He obviously answered, "Yes," for I shut the door, using parts of my hand that didn't have prints on file. I sauntered away casually. The hallway's sole occupants were two girls having an animated discussion about whether President Clinton had had an affair with "that woman," Miss Lewinsky. They barely noticed me.

At the car I retrieved my bag from the trunk and put the picks, gloves and microfilm in it. Since I was headed for a place of worship, I let the Glock remain in the glove compartment for the time being. I left campus and drove toward Church Avenue. In fifteen minutes I was in the parking lot behind the Abraham M. Weiss Synagogue and Jewish Community Center. A dozen or so cars were scattered among the carefully painted stalls, scrupulously avoiding the five unoccupied handicapped spaces.

The building is in the shape of a giant dumbbell with large hexagonal disks at either end. It lies lengthwise on Church Avenue. One of the disks, on the Roman Road side, is the synagogue itself. The other disk is the school and community center. The architect had ceded a little to the Spanish motif of the region, with a generous use of exterior tiles in yellow, green, and ocher shades. But no doubt was left regarding the religious nature of the edifice. A magnificent blue and white stained-glass window in the shape of a six-sided star dominated the wall of the sanctuary facing the main street.

I entered through a double door located in the corridor that connected the religious with the secular parts of the building—the bar of the dumbbell, as it were.

The sounds of tired children, and the stressed voices of equally tired teachers, emanated from the right. Also wafting in from that direction were after-school odors. I'm not sure what ingredients comprise this particular smell: perhaps a combination of microwaved snacks, watercolor paints and the occasional missed toilet appointment.

I assumed that the board meeting would take place in the other wing, away from the school. I turned left and walked toward the synagogue proper. If it was like a church, there would be, in addition to the actual place of worship, administrative offices, a conference room or two, and perhaps a small library. The corridor ended at an antechamber. On the right, three sets of double doors opened into the sanctuary. On the left, a passageway led to other parts of the building. The walls were bedecked with plaques that bore various inscriptions in both English and Hebrew. Scattered around the periphery of the room were half a dozen short benches upholstered in a sturdy green twill fabric.

I ventured into the passageway and stuck my head round the first open door. A middle-aged woman was behind a desk talking on the phone. An engraved brass name sign on the desk read Sylvia Akrich. I assumed she was the professor's wife. She put her hand over the mouthpiece. "Can I help you, dear?" She had an eastern accent, maybe New York City.

"I'm wondering if I'm too late to catch Mr. Akrich. I understand he's in a board meeting."

"No, they haven't let out yet. They usually go right to five."

"Is it okay to wait for him? His secretary at the school said it was, but—"

"It's fine, dear," she interrupted. "They'll have to come down the hall when they leave. You can catch him in the lobby." She returned to her phone conversation.

I returned to the area outside the sanctuary and took a seat. There was nobody around this time of day. Only the sporadic wail of whining children broke the silence. I was too hyped-up to sit still for long. I tested one of the doors to the sanctuary. It was open.

I hesitated before entering. I'd never been in a modern synagogue before. They are in short supply in Germany and Turkey, the two countries where I'd grown up. It might be interesting.

I slipped inside and let the door close behind me. It wasn't as different from a church as one might have thought, leastwise in its atmosphere of spirituality. It lacked the symbols of Christianity—the Cross, the images of Jesus, the Apostles and the Saints, the depictions of the life of Jesus—of course. In their place were portrayals of scenes from the Old Testament: God creating the universe; Moses parting the seas; Moses holding aloft the tablet of the Ten Commandments; the Israelites in battle dress; Daniel in the lions' den; Samson bringing down the house.

The auditorium lacked the nave and transept form of many churches, and there were no chapels off to the side. No narthex, apse or sacristy, either. A large, ornate cabinet stood against the far wall of the pulpit where a church might display a large cross. Above it, light streamed through the star-shaped window, bathing the dais in a multi-colored ethereal glow.

The solemn silence was soothing. I could have sat for a while, relaxing, and thinking. I didn't want to miss Akrich, however. I went back to the lobby and listened for footsteps. Nothing.

I paced a little, stopping to read some plaques. They were all of different sizes and shapes and commemorated the various weddings, funerals, bar mitzvahs, bat mitzvahs, and major donors. I read some of the plaques, just to pass the moments. One had a long list of bar mitzvah celebrants: Louis Aaronsen, Dennis Abrahmson, David Augeberg, Evan Benjamin, and on and on.

Another plaque with fewer names was for bat mitzvah graduates: Brawna Arkady, Roberta Blumberg, Francine Brown and more.

Mrs. Akrich interrupted my musings. "It's five o'clock, dear. I've done my eight-to-five and I'm going home. I'm sure Julius'll be along in a few minutes. They don't like to stay late. Have a good evening."

I thanked her and returned to my reading.

On another wall, weddings were remembered: Sidney and Lorraine Adelman, née Ginsberg; Gerald and Anne Agee, née Verango; Julius and Sylvia Akrich, née Maas. That stopped me in my tracks. Akrich married a Sylvia Maas. I started looking for the name Maas. I found Richard Maas's name on a plaque honoring major donors, and on another one mentioning past presidents of the congregation. My mind shifted gears. Is Richard Maas the brother-in-law of Julius Akrich? Cousin-in-law? Is this the missing link in a chain of murdered students, a thieving professor, and the drug Nandrolex? I needed more time to plan my confrontation with Akrich. The sound of men's voices drifted into the lobby, becoming louder. I bolted for the exit.

Chapter 21

I walked rapidly down the central corridor. Groups of parents and children were coming from the opposite direction. I slowed to a businesslike gait. I didn't think Akrich would recognize me from behind, especially as he had no reason to expect to see me.

I slipped in front of a mother whose child had shifted into reverse and was trying to return to the school. The tug-of-war was going poorly for the mother, who kept pleading, "Now Daryl, now Daryl," as she permitted the child to pull her slowly back from the door.

In the parking lot, SUVs and "momma-vans" were arriving from all directions. Others, laden with children, were trying to depart, creating a chaotic traffic pattern. Everyone crept slowly to ensure the safety of the loose kids who helter-skeltered about.

My mind was racing. I had a link between Akrich and Wellex, but I wasn't sure what to make of it. Akrich couldn't have killed Judy. I knew where he was when Judy died. I hadn't verified his whereabouts when Troy had been murdered. That was a question for later.

When I reached into my bag for my keys, I felt the spool of microfilm. According to the plaque, Akrich had married Sylvia the year following Starry Night's death. The fact that he'd had a large wedding at the synagogue meant his courtship wasn't a whirlwind affair. He had most likely known his wife, and the Maas family, for a considerable time before the wedding. I wondered if they were acquainted at the time Starry Night had died, or when Akrich had photographed the notebooks.

I exited the parking lot onto Roman Road and headed away from the synagogue. Two quick right turns and a left onto Church pointed me toward downtown and the Santa Barbara police headquarters. I intended to file a missing person's report on Lucy and test the waters at the homicide division. I also needed to find out if Charles had had any luck with the coroner. Homicide was unlikely to take action on my account alone.

Charles answered on the first ring. I related my day's experiences succinctly, ending with my suspicions about Starry's demise. "I wish you could have autopsied her," I said, wistfully.

His response surprised me. "It may not be too late."

"C'mon, she's been dead and buried for some twenty-odd years."

"You'd be surprised what we can do."

"Charles, how can we get a court order for an exhumation? We can't even convince the authorities when we have a fresh corpse to examine."

"Who said anything about a court order?"

"Are you suggesting something illicit? Something that might cost us both our licenses?" I tried to sound incredulous.

He wasn't buying it. "You're right, love, we'll have to be exceedingly careful. I'll come round at six."

As simply as that, I launched into the weirdest, most macabre night of my life as a private investigator.

I stopped at the police station and filed the report. I debated with myself about walking over to Homicide, but I decided not to, because time was short, and I thought I'd have stood a better chance if I'd been able to take my brother John with me. He knew most of the homicide detectives and would vouch for my sanity.

There was a message on the answering machine when I got back to John's. I hoped it was from Lucy, or one of the Worthingtons with news about her. It turned out to be Professor Gribith. "Dagny, Bill Gribith from UCLA. Do you remember I said something was nagging at my memory? I thought of it. I think Julius married somebody whose brother was in the pharmaceutical business. I believe it to be Wellex, but I'm not positive. I don't know if this helps. Let me know how things turn out. Bye."

"Thanks, Professor, that does help," I said to the machine. I hadn't doubted that Sylvia Maas was related to Richard Maas, since she was married in the same synagogue that he belonged to, and Maas isn't all that common a name. But given what I was about to do based on that relationship, I was more confident now, having had independent confirmation. It was also helpful to know that Richard Maas and Julius Akrich were almost doubtless brothers-in-law.

It was a quarter to six. I could feel my shoulders sagging. I'd already put in a twelve-hour day, which had included jogging, fruitless interviewing, and breaking and entering. I could have fallen asleep on a bed of nails. Instead, while water was boiling for instant coffee, I packed an overnight bag with essentials. I took my coffee upstairs where I stripped and took a two-minute shower. I dribbled some cold water into the coffee so I could gulp it down, and then brushed my teeth. I dressed in my nighttime skulking outfit: black jeans, a black T-shirt beneath a black turtleneck, a pair of black sneakers. I grabbed a black hooded sweatshirt and threaded it through the handles of the small black bag.

Charles was prompt to the minute. A quick hug, and off we went to dabble in one of the world's oldest professions: grave robbing. Once on the 101, Charles engaged the cruise control and asked me to bring him up to date, sparing no detail. I did. He was fascinated by the breaking and entering, and the discovery of the microfilm evoked a wide grin and a high five.

"We're in luck in one way," Charles said, when I'd finished. "The moon's in its fourth quarter. It won't rise until about two in the morning. Perfect for a midnight excursion. Do you know where she's buried?"

"Tommy said the Churok burial grounds. I got the impression it was somewhere out of town. I hope it's not in the middle of some village."

"All I hope is that she was buried in a relatively dry place."

"Oh, I get it. Less decomposition." I wrinkled my nose.

Charles noticed the gesture. "It won't stink. The soft tissue and fluids are long gone. We'll find some bones, and with some luck, a fingernail or two."

Charles drove hard and by ten after eight we were at the Makrui town limits. I didn't think it wise to ask directions to the cemetery. It would be impossible not to leave traces of digging, and someone would remember two strangers asking questions. I had Charles pull into the same quickie mart I'd been in two days before. While he filled the tank, I went inside and purchased a map of the locale. Back in the car, we drove a couple of blocks and pulled over to study the map. About ten miles east of Makrui, just off the main road, was a shaded-in patch similar to the ones designating recreational areas and parks. Small black lettering read CNBG Cem.* The footnote was *Churok Nation Burial Grounds Cemetery.

Dusk was on the edge of becoming night when we found the cemetery. It was a mile or so from the highway, reached by an unpaved service road that forked into a loop that circled its periphery. The isolation was both good and bad. Good because we wouldn't be observed by passersby; bad because if someone did come up the road, we couldn't slip away unseen.

The grounds were large, at least forty acres. We got out and looked around. The gravesites varied from majestic to humble. Some had vertical headstones as tall as Charles, and were elaborately engraved with mysterious glyphs. Others were marked by a small brick of granite with the bare essentials: name, year of birth, year of death. One brought a lump to my throat: a small headstone in the form of a bunny rabbit marked the final resting place of a four-day-old infant.

If we had to find Starry by examining every grave, it might take all night. I thought to check just the ones with vertical headstones. Starry was an important person. She'd have a gravesite commensurate with her status.

It was already too dark to read the smaller letters. Charles went to fetch a couple of torches while I surveyed the necropolis. A black, polished, granite monolith loomed in the center of the circular grounds. It would make a good starting point for our search. Our path would spiral around and away from the central point in ever-widening rings as we methodically checked headstones.

I stood staring at the central monument amid an utter stillness broken only by the occasional car on the highway a mile away, or the clickety-clack of a distant train. Charles returned with several flashlights, spare batteries, and a good-sized lantern. Together we walked toward the center while I explained the plan in a low voice.

The air was bone dry with little inclination to hold the heat of day. The once pleasant nocturnal breezes now chilled me from the outside, while the enormity of what we were doing chilled me from within.

We reached the monolith. It marked the graves of a husband and wife named Hunter. He had been born in 1875 and had died in 1940; she had been born in 1880 and had died in 1952. No inscription indicated what either had done in life to merit the beautifully polished seven feet of granite that watched over their double tomb. The name Hunter appeared frequently on the headstones closest to the monolith. The further away from the center, the less frequently the name appeared.

Many of the headstones were engraved in the Churok language. I had to hope that the grave marker of Starry Night would have her English name on it somewhere. We only read the headstones of graves whose occupants had died the same year as Starry. Mostly we had to be careful not to leave any gaps of unexamined headstones, a heedfulness that grew more difficult as the spirals became wider and the night darker.

We moved counterclockwise keeping about five feet apart. Charles was on the inside, scanning the headstones to his right between himself and me. I scanned the headstones to my right. We weaved in and out in an attempt to cover a ten-foot swath with each cycle. After each cycle, we moved outward five feet and repeated the process. This gave us double coverage, with Charles going over what I had supposedly seen.

Forty acres is big. Developers can squeeze a hundred good-sized homes onto forty acres, including streets, easements, and recreational areas. After an hour, the flashlights dimmed.

"Batteries have gone flat," muttered Charles.

We replaced the worn batteries and continued. We were on our thirtieth or so spiral, still less than halfway finished, when Charles gave a little cry. He was staring down on a grave covered with a slab of white marble. I remembered having walked past it on our previous pass, but having ignored it because there was no standing headstone.

"Pay dirt," I exclaimed.

"Quite, as it were," said Charles. The slab bore a long inscription in Churok, followed by a shorter one in English: Here rests the body of our sister, known to many as Starry Night. May her soul shine with the stars. "I just caught a glint of the name out of the corner of my eye. Jolly lucky it's white and reflective."

My exhilaration at the discovery quickly turned to dread. "Now what?" I whispered, as if I didn't know.

"Where are we?" said Charles. "All this moving in circles has me disoriented. Can you see the car?"

We swept the road with our lights. "There," I said.

"You stay here. I'll get the tools. I'm going to move the car off the road where it won't be seen if someone drives through. Should've done before. Here's more light." He handed me the lantern, which I switched on to its low setting.

He patted my butt for reassurance and moved off toward the car. Christ, I thought. *I'm alone in the middle of a graveyard an hour before midnight, up to no good, and I'm a heathen to boot. What won't I do to see justice served?* As we were spiraling, I kept thinking of the monstrous crimes of murder that drove my actions. Ends may justify means when dictated by reason, or so I argued to myself.

Charles started the car and drove it well into the desert so that it wouldn't fall within the range of the headlights of any car driving through. Maybe the cops came by here once or twice on their rounds. The lights of Charles's car went out at the same moment that the first beams of light from another car became visible down the road. I quickly doused the lantern and hunkered down, putting a gravestone between me and the new light source.

Music streamed across the graves—Supertramp. I had received their album Crime of the Century for my ninth birthday and I knew every note and every word of every song in it, even these twenty years later. The car went to the farthest end of the road and stopped. I was making like the Tell-Tale Heart. I crawled behind another headstone. From the car came the sound of a couple of tops being popped, some talking, silence except for the music, giggling, and heavy breathing. I was getting the picture.

The periods of no talking became longer, replaced by even heavier breathing and now some moaning. Supertramp was well into the title song, the last cut on the album, and the relentless streams of massive chords from the keyboard charging to a climax. They timed their sex to the music—whether intentionally or not, I couldn't tell. The last strains of "Crime" accompanied the post-coital murmurings of the lovers.

The car started up and slowly completed its circuit of the cemetery and was lost to sight. Thank goodness for the quick and the horny. Though it seemed longer, the whole business had lasted but twenty minutes. Only when their car revved onto the highway did I dare show my light. Another light winked back and came toward me.

It was midnight when Charles inserted the tip of a shovel under the marble slab that had protected Starry's remains for all those years. The dryness of everything heartened Charles as he went about the task. We had survived the invasion of the sex-starved and were hoping for no copycats. We had some heavy labor in front of us and the thought of it took our minds off the ghoulish business at hand.

I grabbed the other shovel and between us we pried the slab up a few inches. "Now the other side," said Charles. "Then it should come right up." We repeated the action and the slab came loose. We moved it off to the side. Then the digging began. The earth was packed solidly; it was dry and hard, but not rocky. We used a pick to help us get through the first foot and from that point the job was easier.

The big thrill when digging for buried treasure is to actually feel the sought-for object. We were standing about three feet inside the grave, sweating, filthy, and exhausted, when I pushed in the tip of my shovel and it scraped against wood. We widened the pit to accommodate the length and width of the casket.

"Keep your feet on the edges," warned Charles. "The top may be rotten. You wouldn't want to fall through."

We toasted with water. Then, between us, we finished half the gallon Charles had had the foresight to bring. Thirsty work, grave-digging.

After another half hour, we had removed as much dirt as we could. The entire top of Starry Night's coffin was exposed. We climbed out and looked back down into the excavation we had dug. "There's no way we can lift that sucker out of there," I said. I was too bone-weary for reverence.

"We'll try to get the top off. It's screwed down but I bet half the screw holes are rotted. Back in a jiff." Charles plodded off to the car for some tools and I noticed that he now cast a long, thin shadow.

While we'd been working, the moon had come up over the hills to the east. Only night people are treated to the spectacle of a rising moon in its waning quarter, its body bloated, its mien a doleful orange, its crescent inverted, its ascent a desperate flight from the overtaking sun that soon would engulf the moonglow in the brilliant dawn of a new day.

The moon has a special meaning in my life. I was born on the day that Neil Armstrong took a giant leap for mankind and stepped out of his earthly craft onto the moon's surface. I'd grown up wanting to be an astronaut, but was unable to pass NASA's rigorous physical examination. The army, at least, was once glad to have me, but they, too, had rejected me after my cancer surgery.

Charles returned with a valise, which he put aside, and a portable electric drill into which he fixed a Phillip's screwdriver bit. We switched the lantern on to its highest setting, and lowered it into the grave. Charles followed it in, careful to mind where he placed his feet. When he was properly balanced, he went to work on the screws. Some came out immediately. If one was recalcitrant, he chiseled away the half-rotted wood surrounding it. When all the screws had been removed, the top was ready to come off. Charles climbed out of the grave. He lay on his stomach and reached back in with a crowbar to pry up one corner of the casket's lid. He repeated this at each corner. "She'll come up now," he muttered with satisfaction. "Would you get the lantern, please!"

I pulled out the lantern and set it aside. Charles grunted, strained, and lifted. The lid creaked but wouldn't come clear. Some of the wood must have fused over the years.

"Give me a hand here, love; grab that claw hammer."

I lay down next to Charles and reached as far as I could into the grave and managed to hook the claw under the lid. Our combined strength was enough to break the seal. Slowly, with a rasping, grating sound that set my teeth on edge, the end of the lid rose toward the open air. We were able to get our hands under it and muscled it up until we could get to our knees, and then lifted some more until we were able to stand. Together, we pulled it fully out of the grave and set it atop the piles of dirt.

We got down on our bellies again, heads in the grave. I chanced a sniff. Charles was right. An inoffensive earthy smell prevailed. Charles lowered the lantern into the grave, fully illuminating the contents of the open coffin.

Chapter 22

I had steeled myself for the sight of a human skeleton, gray and decayed. Instead, I beheld the rainbow hues of Starry Night's burial clothes, faded but still colorful. There wasn't much left of these, and beneath them lay the bony remains of the corpse, which had been laid to rest on its side. Charles bellied forward until he could bend at the waist and reach into the coffin. He felt around for a moment and pulled himself up with a grunt of satisfaction.

"This may work, Dagny. It's very dry. The skeleton is well preserved. I don't think water's ever seeped in."

"Can you tell anything?" I asked.

"No. I'm going to have to climb in."

He got his valise and the lantern and eased himself into the grave, careful not to step on the remains. Edgar Allan Poe would have loved this. Charles switched the lantern to its brightest setting. I had stopped being nervous about being discovered. There aren't many people around a graveyard at three in the morning. Still, the lantern shone so brightly that even in the confines of the grave it produced a glow visible at a distance. I wondered if anyone lived in the hills to the east. They appeared desolate, but you never know. Someone could be looking down on the phantasmagoric sight of a white aurora streaming from a grave. What a ghost story!

Charles opened the valise. It contained a field microscope, stainless steel surgical implements, a laboratory squirt bottle, some cloth, disposable latex gloves, and a surgical mask. He donned the mask and a pair of the gloves and removed all of the other items. He closed the valise and laid it down at the edge of the pit. He set the microscope on top of the flat surface and made some adjustments. It was self-illuminating.

He bent over, disappearing from view. He grumbled and stood up. "I can't see a bloody thing because of my own bloody shadow. Would you hand me that torch? Wait, put some fresh batteries in it."

I did so and watched him go gingerly down on his hands and knees, straddling the corpse as if he would make love to it. He studied the bones of her left hand, some of which crumbled when touched. Then he searched the ground and found something, which he laid aside. He repeated the routine on her right hand. He turned 180 degrees. He examined both feet as he had done the hands. Finally he collected his treasure, exhaled loudly, and stood up.

He squirted the finger- and toe-nail remains repeatedly until they were clean and patted them dry with the cloth. He placed one of them under the microscope and bent over the instrument. He made some adjustments, shifted the object slightly, and made more adjustments. He continued in this way until he was satisfied. He repeated the ritual with the next object, then the next. The fourth one pleased him. His head rose and he gave a thumbs up sign with his free hand. He continued until he had scrutinized all the nails, seven in all.

"You must see this, Dagny." He placed an object under the lens and turned the microscope towards me. "Focus with this knob." I got down on my knees and squinted into the tube with my right eye.

"I can't see a damn thing," I complained.

"Try keeping both eyes open. It takes a moment to get the hang of it."

"What am I looking at?"

"Her right thumb nail magnified five times."

I persisted and got an image. I turned the focus knob until it was clear. I could make out the root of the nail, eaten away at the edges, but mostly intact. The whitening was evident, though faint and mottled in appearance.

"I could only find one other nail with hints of the white striations. You're looking at the best one, but 'twill serve."

"So Starry Night was murdered! But why? For her notes? For her office? For her inheritance? And why Judy and Troy, all these years later? Akrich couldn't have killed the others, even supposing he did kill Starry. I wish I knew more about the circumstances of her death." I was thinking chaotic thoughts aloud.

Charles looked puzzled, but all he said was, "Let's get to work and cover our backs. Maybe while we sweat we'll get some ideas."

"Good luck. I'm too tired to think worth a hoot, but hand me a shovel."

Charles put his instruments away. He wrapped the nails in a piece of cloth and put those in the valise, too, along with the used exam gloves. We doused all the lights. The moon, now at ten o'clock high, gave sufficient light. I leaned over the grave one last time and surveyed the disarranged bones. Rational though I try to be, I found the sight of the open coffin and its ghastly contents disquieting. I apologized silently to Starry's spirit, and promised to make her murderer accountable.

Charles started shoveling. "Wait," I cried. "We're forgetting the lid."

"We'll have to fill the coffin with dirt, otherwise we'll never get it all back in."

We shoveled until a foot of earth covered her coffin. Charles tamped the dirt with his feet, another inescapable profanation. We replaced the lid with the domed side down so it wouldn't collapse at some later time and cause a cave-in. By four o'clock we'd replaced all the earth, tamping as we went along, so there was enough room on top to replace the marble slab. We used a square-tipped shovel and a broom to cover traces of our deed.

"This is a patchy job at concealment," said Charles, "but it will have to do."

We risked the lantern one last time so that we could scour the gravesite for any artifacts we might be leaving. I didn't want to be betrayed by any subconscious feelings of guilt into leaving behind clues to my identity.

We walked back to the car, satisfied that we'd covered our tracks as well as possible. By the time we had gone a hundred paces, I couldn't tell where her grave was among the thousands. We threw the digging tools into the back of the wagon, covered them with blankets, and arranged everything as if we were campers. Charles started the Subaru. We crept onto the road, lights off, and glided darkly toward the main highway. There was no traffic. We were in no man's time, that sliver of night that's outlasted revelers and foreruns the most zealous of early birds.

"Can you drive?" I asked Charles. "I'm so tired I could've crawled in next to Starry. I don't think we can pull into a motel without attracting attention."

He nodded. "Sure. I want to push off and put some miles between us and the cemetery. I'm so hopped on adrenaline I'll be awake for hours. You sleep. If I need a snooze, I'll pull off the road."

I didn't need urging. I dropped the seat back to forty-five degrees and made a pillow of my jacket. Half my sleep the past week had been in cars. I must have drowsed the length of California and back. As I sank into semi-consciousness, lulled by the engine's hum, I thought, *Have I solved a murder? Have I found a murderer? No matter. No way in hell to get an arrest, let alone a conviction.*

I awoke when the car stopped at the bottom of the Castle Avenue exit ramp in Santa Barbara, not far from my temporary home. Every muscle in my body ached. The inside of my mouth had a metallic coating, and when you can smell your own bad breath…yeesh! Charles was smiling at me. He looked haggard. A few craggy lines were trying to take over his boyish face, abetted by his fatigue.

"I'll have you home in a trice. You could use a bit more sleep."

"You don't look so great yourself."

He laughed. "I'm utterly knackered. I need a good soak and a good lie-down."

In a few moments we were parked in John's driveway. Dawn was breaking. Lights were on in one or two houses. An early morning jogger trotted past the idling Subaru. "What now?" asked Charles.

"Bathe, sleep 'til nine, and go see Akrich. Maybe he'll slip up."

Charles leaned over to kiss me.

I gave him my cheek and a hug around his neck. "Nothing personal. I'm saving myself for a bottle of Scope."

Inside, I ran a hot bath. With the water as hot as I could stand, I slipped in so only my head and part of a breast broke the surface. Exhaustion overwhelmed me. The last thing I remembered before dozing off were billows of muddy hue spreading out from my body.

The chill awakened me. I'd slept nearly an hour. The bath was lukewarm. I debated adding some hot, but the tint of the water and my wrinkled fingers suggested soap, shower, and a dry bed. I don't remember getting from bathroom to bed but somehow I was wrapped in a blanket when the phone rang.

I jerked awake. The clock read ten after nine. I'd forgotten to set the alarm. I reached for the receiver, nearly knocking over the blinking answering machine. I'd been too out of it to check messages earlier.

"This is Dagny," I croaked. Good, I remembered my name.

"Dagny, Jeanette Briggs, from Santa Cruz…"

"Hi, Dr. Briggs, how's it going?" I stifled a yawn.

"Just fine. Did you get my message? I left one at your office and one at your home. I haven't been able to get a hold of Dr. Clarke, either."

Uh-oh. Charles and I caught in the act, but not the act she most likely had in mind. "Oh, dear. I was out on a case and haven't been to my office, and my machine at home is acting funny. What's up?"

"Wellex makes an anesthetic called Welnarkothal. When it's mixed with equal amounts of Nandrolex, the Nandrolex acts as a catalyst. A small amount of the mixture could anesthetize an adult human almost instantly. That's what we finally determined was in Troy's blood. It was a tough one. I had staff working half the night."

I could dig that! "That's great, Dr. Briggs! Could a tranquilizer dart hold enough of the mixture to knock someone out?"

"I should think so, yes."

"How long would they be unconscious?"

"That depends. With small doses, a matter of minutes, perhaps as much as ten minutes."

"Really?"

"I've done some experimentation on my own—on lab animals, to be sure, but the results scale up pretty reliably."

"Can a person buy this stuff? Or get a prescription for it?"

"Not that I know of. I guess a medical facility could order the ingredients, but as far as I know, no one's ever tried combining them."

"How did you figure it out?"

"It occurred to me to look for drugs from the same pharmaceutical company. You're the one who reminded us of Wellex. Once I knew I was looking for Welnarkothal, I could analyze it chemically and devise a test for its metabolites. It cost us a pretty penny in lab fees, but I wouldn't be surprised if the coroner goes for a murder one rap."

That woke me up. "Would the mixture contain enough Nandrolex to cause the white lines?"

"That side effect doesn't always occur, but the mixture is fifty-fifty, so the recipient of the dosage would be receiving ten, twenty times the normal dose of Nandrolex. That'd raise the likelihood of collateral activity."

"Is that a yes?"

"It's a *probably*. I don't know for sure. I'll tell you what I think, though, for what it's worth. There are a lot easier ways to kill yourself than strangulation by hanging. These were bright, young, well-informed kids. They'd have access to drugs that'd do the job painlessly and efficiently. A handful of Valium and a half pint of vodka, or whatever. I just don't see them choosing to hang themselves like some Russian in a Dostoyevsky novel."

"Me neither, Dr. Briggs. Thanks for your opinion, and for the info."

"What'll you do with it? Do you have suspects? I'm sure the homicide people up here will want to talk to you."

"All I have are puzzle pieces. I don't have the picture on the box to guide me. I'm not even sure if all the pieces belong to the same puzzle."

"I promised Dr. Peters I would call Dr. Clarke and tell him what we found. Can you pass the information on to him?"

"I'd be happy to take care of that for you, Dr. Briggs. Thanks again, very much."

"Good luck, Dagny."

I forewent jogging without a pang of remorse. I'd had enough exercise the previous night to last a month. I was too sore to even think about running. Besides, I was ravenous. All I could think about were Egg McMuffins, hash browns, and coffee. I loaded up at McDonalds and brought the food with me to the office, devouring well-oiled hunks of potato on the way. I was still wary when out, but the total absence of anything sinister since I started taking precautions had blunted my vigilance.

I postponed eating the rest of the food until I'd brewed a pot, thus affording myself the supreme pleasure of washing down mouthfuls with fresh coffee. Not one of the new phone messages was from Charles, or about Lucy, so I left them for John to deal with when he got back.

I busied myself updating my computer file on the case, using code words and phrases to describe the previous night's quasi-legal activities. At the same time, I was preparing to meet Professor Akrich. Using the stolen microfilm, I would try to bait him into an indiscreet remark.

It was a near certainty that he had murdered Starry Night. He'd have rendered her unconscious using the mixture that Dr. Briggs had described, and then most likely have suffocated her with a pillow. There'd be no evidence of a struggle. The possibility that Starry took Nandrolex and truly died of natural causes was too remote for consideration. Since Akrich had been living in her house when she died, a different murderer was impossible without Akrich's complicity. My gut argued that he had to be involved in the other murders, perhaps through accomplices. He could probably tell me where Lucy was, dead or alive.

A little after ten o'clock, I called the university and asked for his secretary. He was in a faculty meeting from 10:00 to 12:00. "He goes to the Faculty Club for lunch at noon," she explained, "but he usually drops back by his office to check messages. I'll tell him you called, Miss...?"

"Maas. I'm a cousin of his wife. Sylvia said I might catch him for lunch, but I'd like to surprise him, if you wouldn't mind."

"No problem at all. Mum's the word. Do you know where to come? You can waylay him right at noon."

Her wording was apropos. "Third floor of Pearson Hall. I've been before. Thanks very much. Remember, it's a surprise," I said in my cutest voice. She promised again.

I had some extra time but I didn't want to work on anything but this case. I was still feeling a bit smug from my raid on Akrich's office. Why not his home? Somewhere was evidence that would tie him to these crimes. He was busy on campus for a few hours, and I knew Mrs. Akrich worked. Did they have children at home? I doubted it, at their age. I was becoming a serial felon. First a B&E, then grave-robbing, and now another B&E, all in a 24-hour period—a day in the life of a P.I., not! Delivering subpoenas was looking better each moment.

The phone book listed Julius Akrich on Houston Road. I recognized the street. It's off Orchard Drive, in an area of expensive homes on the bluffs overlooking the Pacific, convenient to UCIV. He couldn't live there on a professor's salary, but the Maases probably had money. It's not a great neighborhood in which to break and enter. With the rich, there's always somebody showing up to clean the house, keep the grounds, and wash the windows, not to mention those pesky alarm systems. But I had my methods. I was confident that I could gain access without creating a disturbance. What was that saying? "Man plans, God laughs."

I called the Akrich's telephone number before I left. A machine answered. So far so good. Twenty minutes later I was parking in an inconspicuous place on Orchard. The Akrich estate is at the end of the west cul-de-sac of Houston Road. The house itself stands deep in a wooded lot of several acres, presumably situated for a favorable view of the ocean.

I had stopped at home and changed into a faux uniform of blue denim trousers, a blue work shirt, and a blue baseball cap. My plan was to walk boldly up to the front door, ring the bell, and knock a few times. Then I'd walk noisily around the house and repeat the process at other doors, making sure the property was unoccupied. If anyone was there, I'd pull a lie out of my hatful of prefabricated fibs. I locked my handbag in the car in favor of an official looking clipboard.

I was halfway to the front door when a man stepped out of the bushes and pointed a .45 caliber automatic at my belly button. "You can die now, or you can die later." My hands rose reflexively. The clipboard clattered as it struck the ground.

Chapter 23

Part of my training to be a medic in the Army was to study the effects of gunshot wounds. With a .45 the point of entry is small, no larger than your index finger. The exit wound, if the bullet gets that far, is the size of a man's fist, a tangle of blood and guts to make a surgeon weep. The War Department first issued the gun to U.S. soldiers fighting in the jungle in the late 19th century. Machete-wielding fanatics, who neglected to fall down when shot, motivated its deployment. They would hurl themselves fearlessly into the teeth of our boys' gunfire. The high velocity rifle bullets passed through their naked torsos and on they came, surviving long enough to bring about a dismaying number of amputees. The heavy, slow .45 slug was designed to remain inside the target body, thereby imparting all of its momentum. It could stop a charging man in his tracks. No degree of fanaticism can defy the laws of physics.

A small close target—me, in this case—is insufficient to stop the slug completely. As it slows in the body, it bulldozes a mass of vessels, organs, sinew, and bone to the surface. I was hoping to avoid a jumbling of my insides.

He was a well-muscled man just under six feet tall, medium complexion, wavy brown hair cut short. He wore a Gold's Gym T-shirt, off-brand jeans, and a pair of New Balance cross-trainers. I didn't think he was a professional thug. Nobody uses those old forty-fives any more. They are inaccurate at ranges greater than ten feet, and they tend to jam. The National Rifle Association got a hold of thousands of surplus models back in the sixties. It sold them cheaply as incentives to join the organization long before the advent of gun control laws.

"Won't the professor be surprised to find another little chickadee prying into his business? Maybe now he'll get on with what needs to be done."

"Hey, I'm just here selling magazine subscriptions. If they don't want any, I'll leave. The hardware isn't necessary."

"Uh-huh. P.I. work a little slow so you're moonlighting, right?" He motioned me to precede him. There was a narrow gravel pathway winding away from the main house to the right. Tall bushes on either side guaranteed privacy. Along this he urged me with sharp nudges, the gun now pointed at the small of my back. Thankfully, these surplus automatics are heavy-triggered even when cocked. I didn't think I'd be shot by accident.

At the end of the path in a small clearing was a tiny cottage. It had a pitched roof of red Spanish tile and light brown shingled siding. The path led to the front door, on either side of which were wood frame windows with their shades pulled tightly closed. Beneath each window was a shelf for potted plants or flower boxes. Several clay pots stood on each, their contents dead or dying.

"Down," he commanded, cocking the hammer of the .45 with an ominous click, and at the same time pressing on my right shoulder with the gun's barrel. This is the moment that James Bond would have disarmed him with some slick martial art. I'd had my army MP training and I knew some tricks, but trust me, it doesn't work with a cocked pistol aimed at you. I thought of asking him to shoot me in the head. I hate having large holes in my body. A large hole in my head would be just deserts for blundering into this mess.

I sank wordlessly to my knees under the pressure of the gun barrel. He pushed me down flat on my stomach and put his foot on my back. I closed my eyes and scrunched my face. He fumbled around in his pockets. The sound of keys; the sound of a key in a lock; a dead bolt thrown open; another key in lock sound; a knob turning. The door to the cottage creaked open.

He removed his foot. "Get in!"

I scrambled to my feet, not all that sure I was happy to be alive. I'd rather be murdered than raped and murdered, and there was something sexually domineering about that foot.

Inside, the cottage was dark. With my sun-shrunken pupils I could barely discern the outline of the walls. The measly light that seeped around the shaded windows was the only illumination. There were no other windows in the cottage, which appeared to consist of one large room. I suddenly felt a sensation. There was somebody in the room. I didn't hear or see anything, consciously. My life-form detector had gone off.

He switched on a light. I was in an L-shaped room. To my right, separated by freestanding shelves, was a kitchen. To my left was a living area with a shabby sofa and two decrepit stuffed chairs. In the back, divided from the living area by cords of bamboo beads—like the ones that separate the restrooms from the dining room in cheap Chinese restaurants—was, apparently, a bedroom. I tried to peer through the curtains, but it was unnecessary.

"Back there," he urged me with a nudge. My fear of rape yielded to a worse fear: gang rape. There was someone waiting in the bedroom. I hesitated and the nudge became a shove.

"Go!"

I pushed through the bamboo curtain and gasped when I saw the bed. Tied securely to the bedstead, gagged, and blindfolded, was Lucy Navarro.

"Vagmy," she said through the gag, and tears dribbled out from under her blindfold. Somehow, she recognized me. She must have been here for days. Restrained and blinded, the other senses become keener. She may have recognized my footfall, or even my smell. My outrage surmounted my fear. I turned on my antagonist with spumes of withering curses, holding my ground as he moved toward me, the cocked .45 aimed at a point over my left shoulder. He swung the weapon hard against my left temple.

A sheet of pain engulfed me. I went down, stunned and helpless in agony. I wasn't knocked out; I just wished I was. He opened a door beside the bed and dragged me by the collar into the bathroom. He cocked his fist to strike me again, but thought better of it. For whatever reason, he was apparently under orders not to kill.

The door closed, secured by three dead bolts. The pain in my throbbing head resonated throughout my body, welling up and receding with each heartbeat. I was going to be sick. I barely got my head in the toilet, whose malodor hastened the emptying of my stomach. That somehow made me feel better. I began pain control procedures. Shallow breathing, slow movements, positive thoughts. Yes! I was alive! Lucy was alive! The latter thought thrilled and energized me.

Inhale, exhale, inhale, exhale. The pulsing of pain behind my eyes subsided and my head began to clear. I was taking stock. The bathroom was windowless. The pittance of light from the crack under the door was barely enough for me to pick out the commode, sink and bathtub. The floor I was lying on was everywhere damp, and in some places slimy. It stank of stale piss and vomit.

I took a deep breath through my mouth and got to my knees. Minor head rush. Then to my feet. Major head rush. I put two hands on the sink and lowered my head. I turned the handle, not expecting anything. Out came a stream of cold water. I rinsed my hands. When they felt clean, I splashed the cool water on my face and head. I cupped water to my mouth for a long drink. Tenderly, I explored the side of my head. The goose egg was there, but I've had worse. I was feeling sufficiently better to begin worrying all over again.

He probably didn't have any rope handy, I thought, and had likely gone off to fetch some. I listened at the door. Lucy's breathing was labored. She'd been crying, which meant a stuffed nose and breathing past the gag in her mouth. There was no other sound. I had to risk contact. I needed to know if Mr. Gold's Gym was there.

"Lucy," I called, "I'm all right. If you hear me, make a sound." A muffled vocalization came through the door. I listened for a reaction from a third party. None. "If he's there, remain silent, otherwise say something." Another vocalization. Maybe he forced her, but I had to assume he wasn't there. "Are you okay?" Her response sounded more like uh-huh than unh-unh, but it was a stupid question.

Just for form I tried my shoulder against the door. Solid. The walls, too, were impenetrable. In modern houses a person can walk—or at least force their way—through the walls. Joists are often sixteen inches apart and the gypsum dry wall of today's construction offers little resistance to determined kicks. This cottage was probably built in the 1950s, perhaps for a groundskeeper or some other servant type. The lath and plaster construction of the time was as substantial as that decade's Packard automobile.

With not entirely heartfelt bravado I called out, "Don't worry, Lucy, I'm gonna get us outta this place." Then as an afterthought, "But first I need to pee."

There was a muffled giggle.

The story goes that Newton conceived the theory of gravity when an apple conked him on the head. My guess is he was sitting on the pot (literally) when it happened, inspired by a plop rather than a conk, but that wouldn't go over well in schoolbooks. I have friends who swear they do their best thinking in the bathroom. An inspiration came to me as the last few drops made their tiny splash.

I stooped and reached behind the bowl of the toilet. My hand found the water valve but I wasn't strong enough to twist it closed. Back on my hands and knees I went. I would have to forego squeamishness to carry out my plan. With two hands on the valve I just managed half of a clockwise twist, then another and another until it shut. I flushed the toilet, holding the handle down until the water tank emptied completely. I removed the top of the tank. The darkness mercifully concealed what was growing inside of it. I moved around to one side of the tank, took hold, and began to rock it back and forth.

At the end of each swing the bolts and drainpipe holding the unit in place groaned. I put every thing I had into it. I threw my weight forward for *to*, then stooped and leaned back for *fro*. At about the eighth repetition the entire unit busted loose with a tremendous crack. It was during a fro cycle and I went down hard on my butt. Dribbles of slimy tank water splattered over my entire front.

In the silence that followed, I waited for the dead bolts to be thrown. Nothing. I shouted to Lucy, "I'm okay. I'm breaking the fuck out of here." She squealed back in what I took to be delight.

Some further illumination came up through the hole from under the house. As I had hoped, the continual dampness had rotted the floor and supports. I started kicking and stomping furiously, breaking away hunks of plywood until I had cleared out an area between two floor joists. They were fourteen inches apart. Every calorie I had ever denied myself now paid its dividend. I squeezed between the joists into a mucky, yucky, this-is-worse-than-eating-worms crawl space.

I had learned to belly crawl in boot camp, often through mud, or thick undergrowth not guaranteed to be snake- or spider-free. Nobody liked it, but we all learned to control our instincts of repulsion. I began to crawl in the direction of the most light, hoping for an egress. Pipes and electrical wire were visible in the murkiness, so there had to be a way for plumbers and electricians to get down here.

The light crystallized into a square shape that came from a subsurface access. A mesh of corroded metal separated the crawl space from a cement-lined entrance pit. I bellied up to it, spun around, and kicked it out. I scrambled through to freedom. Muck covered me. Some had gotten in my pants as I crawled. As I rose to my knees, I could feel it oozing down my belly and the insides of my thighs.

I was on the side of the cottage next to the bedroom. The main house was barely visible through some trees. In the opposite direction, toward the rear of the cottage, a wooded area and freedom beckoned to me. I considered immediate flight. I rationalized that once I escaped they wouldn't dare harm Lucy. But I wasn't convinced that I was dealing with rational people. The penalty for kidnapping is only slightly milder than the penalty for murder, and murder eliminates a witness. I had to free Lucy.

Though it felt like hours, I'd escaped in less than 20 minutes. I had no idea when Gold's Gym would return. I peeked around the corner, scanning quickly in all directions, holding my breath and listening intently. A few woodsy sounds, some auto traffic, an airplane overhead. No footsteps. No sign of him. I moved soundlessly to the front of the cottage, thinking to force a window. A little voice said, "Try the door." I love these little voices. The sucker was unlocked. I opened it slowly, planning to make a dash for it if he was there.

He wasn't. I moved quickly to Lucy, removing her gag.

Had I expected her to say something maudlin like "Oh, Dagny, thank God you've come," I'd have been disappointed. The first words out of her mouth were, "There're knives in the kitchen." I didn't delay. I jerked open drawer after drawer until I found a serrated steak knife. She was bound hand and foot to the bed frame with nylon rope strong enough to tow a car. It took a long minute to saw through and remove all her fetters. I didn't want her encumbered as we fled.

"Can you walk?" I asked, cutting through the last strands.

She stood up shakily, balancing herself on a bedpost. She rasped, "Let's fuckin' book." She stumbled through the bamboo curtain. I supported her by the elbow until we reached the door. She shrugged herself free.

I said, "Okay, then. We'll turn left out the door, then left again to the rear and into the woods—no hesitation. Are you game?"

Lucy took some deep breaths, bit her lip, and nodded her assent.

I opened the door a smidge. Still no sign of him. "On three," I whispered. "You go first. One, two, three." We sidled out the door. I gave Lucy a gentle push of encouragement, then pulled the door closed silently behind me and followed. Within seconds we were high-hoofing through the woods as noiselessly as we could.

Our shadows were in front of us, and as it was nearly noon, it meant we were heading north. I turned to put the shadows on our left. East, in a half a mile, was the road. I was out of breath, as much from anxiety as from running. Lucy was faltering, too. I slowed us to a walk, finger to lips indicating we weren't out of the metaphorical woods yet.

We came to a chain link fence, Akrich's property line. It was a five-footer topped with nasty v-shaped brads of sharp wire. There was no horizontal support beam at the top, so it was impossible to climb over. If we turned left, we'd be moving away from the house and from danger, but we might encounter more fencing and find ourselves cornered. To the right was Houston Road, but that way would take us nearer to the house and danger.

I scanned up and down the fence line. "This way," I said. Lucy vacillated. "The ground slopes down," I hissed. "Should be a place to go under." She caught on. We walked quickly to our left and came to a place where the fence no longer touched the ground. I stooped and grabbed the bottom links, tugging upward. Lucy bellied under. Then she pulled the fence bottom the other way, toward herself, but it wouldn't go as high in that direction. I couldn't quite squeeze under. Someone was crashing through the woods. The jolt of fear gave Lucy added strength and she eked out another two inches. I wormed my way under, lacerating shirt and skin on the prongs.

We sprang to our feet, running full out. I heard the fence rattle, and the sound of metal on metal—the gun barrel scraping the chain link. I tensed for shots, but none came. He must have known his weapon was not accurate at that range, and the gunshots risked unwanted attention.

We were on another estate. The main house was off to our left. I thought of running to it, but if it was unoccupied we would be trapped. A car flashed by us in the distance. It must be Orchard Drive. I slowed to wait for Lucy. She was flagging, her breathing labored, but jogging gamely.

With fifty yards to go she stumbled to her knees. I went back, hooked her elbow, and helped her up. I said, "La coche es próxima."

"El coche esTÁ próxiMO, damn it," she gasped. "I'm going to make it if only to fix your wretched Spanish." She began to walk, then broke again into a jog. Moments later we emerged onto the road a few dozen feet from where I had parked. We sprinted to "el coche" like marathoners to the finish line. It cranked and started. I pulled a U-turn on two wheels that would have made Steve McQueen blanch, and sped away.

We said nothing for a short while, inhaling deeply to catch our breaths. Lucy broke the silence. "Well, Dagny, long time no see. What've you been up to?"

"Quite a bit as it turns out. What about you?" We broke into peals of laughter at our mock formality. We might have been girls out having a lark, except for being more filthy and disheveled than Haitian street urchins. "Did they hurt you?" I asked.

She knew what I meant.

She shook her head. "He might've, but that wouldn't jibe with suicide. I'm not sure why they kept me so long."

"Why'd they keep you at all? Tell me your whole story, and then I'll tell you mine." As she began, I set our course for police headquarters.

Chapter 24

Today is Thursday, right? said Lucy. "I tried to count the days, but it was confusing."

"You did a good job; it *is* Thursday."

"Since you were going to Frisco last weekend, I decided to visit some friends in La Jolla. I'd borrowed a typewriter from one of them when she lived here because I had to fill out a bunch of application forms that weren't online. When she moved I forgot to return the damn thing, so I stashed it in a kitchen cabinet. I figured to return it the next time I visited, but I forgot to. This time she reminded me, so I needed to retrieve it. I went into the apartment alone because I was tired of being a wuss. When I pulled out the typewriter from inside the cabinet where I'd stored it, I found a bunch of loose-leaf binders hidden behind it. I grabbed them and the typewriter and got the hell out."

She paused to catch her breath. I was riveted to her narrative.

"This means something to you, doesn't it?"

"It may be important. Please go on."

"The notebooks, they were all in Churok. I spent an hour leafing through them, enough to realize that they were Judy's research data. I thought if I showed them to Professor Akrich, he'd see that she hadn't plagiarized anyone. I practically ran to his office with them. He was at lunch so I waited. He had an appointment at one o'clock but I begged him to see me. He was surprised because I'd left him a phone message earlier saying I'd be out of town. Anyway, when I showed him the notebooks he about freaked. I mean, like, he was speechless. Then he recovered and tried to be cool. He said the notebooks were very significant, that they could exonerate Judy. He asked me to leave them. But I had this funny feeling. I told him I'd rather keep them, if he didn't mind. He said he did mind. He went through this rigmarole about the notes belonging to the university and I'd really get lots of credit for finding them. Meanwhile, I'm getting these weird vibes, and I'm wondering why were they hidden in the first place. So I snatched them up and split."

"Did he make any attempt to stop you, I mean, physically?"

"No, not really. I can't imagine that. But even before I was out of the building I felt like I'd just pissed away my whole career. I thought about going back and apologizing and turning over the notebooks, but in the end I just tossed them in the trunk of my car. I was hoping my buds in La

Jolla would have some insights. But I never got there," she squeaked, and began to weep.

I reached over and patted her knee. "What happened then?"

"I was taking Storke to the 101 when two assholes in a Firebird cut me off just past the fire station. I ran into the curb. They stopped and one of them runs over to me all apologetic like. Then he puts this little tube to his lips and the next thing I know I'm on the floor of his car, held down by that fuckwad that clobbered you. They took me blindfolded to that cabin and tied me to the bed. I got two meals and two trips to the john a day. God, the boredom was torture. I felt I was there for months, but I kept track of the days."

"What about the phone call to the Worthingtons?"

"Oh yeah, I forgot. They made me call my friends in La Jolla and make up some bullshit story why I wouldn't be there. I let slip"—she put finger quotes around the word *slip*—"that if I didn't check in with Doris and Ernie they'd be alarmed. That's when they said it wouldn't matter because by then I'd be just another suicide statistic. But later they made me call anyway. Did you understand my message?"

"Charles finally figured it out. We were worried sick about you. I was considering putting a gun barrel in Akrich's mouth and forci—"

She interrupted. "What did Professor Akrich have to do with this? Those guys must've been the ones that got Judy and Troy."

"Do you know where you were held captive?"

"Wait a minute. I thought the street you were parked on was familiar. Oh shiiiitt. It was on his property. But why? I don't get it."

I took the onramp for the 101 east, concentrating on merging with traffic before I answered. When we reached cruising speed I pulled the microfilm out of my handbag. "These are your notebooks," I said, brandishing the pilfered spool. "Judy didn't write them, I'm afraid. She stole them. And she wasn't the first to steal them."

I filled Lucy in on Starry Night, Professor Akrich, and the elusive notebooks. She hung on every word, her emotions ranging between admiration and horror. When I told her how I got the microfilm she exclaimed "You go, girl," and jabbed a fisted arm in the air. Even as I was telling my tale, I was fleshing out a theory to explain the facts as I knew them.

I pulled up by the red curb in front of the main door into the Police Department. "Let me call John's and see if he's back. I'll get him to meet us here."

I phoned the house and got the machine. I thought I might as well check messages. There was one: "This message is for Dagny Jamison.

This is Reginald White. I'm chief counsel for Wellex Pharmaceuticals. I understand that you believe a Wellex product may have been used in a crime. I'd like to discuss the matter with you. This is Thursday morning, ten a.m. My afternoon calendar is clear. If you get this message, and you possibly could, would you come to my office at company headquarters at two o'clock this afternoon? The receptionist will be expecting you. I already left this message at your office. Thank you."

It was quarter after one. Barely time to get home, clean up, and drive to Wellex. I knew I should go inside with Lucy and turn the entire case over to the authorities. But the temptation to fit one more piece into the puzzle that now obsessed me was too great. I explained the phone message to Lucy and sent her into the police station. "You go in there and tell them the whole story. You'll have to file kidnapping charges against Akrich. Don't hesitate. We're talking capital crimes here. Tell them where I'm going. And don't leave the station until I get back. Believe me, we're in terrible danger."

I watched Lucy pass through the double doors. I drove home with extreme caution, the Glock with a chambered bullet resting between my legs. Alert, pistol in hand, I parked and dashed inside. Immediately on closing and locking the front door I began to strip, reaching total nudity and the washing machine at the same time. I loaded the washer and climbed the stairs buck-naked. I was mud-streaked from tip to toe. I took a hot shower that managed to exceed in pleasure my hot bath of a mere eight hours ago. If I am reincarnated as a pig, I'll have a trotter up on wallowing in dirt.

I couldn't afford the luxury of a soak. I scrubbed myself clean and dressed quickly. I aimed to get what information I could from the Wellex lawyer, and to return at once to the police station to file my own kidnapping charges. The sooner the cops were on this case, the better. The silent, anesthetizing darts frightened me.

I'd formed a partial theory while Lucy was narrating her misadventure. Akrich had photographed Starry Night's notebooks. I had the proof. He'd been "discovering" all these facts about the Churoks, culled from the notebooks. He published them as original research to advance his career. Starry had to be eliminated as the one person who might have uncovered his perfidy. With Tommy in charge, Akrich had good reason to believe that the notebooks would remain under wraps. For over twenty years they did. Then Judy Raskin appeared on the scene and somehow gained possession of them.

Judy, I feared, was into blackmail. It couldn't have been for money— she was well off. It had to be for some kind of academic favor, maybe

Akrich's approval for work not done. Or maybe she wanted to force him to acknowledge his plagiarism, apologize to his colleagues and the Churoks, and remove himself from academia. Who knew what else? The human heart is a many-chambered vessel. Whatever the cause, it cost her her life.

Akrich must have planned Judy's "suicide." He knew her well enough to be sure that she would retreat to her home to recover from the shock of his accusation. I didn't know when, or by what means, he'd been able to hire hit men to carry out the murder. There was more to the man than the pious professorial façade revealed. He undoubtedly provided his minions with the incapacitating cocktail of Welnarkothal and Nandrolex, and Judy's home address. The delivery system, evidently a blowgun, had come from his collection of Indian artifacts. I'd seen several of them in his office but their significance had been lost on me. The advantage of a blowgun over other weapons was that it would go relatively unnoticed. It could be disguised as a walking stick or pipe, and it was silent.

By letting out that Troy was Judy's accuser, Akrich frightened the poor bastard into fleeing, where he could be conveniently disposed of. He must have felt certain that Troy was aware of the notebooks, or was even part of the blackmail conspiracy. I didn't think he had been, based on what I knew of him, but I wouldn't have bet a large sum either way.

What a rush the professor must have had when Lucy walked through his office door with those very notebooks. Here was an opportunity to destroy the evidence forever. Had he been a better actor, he might have pulled it off.

The missing puzzle piece was how Wellex fit in. Was someone like Richard Maas a willing co-conspirator? Could he have provided the drugs? And if so, why? Brotherly-in-law love seemed too weak a relationship to risk being an accessory to murder one. Over the years, Akrich must have met plenty of Wellex employees. Bribery, persuasion, or alcohol may have coaxed out the formula, possibly under some innocent-sounding pretext. He didn't need Maas for that.

These thoughts rattled through my head as I drove to Wellex. I'd called the company and asked for Reginald White, wanting to make sure the call wasn't a ruse. I got his secretary who verified the appointment.

At ten till two I pulled into Visitors Parking. People were pouring out of the building. I thought momentarily that it was an emergency, but they looked happy, not annoyed or worried. It dawned on me that next Monday was the Independence Day holiday since the Fourth was on a

Sunday. Wellex was giving its employees the afternoon off so they could get a jump on the long weekend.

I walked upstream against the flow of people, once nearly bumped into the reflecting pool by the eager crowd. I announced myself to the receptionist cop and signed in. He said he was expecting me, gave me a visitor's badge already filled out, and, surprisingly, directions to Mr. White's office. With everyone going home, there was no one to escort me.

The bustle of yesterday was absent. The halls were nearly deserted as I made my way toward the rear of the building. I turned right at the corner where Richard Maas's office was located. Reginald White's office adjoined it. The door was open but no one was visible. I always feel foolish knocking on an open door, and even more foolish saying things like, "Yoo-hoo, is anyone here?" but I did both. No response.

White's office was neat as a pin, the desk cleared of all work. Only the requisite computer and family photos were visible on the surface. My snooping instinct began frothing. I yoo-hooed again. Still no response, so I treated myself to a walking tour of the office. There were shelves full of law books and company notebooks, nearly all of which were labeled Proprietary and Confidential. Security was shockingly slack. I could have helped myself to any number of company secrets. Several works of art hung on the opposite wall. In the center of the wall, a large Ansel Adams photograph of a woodsy hillside bore the caption: Wellex, harnessing nature's pharmacy for better health. Similar art to the left and right bragged of various Wellex products derived from natural sources. A door on the left wall toward the rear of the office was to a private washroom. I remembered seeing one on the right wall of Maas's office. They probably shared plumbing.

I stuck my head out the door and looked around. Not a soul. I backtracked past Maas's office and looked up the corridor I had just come down. A couple of stragglers were walking toward the exit. Maas's door was open with no sign of him, either. I didn't like the man but perhaps he'd be in a more cooperative mood since I had an official invitation. I peered into his office. No one there. Maybe they were all in the same meeting. It was just coming on two o'clock. I started to return to White's office but Maas's was more interesting. He had stuff on his desk. Maybe a quick peek, just to hone my spying skills. If he showed up I could always say I was looking for Mr. White.

I walked casually around to his side of the desk, scanning the top for anything interesting. My eyes wandered to his computer monitor, and then widened. Something looked familiar. At the bottom of a screen full of ordinary writing was something reminiscent of the coded writing on Akrich's computer:

yjr hot; rdvs[rf/ yjr [/o/ od pm yp ,r/ fp dp,ryjomh/

My subconscious had been hard at work the past twenty-four hours. I knew immediately that it looked like touch-typing when your fingers stray off the home keys. I've done it a zillion times. You end up typing the letter next to the one you want. I studied the first word, *yjr*. It could be *ukt* or *the*. Aha! It's off one to the right. I set my hands on his keyboard on the home keys, then moved my fingers one key to the left. Pretending I was on the home keys, I touch-typed the actual message:

the girl escaped. the p.i. is on to me. do something.

Holy shit! I got out the message I had copied in Akrich's office.

sltovj.

yjrtr od s [tobsyr ombrdyohsypt mpdomh stpimf/ esyvj upitdr;g/ jrt ms,r od fshmu ks,odpm/

=,ssd

I could almost read it. The top line was *akrich*, the bottom line *maas*. The two last words of the message were my name. I didn't take the time to decode the rest. I most definitely didn't want Richard Maas catching me here. I'd be shot dead as an intruder.

I walked as calmly as I could to the door and looked out. No one was in sight. I edged along the wall and peeked up the corridor leading from the lobby. Uh-oh. Three men had just entered the passageway and were approaching purposefully all abreast. I was sure the one in the middle was Maas. On his left was someone whose silhouette reminded me of the Gold's Gym thug.

I needed people. The old song ran through my head: "People, who need people, are the luckiest people in the world." I wasn't feeling lucky. In the hopes that Reginald White was not a part of Richard Maas's gang, I ducked into his office, realizing too late that if I was wrong about him I was dead.

He wasn't there but my eye caught a reddish gray rivulet just beginning to seep from under the door of his lavatory. I stumbled back reflexively, muttering oaths not learned in Sunday school. As I turned hurriedly to leave, I lost my balance for an instant and brushed against the Ansel Adams. It wasn't hung very well and crashed to the ground, the frame's glass splintering into a thousand fragments. The noise shocked both my body and brain into action.

My body spun out the door, pulse accelerating. I began a quick jog in search of an open office and human life. I didn't think I'd be offed in front of witnesses. My brain was undergoing a revelation. These natural source drugs of Wellex. They got their ideas from the Churoks. Specifically, through Starry's notes. Wasn't one of the subjects of the notebooks medicine? The notes guided them to the botanicals. They refined the extraction methods. They patented everything using chemical formulae. The Churoks were none the wiser and out of the big money loop.

So it was a high stakes game, after all. That was the part I hadn't understood. That was why my thoughts had kept going back to the gold mine. The Wellex patents might be worth millions, tens of millions, who was to say? If Starry's original, copyrighted notes were disclosed, Wellex would be sunk under a deluge of lawsuits.

Now my job was to escape these pirates, whose creed was "Dead men tell no tales." I passed several closed doors without seeing a soul. I took a right up a short passageway that ended in a tee. I chose left and that ended in a tee. If I went left again I'd likely run in to Maas's goons. Right was a dead end terminated by a door that said, To Animal Facility. I had no choice. The knob turned and I darted in. It was a stairwell spiraling down clockwise. I tucked my handbag under my left arm, and using my right arm on the banister as a pivot, descended three steps at a time.

I recalled seeing another access to the animals nearer the lobby. If I got to it, I'd be behind my pursuers and could escape. I burst through a double set of swinging doors and found myself in a vast laboratory. There were floor-to-ceiling shelves of chemicals, huge tables containing sinks, desks, bookcases, and long rows of animal cages. The smell took away my breath, of which I had little to spare. An orchestra of beagles began an ear-shattering dissonance of yelping, baying and howling. The screeching of monkeys joined in, as if on cue. To my frustration, no human was in sight. The racket set up by the animals gave away my presence. My pursuers would quickly figure out where I'd disappeared to and follow me in here.

I'd lost my sense of direction in the stairwell. Casting about, I saw what I thought was an exit a good two hundred yards away. I cantered toward it, stopping only to throw open cages left and right as I passed them. The prisoners didn't hesitate. Dozens of beagles scampered out onto the cement floor. The dogs, not liking to soil their crates, took immediate advantage of their freedom by laying down a carpet of fresh feces. The monkeys that I released had taken to the heights and were pulling down bottles of reagents, which crashed to the ground, adding their pungency to the malodorous air.

Two men burst through the double doors behind me and stopped, taken aback by the teeming animals. They didn't wait long to resume the chase. Behind me, over the animal cacophony, a man cried, "Oh shiiiiit!" I looked back. One of the goons had slipped and fallen in the gooey mess. The beagles swarmed around him. The other man had a blowgun aimed at me. I froze in terror. One of the monkeys, mistaking the blowgun for a tree limb, tried to swing from it. The dart skidded along the floor in front of my feet. I turned and ran, weaving from side to side, bobbing my head to throw off his aim.

A monkey grabbed me around the neck. I shrieked and nearly fell. At the same instant, Richard Maas appeared about twenty feet in front of me, blocking my escape. Instinctively, I grabbed the monkey with my free right arm, its weight balanced in the palm of my hand. I threw it with all my strength at Maas's head. He jerked back with a scream, falling to his knees and covering his face with his hands. An angry monkey can tear up a lot of flesh in a short time. I sprinted past him.

It was an emergency exit. A sign warned that its use would trigger an alarm. How I wanted that alarm! I glimpsed a blinking red light on the round push-handle of the door. I felt a sting in my left arm. I had to reach the light. I focused every atom of will on that one small red undulating point, forcing it to grow larger. I was running in deep sand. The sand became oil, rising to my waist. My legs were, oh, so heavy. The red dot became a small circle. My peripheral vision went south. The circle in front of me grew. With one last desperate lunge, I threw myself at its redness. I was weightless, soaring, and falling. Like an aperture stopping down, my remaining vision spiraled and shrank into the red circle, and there was only redness, then nothingness.

Chapter 25

When I awoke, the band was playing "The Stars and Stripes Forever." It wasn't harp music so I wasn't in heaven; and it wasn't accordion music, so I wasn't in the other place. Then I thought that I was back in the army—how the army band loved to play that song. But no, I wasn't wearing khaki. It had to be good old civilian Earth.

As told to me later, I had exploded out the side of the building into the middle of the Wellex holiday picnic, and had landed unconscious at the feet of Mr. Gerald Wolfe, the company president. He was not a man to abide surprises.

An immediate investigation had revealed Richard Maas clutching his face in agony. He was only slightly better off, perhaps, than chief counsel Reginald Smith, much of the contents of whose head were found splattered on the walls and floor of his private lavatory. I had had an earlier acquaintance with the .45 caliber murder weapon.

Reginald's files contained documents indicating he knew of the crimes of Maas and Akrich. The source was Judy Raskin, whose intent was for the Churoks to receive a just and equitable settlement.

Richard Maas had masterminded the scheme of stealing the Churoks' knowledge. He had become aware of the contents of the notebooks during family gatherings in which Akrich had discussed his work. The promise of both academic fame and wealth had lured Akrich into conspiring with his brother-in-law. Both men had profited handsomely from Starry's purloined notes.

At his arraignment, Akrich claimed that he had no prior knowledge of the murders, and had been shocked when he had learned about them. He pointed out that the two murderers were, after all, in the employ of Maas. He further swore that he had conspired with Lucy's kidnappers only to save her life, which he had done by threatening to expose the conspiracy if she came to harm.

There was a ring of truth to this part of his defense, otherwise the hangman would have come for Lucy, too. My guess is that Akrich had seen too much killing and couldn't stomach any more. Fortunately, my rescue of Lucy had cut short the debate over her fate.

An unforgiving district attorney wasn't buying any of it. He had indisputable evidence for a grand jury showing that Akrich had trumped up his accusation of Judy's plagiarism. He convinced them that Akrich had set Judy up, and the jury indicted him as an accessory to her murder and as an accessory to Lucy's kidnapping as well. Though Akrich had lied to Troy to scare him away so that he might be killed, the grand jury found the connection too tenuous for indictment on charges pertaining to Troy's murder. The murder of Starry Night was never broached.

The grand jury indicted Richard Maas and his two henchmen on three counts of murder and one count of kidnapping. Maas was allowed to undergo extensive plastic surgery while in custody. The State undoubtedly feared that his wounds would evoke sympathy from a jury.

The gold mine was indeed as valuable as the crabby assayer from Mojave Analytical had claimed. The law firm that represented the Churok Tribal Nation, acting on behalf of Tommy, attempted to locate the two partners from Guatemala. They were traced to San Diego where it was discovered that they had participated in the Heaven's Gate mass suicide a year and a half earlier. They thought they were shedding their cloak of mortality and ascending to an alien space ship hiding behind the Hale-Bopp comet. The State of California is rather prosaic about such things. It considered them merely to be dead.

Thus Tommy inherited a fortune through fake suicide and real suicide. He wanted none of it. He signed over every troy ounce of gold to his people's government. Substantial though the gold mine income would be, it was dwarfed by the Churoks' settlement with Wellex, a figure never released to the public, but assumed to be in the hundreds of millions of dollars.

The firm of Jamison & Jamison submitted a bill of $2,355.78 to Lucy Navarro with a copy to Tommy Greatoak. Lucy paid to the penny, even before she learned about her $50,000 scholarship from the Tribal Government of the Churok Nation to advance her studies.

Charles and I made our own fireworks that entire holiday weekend, outshining by far the rockets' red glare.

Epilogue

The night after writing the last words of this case, The Dream came. This time I was hand-in-hand with Charles on the beach, and I was myself as I am, not as I was before cancer. The last rays of a coppery sunset had just sunk into the Pacific. We were strolling toward the red sky left behind by the setting sun. Charles held me, and kissed me. I awoke smiling, with the feel of his kiss on my lips.

The Dream has never returned.

www.ingramcontent.com/pod-product-compliance
Lightning Source LLC
Chambersburg PA
CBHW020435180626
46812CB00003B/1246